# Arthur: The Beginning

Walter Stoffel

DIAMOND PUBLISHING INTERNATIONAL
*Canadensis, Pennsylvania*

Arthur: The Beginning / Walter Stoffel —1st ed.
ISBN 978-0-9861500-4-3
ISBN 978-0-9861500-5-0

PRINTED IN THE U.S.A.

Published by Diamond Publishing International

www.walterstoffelauthor.com

Book design and layout by Nancy Cavanaugh, Cavanaugh Interactive.

# Acknowledgements

THERE ARE LOTS OF people to thank. Barbara's Writing Group (an association of fellow authors) guided me through the early pages of *Arthur: The Beginning.* Oli Landwijt and Professor Meghann Ryan provided their editing expertise. Nancy Cavanaugh professionally designed this book and created Arthur's presence on the Internet. Joanna Martinez did a fantastic job producing the original artwork for the book cover. Mary Shafer provided invaluable consulting advice. The author's photo was taken by Nikki DePaul of 27Rose Photography.

I'd like to give a special thank you to the readers of *Lance: A Spirit Unbroken.* There's not enougroom here to name them all but their enthusiastic reception of my first book gave me the heightened incentive and sense of purpose that resulted in *Arthur: The Beginning.*

# Dedication

*Arthur: The Beginning* is dedicated to the eternal human struggle to survive, recognizing that some people face a greater struggle than do others.

# Disclaimer

Any resemblance between names in this book and any persons living or dead is purely coincidental.

# Prologue

Bathed in the comfort of a bright summer's day, Arthur Berndt sat on a neighbor's lawn happily playing with toy wooden trains. The picture of contentment, contentment that evaporated when a woman came out from the house and approached him.

"Arthur, your mom just called me. They're home. I'm going to walk you over to your place."

The little boy burst into tears.

"What's wrong?"

"Bee bited me."

There was no bee. With only a four-year-old's limited vocabulary, Arthur had already mastered the art of lying, a vital defensive tool for a child constantly trying to keep out of harm's way. His family operated via an unwritten and unspoken code. His older sisters had known it for years and Arthur, a quick learner, was also on to it. Anything he said or did that made his parents look bad would cost him dearly. The last thing he wanted to do was return home, but no way in hell would he ever tell this neighbor, or anybody else, why.

Playing alone in a babysitter's backyard had been enjoyable, serving as a respite from the struggle his life had already become. During the afternoon, Arthur had experienced a prison escapee's exhilaration. Now he was heading back to his house, an apprehended fugitive. Just like that, the whole pleasant afternoon experience vaporized as if it had never happened.

The lady and the young boy reached Twenty-one Lowell Place and walked up to the front stoop, where Arthur's mother was waiting for them. "Did he behave himself?"

The babysitter tousled Arthur's hair. "Oh yes. He was a good little boy."

Arthur breathed a sigh of relief. He wasn't sure if he had been good; he was never sure. Even on those rare occasions when he seemingly achieved good boy status, it was always short-lived.

Most children want to feel loved. Arthur just wanted to feel safe.

# Chapter 1

ARTHUR'S FAMILY INCLUDED FOUR other members: his father and mother, August and Marquerite Berndt, and two older sisters, Elizabeth and Ruth.

August, born in 1899, grew up in Freiburg, a city located in southeast Germany, known as the primary entry point for tourists into the Black Forest. August's parents, Helmut and Berta, devout Catholics, had nine children, August being the next to youngest. August's father was not a major figure in his life. It was Berta, not Helmut, who ruled the family. She had no compunction about employing physical punishment when called for, and her world called for it often. Although none of her children were exempt from their mother's scrutiny, she singled out August for extra special attention. A switch or belt buckle were the disciplining tools of choice, accompanied with a vicious tongue.

Growing up, August was forced to attend church every day of the week—a ritual he would resent for the rest of his life.

When World War I broke out, August decided he would rather face enemy bullets than his mother's wrath. Just a teenager, he enlisted in the fledgling Luftwaffe and later told tales of aerial dogfights and dropping bombs on the Allies—by hand! He was briefly in the company of the famous Red Baron (Manfred von Richthofen) while at an airfield Germany had established in Brussels, Belgium. In 1918, the war over, August returned to civilian life, rapidly completing the equivalent of a college education (with an emphasis on literature) while holding down various odd jobs. In the dismal postwar economy, a college degree counted for virtually nothing, so his plans to be a teacher faded. His even more ambitious dreams of becoming an actor or a singer (he had a love of opera and a better-than-average tenor voice) also faded away. His mother pushed him to find a position as a government bureaucrat, dull but stable work that promised a pension. That part of the job market had also dried up. August spent the entire decade of the 1920s doing manual labor in and around his hometown. Though no longer a student, August continued to purposefully study English. The idea of heading for greener pastures in America and escaping his mother once and for all intrigued him more with each passing day.

Marguerite grew up in Schopfheim, a small village also in southern Germany. She arrived in this world under somewhat mysterious circumstances, clouded by the mores of the time. What is known is that she was raised in the loving home of an aunt and uncle. An unremarkable student, after completing her basic education she trained to be an au pair. She had a way with children and little difficulty finding employment. Eventually she was referred to a well-to-do widowed attorney who lived in Freiburg and needed a caretaker for his two children. Although an excellent opportunity that promised a substantial pay increase, Marguerite hesitated. She had never left her hometown and feared she would be overwhelmed living and working far from her family. With great trepidation, she accepted the position.

In 1931, August and Marguerite met for the first time, the only occasion they'd be in each other's company in Germany. The two happened to join the same opera appreciation group and met when the organization took in a performance of Die Zauberflöte (The Magic Flute). They enjoyed critiquing the singers, and Marguerite was impressed by August's vast knowledge of opera. He suffered no shortage of opinions: Mozart would have been the greatest operatic composer of all time if he had lived a full life; German tenors were preferable to Italian, the latter too melodramatic for his taste; and, while Beethoven was his favorite composer bar none, he felt it was a good thing he left the opera genre alone after Fidelio. When the evening ended, onstage Tamino and Pamina were saved, and, in the audience, the two blossoming lovebirds promised to stay in touch. They kept their promise, although it entailed a grand total of two letters and zero phone calls.

Less than two months later, and despite his mother's threats, August emigrated to America. When he arrived at Ellis Island, New York, he spoke passable English, but had no job lined up. His brothers, Karl, John, and Joseph, had also ignored their mother's admonitions and crossed the Atlantic some years earlier, before the stock market crash, and found employment. By 1931, job opportunities in the U.S. had dwindled drastically. Although August was the most educated among his siblings, his college-level education counted for little in America. He also had to deal with a lingering resentment towards Germans in general, a leftover from the Great War, which made the job search more difficult. August, like all the Berndts, had a strong work ethic and preferred any work to no work at all. He obtained a janitorial position at the Kings Park State Hospital for the mentally ill, sometimes working the overnight shift to make a few pennies more per hour. He moved in with John and his wife Ella, a temporary solution for August's lack of housing.

The pleading began. August bombarded Marguerite with letters expressing how he missed her and telling her, less than truthfully, that opportunities to work were far better in the U.S. As fate would have it, Marguerite's employment in Freiburg turned out to be temporary. Times were tough and hiring a full-time nanny was a luxury few could afford. Marguerite returned to live with her aunt and uncle, supporting herself with part-time babysitting jobs. Things looked dismal, except for the occasional letter from August. He definitely had a way with words and Marguerite had never been seriously courted before. Maybe that's why she fell in love with a virtual stranger. Other than his being an opera buff, she knew very little about him.

Marguerite boarded an ocean liner and arrived in New York in November of 1931. There she reunited with the man she had only seen once before in her life. To keep things on the up and up, they were married in a civil union the next day. In the eyes of his mother, August's marrying a Protestant was blasphemy. The Catholic Church didn't officially excommunicate him, but his mother did, angrily disowning her son via a letter laced with venom.

Mr. and Mrs. August Berndt also began the process of becoming citizens of the United States.

Just days after their marriage, good fortune smiled on the newlyweds. August was hired by the Radio Corporation of America as a groundskeeper at its 6,400 acre site in Rocky Point, New York. Since 1921, it had been the location of the transatlantic radio transmitter and, in building number ten, color television would be developed in the late 1940s. Just like a government clerk's job his mother had wanted him to have, this position offered stability and a pension, but it was primarily outdoor work and much more to August's liking. He had a green thumb and now he would get paid to use it. He wouldn't be singing a Wagnerian aria in the Metropolitan Opera anytime soon nor lecturing a college classroom about the greats of literature. Reality dictated August's course of action, not fantasy.

The Berndts moved into a small apartment in nearby Port Jefferson, helped financially by the local Presbyterian Church. Marguerite had been raised a Protestant and was very comfortable joining such a charitable congregation. August had not set foot in a church since coming to America. Dragged by his wife to Sunday services, he reluctantly became a quasi-Presbyterian.

In 1932, Liz Helene Berndt was born. Ruth Ann Berndt was born in 1941. The Berndts had planned on having two children. Arthur Robert Berndt arrived in 1944.

# Chapter 2

PORT JEFFERSON, ARTHUR'S HOMETOWN, was a small village on the North Shore of Long Island that offered a scenic harbor ideal for boating and fishing, a highly rated public school system, four distinct seasons of the year and a rural flavor, while sitting just sixty miles from cosmopolitan New York City.

Suassa Park was a small subdivision located within the boundaries of Port Jefferson. It consisted of seventy-five homes situated on three hundred and fifty acres, connected by a network of wide yet lightly traveled roads, some unpaved. There was virtually no through traffic, except for the occasional lost driver. A less impressive fact: Suassa Park was almost entirely inhabited by what were known in the day as WASPS (White Anglo-Saxon Protestants). No blacks or Hispanics need apply. A physician, Samuel Cohen, had to threaten legal action in order to build there. Dr. Cohen was Jewish.

Prejudices notwithstanding, most people thought Suassa Park was the ideal spot to raise children. It had every appearance of being a tightknit community. Everyone knew everyone, or at least they thought so. It was safe for youngsters to play outdoors without adult supervision. Dogs were often let outside to run unleashed. Mail and milk were delivered door-to-door. Many of the houses were separated by large vacant treed lots, and the entire perimeter of the community was surrounded by pristine woods. Younger kids spent the day playing in their backyards, riding bikes, or hanging out in a tree fort situated on one of the wooded lots. One resident graciously allowed the older kids to play ball on an unused field that was part of his small farm.

Although just sixty miles from downtown Manhattan, Suassa Park might as well have been in another world. It had a Norman Rockwell feel to it. For most, a little bit of paradise. For Arthur, a paradise lost.

# Chapter 3

IT WAS A WARM sunny day.

Outside, birds were joyfully singing, celebrating the beautiful summer weather. A occasionsl gust of wind coaxed the dark green oak leaves into dancing, creating their own gentle, rustling music.

Inside, four-year-old Arthur was enjoying a glass of his favorite grape soda.

Crash! The glass hit the floor, spilling its purple contents onto the kitchen floor. Arthur had done far worse than just drop something. He'd done it in front of his father.

"You pig!"

Without warning, August Berndt shoved his son to the floor. Arthur got back up, only to be pushed to the floor again. The young boy scrambled to his feet and ran, his father close behind. This was a footrace the youngster wouldn't win. His father caught up to him seconds later in the living room. August grabbed his son by the neck and crotch, picked him up, lifted "the enemy" overhead and threw him. For just a split second, Arthur thought he was having fun—he was flying! The floor lamp, the sofa, the fireplace—they all went by in a blur. Out of the corner of his eye the young boy saw the television set rapidly approaching. Wham! His head bounced off the corner of the TV. He continued on, slamming into a wall before coming to rest in a crumpled heap on the floor.

When the black curtain lifted, Arthur found himself lying belly down on the floor, groggy. He thought better of getting up. Instead, he decided to play it safe and remain motionless. Not stirring an inch, he scanned the room with half-opened eyelids. He spotted his attacker, eyes glazed over with blind hatred, standing just a few feet away. August Berndt surveyed the room. Spotting the wooden rocking chair, he turned and headed towards it. Arthur knew if he got up and made a run for it his father would only get angrier—and more violent. Better to stay and take his lumps now than run and risk fueling his father's anger to even greater heights. Resigned to his fate, he lay on the floor and braced himself.

His father reached for the rocking chair. He picked it up and headed toward his son. Arthur, sensing what he was in for, remained frozen in place, tensing up to better absorb the chair's impact.

The front door opened and in stepped Uncle Karl. "What the hell's going on here? Gus, Jesus Christ, you don't always have to be so tough on the kid."

"Goddammit, he's a Schweinhund!"

August slammed the rocking chair back down onto the floor, and the two adults engaged in a conversation spoken in German that Arthur couldn't make out. Motionless and facedown on the floor, he could do nothing but wait for whatever happened next.

Finally, Karl said, "Ah, forget it. Come on outside and have another beer."

Arthur lay there and listened, not daring to look. He heard their footsteps heading away from him. The front door opened, then closed. Lying alone and surrounded by silence, the youngster remained prostrate on the floor, unsure the storm was over.

This attack left an indelible scar on Arthur's psyche. Though too young to fully understand the concept of death, for the first time in his life he sensed his father could not only hurt him—he could do something far more final.

# Chapter 3

After a few minutes, Arthur cautiously lifted his head and looked around the room. Convinced both men had gone outside, he struggled to a seated position, remaining on the floor. One side of his head throbbed painfully. Arthur gingerly probed it with his fingers and felt a bump under his hair. Ouch! He quickly drew his hand away and looked at it. No blood. He would live. Slowly, he got to his feet. A bit wobbly at first, he shook the cobwebs off and walked over to the front door. Opening it, he went outside, dizzied by a headache and the dazzling sunlight. He joined his cousins who were having a water pistol fight in the backyard.

It was a warm sunny day.

# Chapter 4

BECAUSE HE LIVED UNDER the constant threat of attack inside his home, Arthur always wanted to get out of the house with a far greater urgency than other young kids. At an early age, he developed the habit of escaping his home whenever possible, both excited and relieved when taking off for whatever the outdoors had in store.

One early summer day he had left his house and was aimlessly walking along Hawthorne Street when he bumped into an older boy, Buddy O'Brien, for the first time. Arthur was now five years old, Buddy almost twelve. During that initial encounter the older boy immediately assumed the role of bossy big brother. Rather than being put off by Buddy's aggressiveness, Arthur was overcome by a need to win his approval—at any cost. He felt the quickest way to do that was to play follow-the-leader. For his part, Buddy had plenty of ideas as to how they could entertain themselves. The two boys began to meet on a regular basis, despite their age disparity.

Something struck Arthur as odd. Whenever he went to Buddy's house, there was nobody else at his home or, whoever was, stayed hidden inside.

Arthur never invited Buddy to his house. There was an indefinable dark "something" about his older friend that even this naïve young boy picked up on and sensed would meet with his parents' disapproval. Bad company, but, to Arthur, better company than he had at home.

Just a few days after they first met, Arthur arrived at Buddy's home and found him in the backyard sitting on the ground next to a motionless cat. The cat's face was disfigured. Arthur asked his friend, "What happened?"

"He died."

"How come?"

"I don't know."

Buddy flung the limp cat into the woods.

# # #

Soon the two boys began a crime spree that quickly escalated in its severity. First, broken spokes and flattened tires on bicycles, then punctured tires on automobiles, next, stolen mail they had no use for (sometimes taking the mailbox itself), and then on to throwing rocks at passing cars. The rock-throwing led to Arthur's first confrontation with an angry nonfamily member.

Buddy and Arthur would arm themselves with as many rocks as they could carry in their hands and pockets and then lurk behind bushes, just off the street. When a car passed by, they'd hurl as many of the stones as possible and then take off deep into the woods. By the time the driver under assault stopped to see what had happened, the boys would be long gone.

So it went, until one particular day when, standing in the woods along Hawthorne Street, they spotted an approaching vehicle. Buddy, farther back in the woods than Arthur, ordered the younger boy to begin the attack. When the sedan was almost past him, Arthur let loose a rock with gusto that fell short of its target. Simultaneously, Buddy threw a large stone with more force. Direct hit on the rear window. It splintered. The sedan screeched to a halt. From the driver's side a man jumped out on the run giving chase. Buddy, with a head start from deeper in the woods, was already out of sight. Arthur began running for his life.

A five-year-old trying to outrun an adult male—it should have been an obvious mismatch. But not to this five-year-old. Arthur scrambled through bushes, poison ivy, prickers and low-lying tree limbs. All the while, the crunching footsteps of his pursuer got louder and louder. Buddy? He was just a distant memory.

Snagged! A hand wrapped around Arthur's chest, yanking him to a halt. "What the hell ya think you're doing, you little sonofabitch?"

Arthur was too frightened to answer. The man grabbed him by the hand, ready to drag him out of the woods. Arthur sunk to the ground and wrapped his arms around his head, ready for a beating.

With a mixture of anger and puzzlement, his captor demanded, "What's wrong with you, boy?" Again Arthur had no answer to offer.

"Get up, dammit!"

Arthur remained frozen in a fetal position. The man yanked him to his feet and the two made the trek back to the car, which was sitting on the road, idling in neutral. The stranger shoved Arthur into the front passenger seat. "Where do you live?"

"I don't know."

"You don't know? Well, then we'll have to go to the police station to find out. Can't have you out here lost in the woods, right?"

"No! I don't wanna go to the police! Who are the police?"

"No police, eh? Maybe it's time you found out who they are and what they do—before you become a bigger brat than you already are. Whadda ya think, wise guy? "

The man forcefully grabbed the youngster by his arm and violently shook him. "Okay. Let's start over. Do you live around here?"

"Kind of." Arthur was stalling for time, hoping to dodge his own execution.

"Listen. I'm not going to put up with any bullshit. You tell me right now, who are your parents? If you don't, I'll beat it out of you. Your choice."

Arthur had never been beaten by anyone but his father. He briefly wondered how a stranger's punishment would feel compared to what he received at the hands of his father. Then, after taking another look at the man's angry face, he decided he didn't want to find out. Better to stick with the devil you already knew at home.

In a trembling voice, the young boy blurted out, "You mean my mom and father?"

"Yeah, your mom and dad. Where do they live?"

Arthur gave up all hope of escaping his fate. "It's the next turn right down the road. The next road, you go that way." He pointed with his finger.

After arriving at the Berndts' house, the stranger marched up to the front stoop, pulling Arthur with him. His mom had heard the car and was waiting at the door, a look of concern on her face.

"Is this your son?"

"Yes. What's happened?"

"Plenty. Your son broke my car window. He did it on purpose, while I was driving, no less. Throwing rocks. This is going to cost someone money and it's not going to be me."

"Oh, I'm so sorry. I truly apologize. Was he with anyone?"

"I didn't see anyone else."

Marguerite directed her look towards Arthur. "Who were you with?"

"Nobody."

"Arthur, did you throw a rock at this man's car?" The young boy remained silent.

She turned back to the man, "Again, I apologize. I'm Marguerite Berndt."

"Jack Stevenson."

"Sorry to meet you this way. This is very embarrassing. He can be a handful, but I know that's no excuse. I am so very sorry. I just don't understand this. I mean, how could he reach your window with a rock?"

"I don't know and I don't care. All I know is I caught him running away. That's proof enough for me."

Marguerite again asked her son, "Are you sure no one was with you?" The youngster shook his head.

"I'll get this repaired and send you the bill. Actually, I live over on Whittier, so I'll just drop it off. Okay with you?"

"Certainly."

"You better keep an eye on him. He's awfully young to be doing this kind of stuff."

"I can't argue with you on that, if he did. I'm just not sure."

"Well, why would he run then? Maybe he thinks it's funny but someone could get hurt. What if my window was open and he hit me?"

"I completely agree. I'll have his father talk to him about this."

The young boy's heart sank. "Talk to him about it" meant his father would find out what he'd done wrong and that would lead to much more than a lecture.

Arthur's fears proved to be justified. Marguerite divulged the entire story to August when he got home from work. There would be no stay of execution; it went off without a hitch.

# Chapter 5

WHEN BUDDY AND ARTHUR met up a few days later, the younger boy dared to stand up to his older partner-in-crime. In a rare display of assertiveness, Arthur insisted his rock-throwing career was over. He was still smarting from the welts and bruises—courtesy of his father—his most recent antisocil effort had earned him.

Buddy was nothing if not creative. If Arthur was no longer up for rock throwing, his pal knew other ways they could entertain themselves. One day the two were wandering through the neighborhood. They had no particular destination, as far as Arthur could tell. The two kept walking until Buddy stopped in front of the Cohen home. The owners were gone, along with their children and two dogs. Buddy and Arthur traipsed through the woods that lay near one side of the house and walked out onto the Cohens' backyard. Buddy, being the taller of the two, used a lawn chair to stand on and peeked inside the house through several different windows. Arthur had no idea what his cohort was up to.

They walked over to the breezeway which had a side entrance into the kitchen. The door was unlocked. In they went, Arthur unsure if they should enter, but afraid to show any hesitation.

Buddy got right to work. He turned over the kitchen table, knocking a vase with flowers to the floor. He picked up the vase and heaved it into the adjoining room, where it flew into a glass cabinet filled with dishes, scattering broken glass onto the dining room table and floor.

The older boy stopped what he was doing, turned toward Arthur and shouted, “What are you waiting for, scaredy cat?”

Arthur, sensing he’d better join in, threw a Hummel figurine into the TV set, destroying the screen. The two boys took a floor lamp and shoved it into the downstairs toilet. Bed sheets were thrown out the window into the backyard. They tried to do the same with a mattress, but it was too heavy, so they left it half on the bed, half on the floor. Every lamp and light bulb they could reach was broken. More Hummel figures were smashed to pieces. Buddy found a saw in the basement and partially cut the legs of several pieces of furniture. Arthur didn’t know if he was having fun, but his partner seemed to be enjoying himself, and that was what mattered.

As the grand finale, all the food was pulled out of the refrigerator and freezer. What wasn’t thrown onto the floor was carried outside by the two lawbreakers. They perched themselves on a picnic bench and, by hand, ate a strange combination of food—bananas, mayonnaise, lettuce, marshmallows, and raw hamburger meat. The banquet over, they went back into the house and briefly admired their handiwork. Then the two boys headed for their respective homes, satisfied they’d done enough damage for one day. Arthur was particularly happy, basking in his mentor’s approval.

The vandals hadn’t bothered to cover their tracks. A nearby resident had noticed them loitering in front of the Cohen home and later, from his porch, seen a sheet flying out of his neighbor’s window. Suspicious, he later checked inside the vandalized residence and found an absolute mess in every room. The Cohens were on vacation and wouldn’t be back for a few more days. Having no way to reach them, the neighbor decided to notify the police.

## Chapter 5

A few days later two men showed up unannounced at the Berndt house. They arrived in a police squad car. Marguerite, a look of concern on her face, greeted them at the front door. "Can I help you gentlemen?"

"Well, I think your son can. You're Mrs. Berndt?"

"Yes."

"I'm Detective McIntyre and this is Officer Burger. Can we come in for a minute?"

"Certainly, but what's this all about?"

"I'll let your son explain it all. At least I hope he will."

Arthur was in the kitchen, finishing a peanut butter and jelly sandwich. The kitchen door swung open and in marched his parents, his sisters, and the two strangers, one in a police uniform. The detective immediately began grilling Arthur in full view of his entire family. Stuck in a small kitchen, surrounded on all sides by disapproving looks, his father glowering at him from behind one of the policemen—the terrified young boy expected that, at any moment, the two strangers would join his father in beating him.

Arthur played dumb, denying it all. His "I didn't do anything" convinced no one.

"Well, that's not what your pal says. We already spoke to Buddy. He didn't waste any time fingering you. Said it was your idea. Ridiculous—" The detective turned to Arthur's parents. "Did you know these two were hanging around together? A twelve-year-old and...exactly how old is your son?"

"Five," replied a distraught Marguerite. She continued. "No, I am...we had no idea. I really don't know the O'Briens at all."

"Well, they have one rott—er, troubled son. No need to go into details. Just not someone for your son to be hanging around with."

August chimed in. "I'll see to it he doesn't."

The detective turned back to Arthur. "Look son, my partner and I aren't leaving here until we get the truth out of you. If we don't, we'll have to take you down to the station to continue this conversation."

In trouble with the law for the first time in his life, Arthur feared getting into a car with these unfriendly strangers but, if they left without him, he'd have to face his father. Those two dark alternatives got the best of him. He broke out in tears.

Detective McIntyre put his hand on Arthur's shoulder. "I'll take that as a confession. Okay, Arthur, that's it. Way better to tell the truth. So you were with Buddy?"

Arthur, still crying, stammered out, "Y-y-yes!" He braced himself, expecting his father to rush at him in a rage. Other than muttering "Goddammit!" August contained himself.

Detective McIntyre had one last question for Arthur. "Can you tell me why you did this? I'm sure your parents wonder why, too."

The young boy offered no explanation for his criminal behavior. There was one: a deep anger at how he was treated at home. But, he sensed accusing one's parents was strictly taboo and nobody would come to his defense if he spoke openly. In fact, he might get into even more trouble. He suppressed his unacceptable thoughts.

"Well, folks, I believe this matter is settled. Dr. Cohen is not interested in pressing charges. He just wants the property damage paid for. Hopefully, you and the O'Briens can settle with him amicably."

"Christ, how much are we talking about?" August asked.

"I don't know the exact details but it'll probably be somewhere around a thousand dollars. I saw the place. Quite a mess."

Arthur had not been paying attention to the conversation. He'd been busy assessing the mood of his father. He sensed his dad was impatiently waiting for the policemen to leave so he could get down to business. Arthur no longer looked at the officers of the law as threats; they had become protectors. He searched for words that would prolong their stay, but found none. He could only silently scream *Help!* inside his head.

"So, Mr. and Mrs. Berndt, will you try to work this matter out with the other parties involved?"

Margaret answered. "We'll do our best to. We don't have a lot of money. This is going to be difficult."

"Understood. A lot of damage. Your son is way too young—." The detective stopped himself and turned to his partner. "Well, Dan, let's get back to the station." Marguerite let them out the front door. These strangers, who had arrived as enemies, left as would-be saviors who were now abandoning Arthur, leaving him at the mercy of his father.

Just as the squad car began pulling out of the driveway, Arthur took off up the stairs towards his bedroom with August Berndt in hot pursuit.

# # #

Upon returning from his vacation, Dr. Cohen initiated a screaming match on the phone with August. "That kid's a punk. He's a goddamn Nazi, a Hitler Youth. You must be so proud."

"Yeah, and you're a Jew bastard trying to make money off me."

"You're an asshole. You better keep him off my property and out of my sight. He's a menace."

A rather uncharacteristic verbal display from a normally reserved physician. For once Arthur's father had met his match and had little to say in rebuttal. Just minutes after that exchange on the phone, he was back in control and got down to the business at hand—he threw an ashtray at his son, grabbed several bottles of beer, and went outside in the backyard to stew. The rest of the Berndt family dutifully honored August's need for some alone time which also served as a lull in the war constantly being waged at 21 Lowell Place.

During his interrogation by the police, Arthur had initially expected the two lawmen to join in with his father and give him a beating right then and there. They hadn't. The young boy's conclusion? His father was more fearsome than the legal system.

# # #

Homeowners insurance paid for most of the damage the two boys had done. The children's parents made up the difference.

Arthur was given strict instructions to stay away from his co-conspirator. Nevertheless, just weeks after admitting to the crime, he made his way to Buddy's house. After all, Buddy was his best and only friend. After knocking on the door, a middle-aged woman he'd never seen before opened it. Upon seeing who the visitor was, her face instantly morphed into a look of disgust.

"Oh, it's *you.*"

Adults intimidated Arthur, and this neighbor was no exception, especially after such a cold reception. The young boy hesitated, and then nervously asked, "Is Buddy home?"

"No, he isn't, thanks to you."

"Can he come out and play when he gets back home?"

"Not with you. And he won't be home for a long time anyway."

"Where did he go?"

"Why should I tell you? It's none of your business. Someplace, that's all you need to know, you brat."

The lady broke down crying and slammed the door shut, leaving Arthur standing alone on the stoop. He turned around and headed back home, wondering where Buddy was and feeling friendless.

# Chapter 6

SEPTEMBER, 1949. TWO MONTHS after participating in that ill-fated home invasion, Arthur began attending kindergarten. The very first day he sized up the situation as one to his liking. School was a refuge providing rules that, if followed, afforded a decent share of predictability and safety.

Of all the many attractions in the spacious classroom, the youngster immediately took to the sandbox, and, even more so, the slide. The minute his feet hit the floor at the end of a ride he scrambled over to the steps and climbed back up to the top for a repeat performance.

While sitting atop the slide preparing to take off, Arthur spotted a neighbor's son, David, standing in the doorway, clinging to his mom's dress and crying. Mrs. Brand, the teacher, encouraged the young boy to join in the activities, but without success. Though Arthur hardly knew David, he greeted him like an old friend.

"Hey, Davey, come in. This is fun!"

David's mom walked him over to the slide and he began scaling the steps. Arthur let go of the rails at the top and began his journey downward. David quickly followed behind him. One trip and he was convinced, gleefully exclaiming, "Yes. This is fun."

With an expression of relief on her face, David's mom left the classroom, grateful her clinging son had finally taken to his new surroundings.

There was a lot to like about kindergarten: arts and crafts, stories read by the teacher, milk and cookies. Only nap time presented a challenge for Arthur. While pretending to sleep, he'd stay awake to prevent soiling himself. There were a few occasions when he did fall asleep, but fortunately had no accidents, not until that one time, near the end of the school year...

The trouble started when he was stirred out of his sleep by Mrs. Brand's soft voice. "Arthur, wake up. You had a bit of an accident."

He felt the dampness throughout his shorts and panicked. "I'm sorry."

"Well, accidents happen. I'll call home and let your mom know to bring some fresh clothes."

Arthur began crying, at the same time demanding, "No, you can't do that!"

"Well, why on earth not?" That was a question Arthur knew better than to answer.

There he was, soaking wet in a classroom full of his peers. Mrs. Brand wrote something on a piece of paper, folded it and had one of the children bring it to the office. She turned to Arthur. "I'm having your parents called."

"Do you have to?"

"Why, of course. We have to get you dry clothes."

Arthur didn't utter another word. No need to. His forlorn expression said it all. The young boy had been mistaken. Even in school, he couldn't escape from his father's wrath.

"Class, it's time for us to all work with clay. Everyone sit down around the big table. George, why don't you pass out the clay? Arthur is going to work at my desk."

Still in urine-drenched shorts, Arthur struggled unsuccessfully to put a lid on his growing panic. He only went through the motions with his clay; he was too busy picturing the hell he was going to catch at home. The youngster was going to pay an especially steep price for having urinated in public and embarrassing his family. Even worse, what if his dad drove to school to get him? Arthur was sure his father would come after him the minute he entered the classroom. Getting hit in front of his classmates would be a humiliation he knew he'd never recover from. At that moment, Arthur's only wish was to be beaten in the privacy of his home.

Fearfully awaiting the moment his father would come charging into the classroom, Arthur continued to unenthusiastically fumble with the ball of clay in his hand. All the while, he was sure Mrs. Brand would start making fun of him, maybe comment on how awful he smelled. She never did.

Clay time over, George walked around the table, letting each kid place his or her mound of clay into the box he carried.

The classroom door opened.

"Mrs. Brand?" Arthur knew that voice. Mom!

"Yes?"

"Hi, I'm Marguerite, Arthur's mother. I brought some things for him."

"Good. There is a boys' bathroom right outside, to your left."

Arthur walked over to his mom. She took him by the hand and left the classroom.

In the bathroom was a small sink. Marguerite, armed with a washcloth, towel, and soap she had brought from home, cleaned up and dried off her son. She helped him dress in clean clothes, putting the soiled ones in a paper bag she'd also brought with her.

After confirming with his teacher that she was taking Arthur home, Marguerite and her son left the school.

Arthur had escaped the public scolding but still had plenty to worry about. On the walk to the family car, he asked a question he feared the answer to. "Is Dad home?"

"No, he's still at work. He'll get home in about an hour."

Arthur wanted so badly to ask if his father was going to find out about today's mishap, but didn't, too afraid he'd hear the wrong answer. The ride home was in dead silence.

Arriving at their house, Marguerite went to the basement and purposely put the soiled clothes at the bottom of a basket of dirty laundry while Arthur went glumly to his room. He began to half-heartedly fiddle with his Tinker toys, but soon lost track of what he was doing. He was too busy wishing he could disappear from his life for the next few hours.

An automobile pulled up in front of the house and he heard his father's "See you tomorrow" directed at his fellow carpoolers and a "Take it easy, Gus" in response. A car door slammed and off the auto went. The youngster heard his father's footsteps approaching the house. Each step brought August Berndt closer to finding out what had happened at school that day. Arthur closed the door to his room, though doing so guaranteed him no protection. With resignation, he sat on his bed and awaited his fate, heart pounding, palms sweating.

Downstairs, the front door opened and closed. Marguerite spoke first. Arthur listened intently from upstairs.

"How did work go today?"

"All right. Not for Jack McEwing, though. He got the boot today, but he had it coming. He's a lazy sonofabitch."

"Dinner will be ready in about twenty minutes."

"Good. Anything new going on?"

"Nothing much, really."

At the dinner table, the Berndts ate in their customary uncomfortableness, the mother and her three children carefully measuring their words in hopes of not touching off August's ire. After supper, dishes were done and everyone sat down in the living room to watch TV. Sometimes, television temporarily distracted the Berndts from their own dysfunction.

Arthur soon got bored with the fare on the screen and retreated to his room, where he started reading a picture book. He left the door open and one ear cocked to the sporadic conversation going on downstairs. Every time his mother started to speak, he feared the worst. His fears ultimately proved unfounded. By the end of a half-hour talent show on television, his "accident" in school remained a secret between mother and son. He heard his mother announce she was going to bed.

Not believing he could have such like luck, Arthur waited a few more tense minutes before allowing himself to silently celebrate. Finally convinced he was in the clear, his panic melted away, leaving Arthur in a state of giddy exhaustion. Such an indescribably beautiful feeling.

# Chapter 7

OTHER THAN THAT ONE accident while napping, Arthur enjoyed a successful first year. He savored the break from home life attending kindergarten had afforded him. The hours he'd spent in the classroom were a respite from the battle he was fighting—and losing—at home. When school ended in June, the youngster experienced a loss of safety likely not shared by any of his classmates. His regular contact with children his age had sparked a conflict in Arthur's thinking. For the first time in his life, he wondered if there was a different way of living than the one he was experiencing at home. Sensing he had mentally waded into taboo waters, the young boy squelched what seemed to be treasonous thoughts about his parents.

###

Throughout the school year Arthur had pestered his parents—he wanted a dog, a German shepherd, like the one Roy Rogers, his favorite cowboy, had. He asked for one as a Christmas present. No luck. He asked for one as a birthday present. Still no luck. His father was less than enthusiastic: "They cost too much. Make a mess." All year long Arthur had to listen to his classmates talk about how great their dogs were without being able to add to the conversation.

One morning, a few days after the school year ended, Marguerite announced, "I'm going shopping in Patchogue. You kids come along." Ruth and Arthur piled into the car. Since everything outside Port Jefferson and Suassa Park seemed like foreign territory to him, Arthur was especially excited. To the youngster, just getting to Patchogue was half the fun. For this six-year-old, the thirteen-mile journey on Route 112 never failed to fascinate.

Patchogue was bigger than Port Jefferson. It had way more stores. Marguerite parked the car along Main Street. The first stop was JCPenney to buy sandals for Ruth and sneakers for Arthur. Then, on to Swezey and Newins. Mom needed blouses and Dad, socks.

"Kids, we have one more stop to make."

Arthur hoped it would be at the ice cream shop. It turned out to be even better. All three Berndts walked two blocks, ending up in front of the Patchogue Pet Store. Could it be at long last...?

"Mom, are we really...are we getting a puppy?"

"Yes, but only if you see one you like." Of course he would.

"Hot dog!" Marguerite and Ruth laughed at the young boy's unintentional play on words.

Marguerite opened the door to the shop and let Ruth go in. Then she called to her son, who was busy gazing into the store window. "Arthur, c'mon. Follow me. Let's go!"

"Mom. I picked him—I want him."

He was pointing in the window. Marguerite came back down the steps, over to Arthur. There were several puppies frolicking on wood chips and shredded newspaper.

"Which one?"

"The brownish one. He's neat."

"Well, there are two brownish ones. The dark brown and black one or the light brown one?"

"The light one."

They went inside and talked to the proprietor. He advised them that the dog Arthur had picked out was a purebred German shepherd. The dog cost $175. When Arthur saw his mother's reaction to the price, his heart sunk. He was sure his mom would back out of her promise.

"Whew!" Marguerite thought awhile. She would have some explaining to do at home. In her husband's eyes, this would be seen as a frivolous act. She might have to lie.

"Okay. We'll take him. Does he have a name yet?"

"No. He's yours to name."

"I can't take him today. We'll be back on Saturday." Marguerite left a deposit and exited the store with her two children. Heading to the car, Arthur was about as happy as he'd ever been in his life. "My own real dog. I can't wait. How far away is Saturday, Mom?"

"Only four days. What are you going to name him?"

"Bullet."

"Art, Roy Roger's dog already has that name. Why don't you think of another one?"

Arthur got deep in thought. "I can't. That's the only one I like."

"Well, we'll just have to come up with another name you like."

On the ride back to Suassa Park, Arthur wracked his brain but always came back to Bullet. That evening Liz bailed him out. His sister had taken Latin in high school and she suggested Rex. At first, Arthur didn't like the name. He thought it sounded "funny." When Liz explained to him it meant "king" in Latin, Arthur liked the idea that he would have royalty for a pet. Rex it was.

Later that day, Marguerite broke the news to her husband. She waited until he had his second beer and was at his happiest. "We bought a dog today. Cutest little thing."

"I thought we agreed no dog for our son until he stops bedwetting."

"Well, it just doesn't seem like that's going to happen any time soon. It doesn't feel right to deprive him of a dog for that reason. Besides, Rex belongs to the whole family."

August Berndt mulled over his wife's comments and said, "I've only got two questions. Who's going to take care of it?"

"Oh, all the kids are delighted with him. Liz can take him for long walks. I'm sure Ruth and Art will help out as best they can. He's a German shepherd. He'll be a good dog."

"Second question, how much?"

"Well, we went back and forth. Finally, we agreed on $115. He wanted $200."

"Jesus Christ! Well, you did jew him down pretty good. It's July, but let's consider this a Christmas present to all the children and leave it at that. $115. That's a lot of money. I assume he's a purebred at that price."

"Yes. He has papers. I'll get them when I pick him up next Saturday."

Absorbed in a baseball game on TV and about to begin working on beer number three, August said nothing more about the impending family addition.

When Saturday arrived, Arthur, his mom, and both sisters returned to the pet store. Rex looked just as cute and frisky as he had a few days earlier. The pet shop owner apologized that the pedigree papers still hadn't arrived from the breeder, but said he'd mail them to Marguerite as soon as he got them. Done deal.

Arthur was unsure how to handle the puppy so Ruth took him from the store owner's hands and put him into a cardboard box Marguerite had brought along. The four Berndts returned to the car, cardboard box securely in Liz's hands.

On the way home, Ruth got in front with Marguerite. Arthur and Liz sat in the back, Rex in the box between them. The young boy touched the puppy both out of curiosity and affection. Rex lightly gnawed on his fingers, but Arthur quickly realized there was little to fear and let the puppy nibble to his heart's content. Nevertheless, every once in a while Rex got in a good nip with his baby teeth. Arthur would quickly yank his hand out of the box and shake it a bit, before bravely resuming his interaction with the weeks-old pup.

As soon as they got home and out of the car, Marguerite slipped a collar on Rex and attached a leash. She handed the leash to her son and let him walk the puppy around the yard before bringing him inside. Rex piddled outside numerous times, but not enough evidently; he had an accident as soon as he was let back into the house. The kitchen was designated his home until housebroken. After less than a month, Rex was allowed to enter all the downstairs rooms. He had a couple more accidents, then none. When Rex urinated inappropriately in the house, Arthur noticed the punishment his dog suffered wasn't nearly as severe as that he himself endured for wetting the bed.

That summer and fall Arthur and Rex were restricted to playing in the yard. By the time Rex was six months old, the two were allowed to go on short walks together. By then, they had become buddies for life.

Rex made another friend—Nicky. He was a black male dog of various and sundry breeds that lived two houses away from the Berndts. Having no aggressive side, Nicky was the definition of laid-back. He greeted everyone with a human-like grin on his face and a body wiggling from head to toe.

The two dogs hit it off so well that, if one was let out of the house, he'd lie down and wait at the edge of his property until the other came outside. Then the canine duo would take off for the abundant woodlands nearby. Hours later they'd return together, each ultimately heading for his home. Sometimes Arthur joined them on these jaunts, forming a happy trio.

Rex and Nicky became neighborhood fixtures, wandering around Suassa Park, either tending to their business, or hanging out with the local kids. They became unofficial pets for the entire community.

Nicky assumed he was welcome everywhere. He'd often allow himself into the Berndts' garage or basement to sleep if either door had been left open. Luckily, even August Berndt saw the humor in a canine audaciously taking such liberties. Nicky may very well have been the only living creature that never stirred August's ire.

# # #

Arthur was eager to help keep Rex clean. He volunteered to shampoo the dog on a regular basis. He considered it not a chore, but fun. The young boy got a kick out of how Rex, trying to shake himself dry during and after his baths, left both of them soaked. At least when Arthur got himself wet bathing the dog, he didn't have to worry about getting in trouble.

Arthur, with his mother's guidance, taught his dog how to stay, sit, lie down, come, and fetch. Rex proved to be a quick learner.

The family dog was also a quick learner when it came to August Berndt. After feeling the elder Berndt's boot a few times, Rex knew to steer clear of him. In spite of this, when August was administering discipline to his son, the dog became a nuisance, attempting to break up what was going on. To eliminate Rex's interference, August either ordered the dog to go into the basement, barricaded him in the kitchen, or put him outside—a time-out for the dog, but not for Arthur. If slow to obey August's commands, Rex might also get a taste of the elder Berndt's medicine. Once isolated, Rex could do no more than helplessly howl his disapproval over the youngster's harsh treatment. Boy and dog felt each other's pain.

Despite the punishing treatment he occasionally suffered at the hands of August Berndt, Rex held no grudges and made a great family pet, friendly and nonthreatening except when in watchdog mode. Then he became a soldier ready to do battle to the end, a staunch defender of his pack.

Although Rex was technically the family pet, Arthur was clearly his favorite. The two became an inseparable pair. Even before Rex arrived in his life, Arthur had gotten into the custom of escaping from the house at every opportunity, venturing out into the world alone. Now he had a four-legged companion that would devotedly and protectively follow him anywhere.

\# # #

Around the time Rex (or Rexy, the nickname bestowed on him by his youthful master) graduated from puppyhood, he developed a disliking for Joe, the mailman. As a pup, Rex had ignored him. Now, if the dog happened to be out on the lawn when Joe arrived, he greeted the letter carrier with throaty growls, daring him to set foot on the property. The first time this happened Joe retreated, taking the Berndts' mail with him.

Joe was no quitter. He was determined to live up to the postal service's promise of delivery despite snow, sleet, ice, rain—and now, Rex. No easy task since the Berndt's mailbox was affixed to the house next to the front door, far from the road. Back at the post office his coworkers were betting each other on how long it would be before Joe turned in his mailbag and went back to tending bar.

Standard mail delivery morphed into a military action. The next time mail carrier and dog met, Joe arrived brandishing a long buckled strap in his hand. Bracing himself, the determined mail carrier headed for the house, knowing he had to travel the length of the driveway, then the flagstone walkway, and finally, up the steps of the stoop, all while being escorted in a most threatening manner by a berserk German shepherd. He and Rex did an uneasy dance along the way—Joe swinging the strap, and the dog alternately dodging it and lunging at his prey. Joe was able to keep his nemesis at bay, but it only served to further inflame Rex and convince the dog he was dealing with a mortal enemy. Later that day, Marguerite got a telephone call from Joe advising her that if Rex was not kept inside, the Berndts would have to start picking up their mail at the post office.

Never having had any other discipline problems with her dog, Marguerite didn't like the idea of Rex being forced to stay in the house all day until the mail carrier had come and gone. She came up with an alternative course of action that Joe unenthusiastically signed on to.

## Chapter 7

For the next few weeks, the mailman only stopped at the house when Marguerite was inside with Rex. Taking off his mailbag, he waited on the road until Mrs. Berndt and her leashed dog exited the house and walked out to him. He then handed over the mail, and owner and dog went back inside. Rex behaved himself except for a couple of growls during the first days of the experiment. After three weeks, the procedure continued, but with Rex unleashed. There were no incidents.

Then, for another couple of weeks, after being greeted by Marguerite and Rex, and leaving his bag on the edge of the property, all three walked to the mailbox, into which Joe deposited the mail. By the end of this stage of training, Rex was clearly losing interest in Joe.

Finally came the day Rex was given the ultimate test. Joe, upon arriving, took off his bag and started carrying the Berndts' mail up to the house, all the while being scrutinized by their dog, lying on the front yard. Marguerite remained inside, watching events through the screen door. With Joe halfway to his destination, Rex got up and scooted to the front stoop just as Joe was arriving there. Would he let Joe proceed? Joe went up onto the stoop, put the mail in the box, turned around, and headed back to the road. Rex, eyeing him warily, remained in place.

After a few more days of this final stage of training, Rex paid Joe scant attention. Marguerite and Joe concluded that all along it had been the mail bag antagonizing the dog, and not the human carrying it. Rex kept his opinion on the matter to himself.

# # #

Despite several phone calls from Marguerite, the owner of the pet shop never produced written proof that Rex was a purebred. All the other members of the Berndt family were grateful and pleasantly surprised that August let the matter go, apart from calling the pet shop owner a "fuckin' swindler."

# # #

Occasionally, Arthur played a game with Rex. He'd collapse on the ground and play dead. His dog always immediately lay down next to his fallen master. After a while, he'd get impatient and start whining, nudging the boy in an effort to bring him back to life. If Arthur kept up his act, Rex eventually would settle down next to the "corpse," eyes riveted on him with concern. There the two would lie in frozen silence. Every so often Arthur would peek, comforted to see that his dog, motionless, was still staring at him. When Arthur finally sprang back to life Rex would too, jumping up and down, licking Arthur in the face, so happy to have him back. It was a cruel trick to play on the dog, but Arthur was desperate to feel that at least one other living creature in the world cared about him.

# Chapter 8

SEPTEMBER, 1950. LIZ BERNDT began attending Buffalo State University. She would live on campus for the next few years, only returning home to work during the summer. Ruth Berndt entered the fourth grade at the Port Jefferson elementary school.

For Arthur Berndt, fall of 1950 also ushered in a new school year, new grade, and new teacher—Mrs. Spear. With kindergarten out of the way, there would be less time for fun and games. Arthur and his classmates were issued several books geared towards introducing elementary reading, writing, and math skills.

To a greater degree than his peers and out of necessity, Arthur had already honed the skill of "reading" adults, and he didn't like the story written on Mrs. Spear's face. To his great disappointment, Mrs. Spear reminded him too much of home. She looked much harder around the edges compared to his kindergarten teacher. His fears appeared to be confirmed during the first few days of school. Desks had to be kept in perfect order. Mrs. Spear didn't put up with unauthorized chatting among her students and you'd better be ready to respond if she called on you. It was easier to get in trouble with her than it had been with Mrs. Brand. Arthur knew bad reports from school would beget severe repercussions at home. He was determined to keep a low profile, other than getting good grades.

Sometimes first impressions can be deceiving. Though she was on the strict side, it didn't take long before Arthur realized that, just as in kindergarten, he had more control over his fate in Mrs. Spear's classroom than he did at home. Follow the teacher's rules and you had nothing to fear. Some of his fellow students called her "mean" or "scary." Arthur didn't see her that way, because his idea of mean and scary was different from that of his classmates. While Arthur continued to bounce (sometimes literally) in and out of trouble at home, school was proving to be a respite from the never-ending turmoil he faced inside his house.

A significant benefit of being a first grader: no more forced naps, naps which could lead to urinating on himself and abject humiliation. One less worry in Arthur's world of worries.

Throughout the school year, Arthur excelled scholastically. If it wasn't for fellow student Catherine Thomas, he would've graduated first in his class. Their academic competition had begun.

# Chapter 9

THERE WAS ONE ESPECIALLY impactful event Arthur experienced during his year in first grade. On February 13, 1951, Arthur turned seven years old. Normally a cause for celebration. Weeks earlier, he had been promised by his parents that on this special occasion he'd be llowed to wear his favorite cowboy outfit to school. That deal was dead, and he had only himself to blame. Overnight, he had wet the bed. As a result, wearing the cowboy gear was out. First, Arthur tried crying to see if it might bring about a change of heart. When that failed, he switched gears and became mute, refusing to speak. His silence sprung from a bottomless pit of resentment.

Behind schedule because he'd gotten a late start washing his soiled sheets, the youngster had to be driven to school. His mother dropped him off by the school's side entrance. Arthur watched as she drove away. The minute she was out of sight, instead of entering the building, he started walking away from it, bagged lunch in hand.

Jimmy, a fellow classmate, spotted him from their first-grade classroom. He stuck his head out an open window and warned, "You're going to get into trouble!" Arthur said nothing and just kept walking. If he couldn't go to school wearing his cowboy clothes on his birthday as promised, he wouldn't go to school at all. Damn the possible consequences! Anger trumped whatever reason this first-grader might have had.

School lunchbox in hand, Arthur walked down to Main Street and headed for Anderson's delicatessen. There, just like any other self-respecting kid, he bought some candy with the money he otherwise would've used to purchase milk in the school cafeteria. Shopping completed, he left Anderson's and headed onto Old Post Road. He resumed his march past a lengthy string of houses, then the high school, and continued up the steep winding hill that led to Suassa Park.

He reached a house under construction just a short distance from his home. Finding the construction crew's activities entertaining, he parked himself on some lumber to watch. He began to eat his lunch, although it wasn't even ten o'clock in the morning.

Arthur didn't have the sense to realize that a seven-year-old walking around town by himself on a school day screamed of truancy. One of the crew jokingly asked, "Hey, kid, shouldn't you be in school?" Another worker shouted, "Do you want me to drive you to school?" Arthur alibied. "I didn't go to school today because I was sick." Some of the construction crew laughed and one said, "Well, you'd better go back home. In case you didn't notice, it's freezing out here. Where do you live?"

"Right around the corner. I'm going there now." For once Arthur wasn't lying. That had been his ultimate destination all along. The young boy quickly got up and began walking; the workers were getting too inquisitive.

Arthur traveled the two remaining blocks to his house. He figured he could safely hang out at home until three o'clock rolled around, which was about when Ruth and he usually returned from school. His parents arrived home well after three and would have no idea what he'd done.

People rarely locked their doors in the neighborhood and the Berndts were no exception, so Arthur entered via the front door. Rex, surprised his buddy was home so early, greeted him with a combination of jumping up and down, tail wagging, and happy barking.

It felt strange being in the house alone during school hours. Since the TV was at the repair shop, Arthur killed time by listening to the radio. Most of what he heard made little sense to him; it was for adults. He also had a model airplane that he worked on a bit. Later, he took Rex outside in the backyard and played with him for a while, oblivious to the fact that neighbors might see them.

Everything went according to schedule. At ten minutes after three, Ruth showed up from school. Then, his mother and finally, his father. No one but Arthur had the slightest idea what he had pulled off, that he had exacted revenge for his undeserved punishment. Besides righting a wrong, the youngster savored the additional thrill of getting away with something, fooling his parents.

After an early dinner, Arthur went along with his parents to the grocery store. The three were walking down one of the store's aisles when Arthur spotted his teacher heading towards them from the opposite direction. The young boy's heart sunk.

Mrs. Spear initiated the conversation. "You must be Arthur's parents. Is he feeling better?" Marguerite responded. "Oh, did he hurt himself in school today?"

"No, no. He wasn't in school. Shame. The class had cupcakes to celebrate his birthday, but the birthday boy wasn't there."

"Not in school? I...I don't understand."

Her confusion left Marguerite at a loss for further words. August took over. He shot his son a menacing look and asked, "Well, where the hell were you?" and then let loose a barrage of obscenities.

Caught off guard by August Berndt's outburst, Mrs. Spear said, "Oh, I'm sorry..." and quickly headed for a check-out counter.

Grocery shopping came to an abrupt halt for the Berndts. A half-full cart was left behind as the family trio left the store, August threatening to beat the hell out of his son. Marguerite begged her husband to calm down, but Arthur had little confidence her pleas would do any good. They rarely did. Marguerite insisted on driving, convincing her husband he was too upset. After pushing his son into the back seat of the car, August got in the front.

The ride home was pure terror for the young boy. What lay in store for him? He had the cold comfort of knowing he'd find out soon enough. His father kept uttering a nonstop flood of expletives. Even though Arthur didn't know exactly what many of them meant, they succeeded in drowning him in a sickening mixture of fear and shame. Marguerite meekly attempted to calm August down, to no avail.

A car filled with three upset people pulled into the Berndt driveway. Arthur bolted from the car and ran inside the house. He rushed up the stairs past Ruth and into his bedroom, locking the door behind him. He heard his father enter the house and storm up the staircase. Reaching the second floor, he walked over to his son's bedroom door and began pounding on it. Then, he started kicking it.

From below, Marguerite cried hysterically, "August, please come down here. Don't let him make you so upset. It's not good for you."

"Not 'til I'm done with him." As he banged his fist on the door, August screamed, "Get out here, chickenshit."

Arthur dared say nothing, fearing that the mere sound of his voice might further enrage his father. He stood motionless in the middle of a pitch-black bedroom, heart pounding, gasping for breath, and praying for God's help. Only a locked door stood between him and doomsday. If he didn't open it, his father might very well break it down.

Then, complete silence. Silence could be his friend or it could be his enemy. It all depended on what was happening on the other side of the door. His father was calling all the shots.

"August, please come downstairs. We've got to get groceries. The store is going to close soon. There's nothing for your lunch tomorrow."

"Goddammit."

More silence. Thirty seconds that lasted an eternity. Then, the sound of footsteps going down the staircase—at that moment, the most beautiful music in the world to the young boy. But Arthur, still standing inside his bedroom, wasn't taking anything for granted. He waited in the darkness until he heard the family car being started up, backed out the driveway, and driven away.

This time Arthur's prayers had been answered.

# Chapter 10

THE VERBAL OUTBURST BY Arthur's father in front of Mrs. Spear had been a huge embarrassment for the young boy, but later that school year, there was an incident that almost blew the lid completely off the part of his life Arthur fought so hard to keep secret.

One spring day during lunch recess, Arthur was playing kickball. On his turn to kick, he sent a slow dribbler towards the right side of the infield. Arthur took off for first base; the first baseman took off for the ball. After snagging it, he headed for Arthur. The race was on. Would the fielder reach Arthur and hit him with the ball, or would Arthur beat him to the bag? Just before reaching the image of first base painted onto the asphalt playground, Arthur tripped. Down he went, landing hard on his knee. He reached out with his hand to touch the base, just as he felt the ball hit him. Still lying on the ground, he looked around to see if he had been declared safe. Members of the opposing teams briefly debated the matter and the decision was made that Arthur had beaten the ball.

Slowly getting back to his feet, Arthur positioned himself on first base. One of his teammates, Sal, was already waiting at home plate for his turn to kick the ball. That's just what he did, booting it between and past two infielders. When kickball was played by first graders, few balls made it beyond the infield so nobody ever bothered to play the outfield. Thus, this kick had all the earmarks of being a two-run homer. Arthur began running, or rather limping, toward second base. By the time he rounded second and started heading to third, Sal, the would-be homerun hitter, was just a few feet behind, urging Arthur to hurry up. Not up to the task, Arthur slowed down to a painful gimp. At the same time, a member of the opposing team had retrieved the ball and was steaming in from the outfield, ball in hand. Seeing a youngster in physical distress, Mr. Phillips, the playground monitor, came running over from his station by the swings.

Arthur struggled to reach third and then headed for home, his frustrated teammate still prodding him from behind to run harder. He couldn't. Just feet from home plate he felt the ball hit him. He was out. The ball bounced away, allowing Sal to touch home plate and score. An argument ensued between the two teams. It was decided that because Arthur had made the third out, Sal's safe arrival at home plate didn't count. Arthur hobbled over to a low stone wall and sat down, disgusted with himself for letting his team down.

Mr. Phillips, huffing and puffing, reached him. "What happened? Why are you limping?"

"I fell down."

Mr. Phillips had Arthur sit on the ground and roll up his pants leg as far as he could. Although the young boy couldn't completely expose the knee, what could be seen made it clear: Arthur had scraped his knee badly. "Boy, that looks nasty! You're done with kickball for today. I want you to sit the rest of this game out. No. In fact, I want you to go to the nurse's office. Can you make it from here?"

"I think so."

"Maybe I should have the nurse come out here."

"No, it's not so bad."

"Can you get up by yourself? You want some help? Here, let me help you—"

"Nah, I'm okay." Arthur gingerly got to his feet, before the teacher could help him.

"Walk a bit. Let me see how you do."

The youngster took a few steps, slightly favoring one leg but insisting he was okay to walk.

"Okay, Arthur, get to the nurse right away."

Under Mr. Phillips' watchful eye, Arthur completed an uncomfortable trek across the playground and went up the front steps into the school building. Inside, he gimped up another flight of steps and then down the hall to the nurse's office. Arthur knocked on the door and, after hearing a warm "Come in," he opened the door and entered. There at her desk in full nurse's uniform sat Mrs. Cagney. Arthur had never been in her office.

"What can I do for you, young man?"

"I got hurt in the playground."

"Oh, what happened?"

"I fell and hurt my knee or something."

"Well, let's take a look."

She had Arthur sit down and then asked him to show her the wound. The pant leg was too tight to roll up high enough to expose the entire wound, but what she saw impressed Mrs. Cagney. "Oh my, that must hurt!"

"Not too bad."

"Well, we're going to clean that up and bandage it right now. I'll have to ask you to lower your pants. I can't dress your knee properly otherwise."

Blindsided! Panic engulfed the young boy. Arthur suddenly remembered. He had some injuries on his legs that had nothing to do with today's fall. He couldn't and wouldn't explain them to anyone, no matter what. They had to do with private matters that were none of Mrs. Cagney's business. Instinctively he knew these were secrets to be kept in order to protect his family from the rest of the world, and him from his father. Arthur had to keep it together. No crying. He must find a way out of this.

The bell rang, indicating recess was over. Time for the kids to come inside and get back to their classrooms.

"Mrs. Cagney. I think I'm okay now. Can I go to class? I don't want to get in trouble for being late."

"Nonsense. I have to clean up that knee. You'll get a note to let you back into class. Come on, Arthur. No dawdling. I'm ready to dress that scrape."

The young boy knew that if anyone, especially a grownup, treated him nicely it was because they didn't know how evil he was. Mrs. Cagney was being kind to him only because she didn't know the real Arthur. Though he felt undeserving of her empathy, he didn't want that warm comforting feeling he was enjoying to vanish. He knew it would the minute the nurse saw his discolored skin. "*Why, Arthur, I had no idea you were so bad. You must be really bad. I'm sorry. I can't talk to you anymore. Bad boy! You'll have to leave my office or I'll call your parents.*"

He kept searching, but just couldn't come up with an excuse to disobey the nurse's request. There was no way out. As he pulled down his pants, a large black and blue bruise was exposed on one thigh. On the other, an even larger one that blended into another that had yellowed with age. These bruises were proof of his evilness; he had earned them with his misdeeds. They were his badge of dishonor.

When the nurse came over to treat his wound, she took one look and gasped, "That must have been quite a fall you had. Look at those bruises. And there's an old one there too. You didn't do all that damage today. How did you get yourself so banged up?"

There was nothing to be gained by telling the truth. Lying was the key. Arthur began desperately fishing for an alibi and quickly caught one. A dire necessity for secrecy proved to be the mother of this young child's invention.

In a convincing acting performance, Arthur puffed his chest and proudly announced, "I play football on the Jablonskis' field with the big kids."

"Where's this field? I never heard of it."

"It's near my house. I walk to it sometimes."

"Oh, I thought it was some famous ballpark. That game is so rough. I'll never understand how you boys think getting beaten up over a ball is fun. Anyway, you're way too young."

"I am not!"

As she was cleaning the wound, Arthur let out an "Ouch!" After a sincere "I'm sorry," Mrs. Cagney applied a large dressing that covered Arthur's knee. "Nothing to do for those bruises but to let them heal. Why don't you give football a rest for a few weeks?"

"Okay."

"Now, Arthur, let me see you walk across my office."

He forced himself to do it with even less of a limp than he'd had entering her office, hoping to hasten his return to class.

"Thankfully, it looks like you didn't break anything. But I'm going to give you a note to give to your mom. She might want to follow up with your family doctor."

"Okay."

Arthur pulled up his pants and walked over to the nurse's desk. She wrote a brief letter on a piece of paper, put it into an envelope and stuffed it in Arthur's pocket. "Young man, don't lose that note and make sure your parents get it."

"Yes, Mrs. Cagney."

Later that day, on the way home from school, Arthur ripped open the envelope and read the note:

*Mr. and Mrs. Berndt, Arthur had a nasty fall today at school. I cleaned and treated a bad scrape on his knee. In the process I discovered he had several bruises which he's getting from playing football with kids older than him. I'm not sure he should continue doing that. I base that on the fact that he says he usually comes away from those games bruised. You also may want to follow-up with the family doctor regarding his knee. If you have any questions please feel free to contact me at 516-PO3-5555.*

*Sincerely, Lois Cagney R.N.*

The young boy didn't understand all the words, but instinctively knew what had to be done. He ripped the note into pieces and buried it by hand in the woods a couple of blocks from his house. Arthur then walked the rest of the way home, secure in the knowledge he had hidden a family secret from prying eyes. That assurance gave him a twisted sense of accomplishment—and relief.

# Chapter 11

"HEY, DO YOU WANNA play?"

Arthur did. It had been almost two years since his pal Buddy O'Brien had disappeared from his life. He always had Rex to fall back on, but he was ready for another stab at human friendship. "Okay. Whatta ya wanna do?"

"Follow me."

Ending his aimless after-school walk through Suassa Park on a bright spring day, Arthur accompanied the other boy into his backyard. There, under a huge maple tree, sat an elaborate outer space setup that Arthur scanned with wide-eyed fascination—and envy. There were spaceships, spacemen with ray guns, launching pads, and lots of other gizmos, all spread out in a deep rectangular sandbox whose walls consisted of railroad ties.

The two boys looked at each other.

"I'm Warren."

"I'm Arthur."

Introductions over, the two sat down in the sandbox and played with the space stuff. From the start, Warren took the lead, not surprisingly since he was a fifth-grader and three years Arthur's senior. One particular spaceman that had the neatest helmet caught Arthur's attention. He reached for it but Warren quickly snatched it up. "It's my man," the older boy commanded. Case closed. Arthur had to content himself with second choices in spacemen, spaceships, and rocket launchers. Still, these were all toys he had never dreamt existed, so he had little trouble enjoying himself.

The two remained engrossed in play until a lady called out from the kitchen window, "Warren, it's lunchtime. Bring in your friend."

The two boys scrambled to their feet and went inside.

"Warren, who is this young man?"

"This is Arthur."

"Hi, Arthur. I'm Dolores Howell. I'm Warren's mom."

"Hello."

"Should I call your mom to see if you can have lunch with us?"

Arthur hesitated. He couldn't remember if his father was home. What if his dad answered the phone? He'd probably say no. Worse yet, the young boy was self-conscious about his family, especially his dad. He always felt embarrassed whenever his father temporarily came out of his reclusiveness, especially in person, but even on the phone. Arthur sensed there was something strange about his father and, by extension, himself. The more he could distance himself from his roots, the better he could hide his own oddness. After some troubled hesitation, Arthur stammered, "Okay."

The phone call was made. To Arthur's great relief, his mom answered and allowed him to have lunch at the Howells'. He had never eaten at anyone else's place before—except at the Cohens' house, where it had been done illegally.

Arthur had a grilled cheese sandwich and tomato soup with Warren and his mother. Then, the two boys played together a few more hours. Arthur had found a new friend.

# # #

Warren Howell and his parents had moved into their new home a few months earlier. They lived on Hawthorne Street, right around the corner from Arthur. If they got along, it would be easy for Arthur to visit Warren. Just as it had been with Buddy, Arthur didn't want Warren coming to his house.

Very quickly, Arthur became a regular visitor at the Howell home. The two boys played a lot of board games. It was understood that Warren had to win, all the time. This presented a challenge to Arthur. He was an incredibly poor sport himself who cheated to win and, when cheating didn't work, had a fit as the loser. Ultimately, his need for acceptance from his new friend trumped his own need to be victorious. Warren racked up quite a winning streak while Arthur privately fumed.

Eventually Arthur met Warren's dad, Lenny. Lenny was a lot calmer than Arthur's dad. A lot more predictable, too. Safe to be around.

Once the school year ended, the two boys became inseparable, getting together almost every day that summer. Spending so much time in their home, Arthur noticed some things about the Howell family. Mom and dad seemed eager to accede to their only child's wishes. Although Warren already had a lot of possessions, if he saw something else on TV that he wanted, within a week or two there it was in his hands. He often asked for—or even demanded—money from his parents, and usually got it. His parents cleaned up after him. He had no chores. His allowance was a whopping one dollar a week for doing nothing. When the two boys left the Howell house, Warren was never asked where he was going or told when to come back. Arthur wished he could—but knew he never would—get a deal like that.

There were other clear differences between their lives. Arthur noticed that Warren was able to talk back to his parents, without consequences. Sometimes he said bad words grownups used, but didn't get hit. In fact, he never got hit. Also, unlike Arthur, Warren didn't like dogs ("They're goofy looking."). To keep the peace, when going to see his friend, Arthur usually left Rex at home.

A distinction of lesser note: Warren drank Super Coola, the latest thing—soda in a can. At his house, Arthur had to settle for Jud's, the cheaper store brand, which came in a glass bottle.

Warren and Arthur did have one thing in common. Apart from each other, neither had any friends in Suassa Park. Warren was a spoiled loner, Arthur just a loner.

A few times Arthur was invited to sleep over, but he knew better than to take that chance. He did notice that Warren's bed sheets were never hanging outside on the clothesline as the only wash for the day.

# # #

One day, Warren decided to test Arthur's loyalty. It turned out to be blind.

They were walking along Whittier Place. Ahead of them sat a car, parked alongside the front lawn of the Wests' house. Warren dared Arthur to unscrew the car's gas cap and put stuff into the tank—"stuff" meaning dirt. Arthur knew this was something you wouldn't want to get caught doing, but, without asking Warren why he wouldn't do it, Arthur summoned up all his courage and proceeded. The front half of the car jutted out alongside the Wests' front yard and could be seen from their house. The rear half of the vehicle was hidden by a thickly treed lot lying next to the Wests' home. Arthur, barely four feet tall, provided a miniscule visual target, making this a relatively easy crime to commit. Making it even easier, there happened to be a large collection of loose sand near the vehicle.

Warren ducked into the woods and barked directions. "Go find the cap."

Dutifully, Arthur got on his hands and knees and crawled up to the rear of the car. Not sure what to do next, he asked, "Where's the cap thing?"

"Look on the sides of the car."

Arthur did. "I don't see anything."

"Pull on the license plate. That thing in the back with the numbers on it."

"Okay."

Arthur pulled the plate down, exposing the gas cap. Brimming with misguided enthusiasm, he gleefully announced, "I think I found it!"

"Okay, open it."

First, Arthur pulled on the cap. No luck. Then he twisted it. The cap came off and he threw it on the ground.

Warren barked the next order. "Okay, put dirt in it. Put a lot, all you can."

Arthur scooped sand up from the road with both hands and, while holding the license plate down with one elbow, he clumsily threw the dirt into the tank.

"Do it some more."

Arthur nodded and dutifully tossed a couple more handfuls of soil into the tank.

A dog started barking from inside a neighbor's house. Both boys panicked. They took off, Arthur trailing Warren. The two scurried across the street into a vacant lot. They ran and ran until they came out onto the Jablonskis' farm, a safe distance from the scene of the crime. From there they walked out onto Hawthorne Street.

"Does it matter that I didn't put the cap thing back on?"

"Nah."

Enough outside activity for one day. The destructive duo walked back to Warren's house and had lunch.

# # #

Another day, another caper. The two boys had been walking in the woods when they came upon the backyard of a home. They hadn't planned on doing anything in particular, but an opportunity presented itself. Warren eyed the huge bay window in the back of the house and thought it would be great for target practice. But what if someone was at home? Warren sent Arthur through the woods alongside the house to check up front for cars. There were none outside. Arthur then had the audacity to drag a cinderblock over to the closed garage door, balance himself on it, and peek inside. Arthur's report to his commander: no enemy vehicles.

The search began for rocks. They found a few and began chucking them from the woods at the window. It quickly became obvious neither of them had the arm strength to reach the window with a stone from so far away. This called for a more daring approach. Arthur spotted a pile of bricks stacked next to the rear stoop. Just one thrown from close-up would do the job. Warren volunteered Arthur to carry out the mission. The young boy was all too eager to impress his pal. He marched straight over to a pile of bricks, picked up the top one, carried it to within a few feet of the bay window and, lifting the brick over his head with both hands, let it fly.

Direct hit! The window collapsed into a thousand pieces. At the very same time, Arthur heard a shriek from inside the house. He spun around and sprinted across the backyard into the woods. Warren was waiting there, crouched behind a pile of firewood. They didn't know if they should run and risk exposing themselves, or stay hidden.

The back door flew open. A woman stuck her head out and took a few moments to scan the surroundings. Then, she went back inside.

Sensing this might be their one and only opportunity, the two boys made a run for it, retreating into the deep woods they had earlier emerged from. Energized by fear, Arthur was almost keeping pace with his older cohort. The two came to a stop deep within the woods, bending over with hands on knees, to catch their breath. A combination of sheer exhaustion and the thrill of escape prompted them to burst out into uncontrollable gasping laughter.

When their laughing fit ended, the two headed to Warren's house to play Monopoly. The game ended with Arthur in financial straits.

# Chapter 12

DURING THE FIFTIES, THE Cold War between the U.S.and the U.S.S.R. was in full bloom, and it was reflected in the daily life of Americans. News reports about the Red Menace crowded the airwaves. School children practiced air raid drills in class, falling to the floor and squeezig themselves under their desks at the teacher's direction. Bomb shelters were the rage, a symbol of status if you could afford one, mocked as useless by those who could not.

Another feature of the Cold War: the Ground Observers Corps. In 1950, six months after the Soviets' first A-bomb test, the US was guarded by only a rudimentary radar network. Plans were in place to build a much more sophisticated system. Meanwhile America was vulnerable to air attacks sneaking under the existing detection system. The Ground Observer Corps, begun in the Second World War, grew in size throughout the Korean War conflict. In an attempt at greater efficiency, a revamped Ground Observer Corps, now called Operation Skywatch, went into effect. It doubled the number of lookout posts to 16,000 nationwide and would reach a maximum of 400,000 volunteers by the mid-fifties.

After a few hours of training in aircraft recognition and report filing, civilians went on duty at observation posts concentrated along coastal and northern regions. They stood atop buildings, in church bell towers, forest ranger stations, racetrack grandstands—anyplace with an unobstructed view of the sky.

One of those 16,000 observation posts was an imposing tower constructed alongside Emerson Street in Suassa Park, specifically for the Operation Skywatch mission. It consisted of four telephone pole-like columns, each ninety feet high, held together by elaborate wood framing. It had winding stairs that led up to a platform on which sat an observation booth. The booth poked out above the tall oak trees that surrounded it, affording a clear view of Port Jefferson and its environs and, most importantly, the sky above. To a child Arthur's age, the tower was a spellbinding behemoth, overshadowing all around it.

Operation Skywatch functioned round-the-clock and consisted entirely of volunteers who put in designated hours. August Berndt mocked the whole system: "By the time anyone spotted an enemy plane, we'd all be goners." Nevertheless, in a rare display of civic duty, he volunteered as a spotter. It wasn't long before he started coming home telling tales of potential invading aircraft and the critical telephone calls to distant places like New Haven, Connecticut, or New York City, where sat the mysterious-sounding filter centers. He talked of seeing shooting stars and even UFOs.

Arthur was quite taken in by these stories and by his father's official Ground Observers Corps pin. Fascinated, he longed to see what the world looked like from so far up. Of course, to do that, he would be stuck in the booth with his father for three or four hours. One day, the boy's sense of adventure trumped his fear of his father; he asked his dad if he could accompany him on his shift.

"No. You're way too young."

"No, I'm not."

"I say you are. You'd never make it up the steps. That thing was built for grownups. There's just a thin railing, nothing else to keep you from falling off. I don't think you could even reach the railing with your arms. You're a shrimp."

"But—"

"Just wait 'til you get older. Then you can volunteer, if we're not all blown up by then." End of conversation. Nothing a kid hates more than being told he or she's too young.

Over the months, August continued to report at home about his volunteer duty, jazzing it up to impress the rest of his family. His father's stories certainly impressed Arthur. The seed had been planted. It just needed to be fertilized and watered. Arthur's mind took care of those duties.

Warren's father was also an Operation Skywatch volunteer, but his son never expressed an interest in venturing up to the observation booth.

# # #

Once school went back into session in September of 1951, Arthur and Warren made sure to see each other on the weekends. One mid-October Saturday, Arthur and Rex showed up at Warren's house just as lunch was being served. Although he had just eaten, Arthur happily wolfed down a second lunch that consisted of hot dogs, sauerkraut and beans. Rex, having made one of his rare visits with his master to the Howell property, graciously waited outside until they were done.

After lunch, and with Arthur's belly bulging, the two boys hit the streets. As was often the case, they had no destination in sight. During their stroll, they reached the Jablonskis' farm on Old Post Road and saw kids playing football on an untilled field. Taking a seat on the ground near one of the designated end zones, they watched the game. Rex watched too, but he soon got restless and headed for the stables to socialize with the farm animals. Cows, goats, hens, pigs—Rex was on good terms with all of them.

Because he was old enough, Warren was invited to join one of the two teams but he declined. As they watched the game, Arthur asked Warren a few times to explain what was going on and the game's rules, but Warren couldn't answer his questions, insisting, "It's a dumb game anyway." Although the two sides were playing touch football, at times things got quite rough. With tempers already flaring on both sides, an argument broke out over whether the quarterback had been over the line of scrimmage when he completed a pass; it was difficult to determine as there were no yard lines or hash marks. Each side dug in, defending what it felt the ruling should be. The verbal dispute led to some pushing and shoving and then a fight broke out between Billy Chamberlain and Corky Smithers. Billy was the toughest kid in Suassa Park and he lived up to his reputation. He put on a boxing exhibition at his opponent's expense. Landing several close-fisted punches in the stomach, he was kind enough to use open hands on Corky's face. Those slaps landed more with a humiliating than punishing effect. The conflict ended voluntarily when it was clear that Corky was being completely outclassed. By that time, both teams had lost interest in continuing the game and the players dispersed.

Arthur and Warren got up and resumed their walk through the neighborhood. Many houses were already decorated for Halloween. The boys debated stealing or wrecking some of the ornaments, but didn't want to take the chance of getting caught and ruining their own chances for participating in a successful night of trick-or-treating.

They passed by the Willets residence all the way at the far end of Hawthorne Street. Mr. Willets was outside washing his car. He spotted the boys and, looking at Arthur, commented, "You're that Berndt kid, aren't you?"

"Yes, sir."

"What are you doing in this neck of the woods?"

"Nothing."

"You better not be up to no good. I'm warning you. "

"I'm not, sir."

"I work with your old man. He told a couple of us to keep an eye out for you. Don't make me give any bad reports."

"No, sir."

That brief conversation unsettled Arthur and he convinced Warren they should return to Warren's house. They did and watched TV. Arthur even got treated to a Super Coola grape soda. He was surprised that it didn't taste any better than his lowly Jud's did. Maybe not even as good.

After a while, the two got bored and went outside again. It was getting near four o'clock and Arthur was expected to be home by no later than five. Nonetheless, when Warren suggested they look around for something to do, Arthur agreed. Rex, who again had waited loyally outside the Howell residence, tagged along.

Their travels to nowhere in particular took them onto Emerson Street and, ultimately, in front of the Operation Skywatch observation tower. They both looked up at the mammoth fortress in awe. Arthur was so short he couldn't quite see the booth jutting out at the very top. To these two kids, the tower qualified as the eighth wonder of the world, even if they didn't know what any of the other seven were.

Warren got the ball rolling. "I bet you wouldn't climb up it."

"I bet you wouldn't either."

"I bet you first."

"So?'

"So, if you don't, it means you're chicken."

It was easy to get Arthur to do things he shouldn't, if not doing them made him a coward in someone else's eyes. It was clear: if he scaled it, he earned Warren's approval. If he didn't, he earned Warren's scorn.

From Emerson Street, the two trudged up a slope and, reaching its top, ignored a pair of No Trespassing signs and walked underneath the tower.

There was another sign next to the first flight of steps: No children under twelve permitted on tower. Youth volunteers ages 12-18 must be accompanied by an authorized adult. Arthur wasn't sure what some of the bigger words meant. Warren told him not to worry about it.

When they got to the beginning of the staircase, the youngsters looked upwards at what lay ahead for the adventurous soul who dared initiate a climb to the top. Arthur had second thoughts. "I don't know...It's kinda late."

Warren did an amateurish imitation of a chicken clucking.

Arthur got the message. Even though every bone in his body screamed Don't do it!, that warning was quickly trumped by his dire need to impress Warren, no matter what it took.

He walked over to the stairs, put his foot on the first step, and began the upward climb. He noticed right away that the railings on each side of the steps were too far apart; he could not reach both while ascending the tower. He could hold on to a railing on one side with both hands, but that was too scary as there was nothing but three feet of wide open space between the railing and the steps. He panicked at the idea of being so close to either end of the step and falling off. Instead, he opted to crawl on his hands and knees in the middle of each step. Up he went.

Halfway towards his destination, Arthur looked down and could make out the faint images of Warren and Rex staring up at him.

"Keep going." That was the command coming from ground level.

Arthur dutifully obeyed. All the while he battled conflicting fears: that of falling versus that of failure in front of his friend.

When he'd scaled about two-thirds of the steps he stopped to rest. He was afraid to look down from such a height so he simply shouted, "Is this far enough?"

"No. Keep going. Wave to me from the top."

Rex began whining, while Arthur got back to the task at hand. Each step he took ratcheted up the fear to an ever higher level. If the plank under him creaked, Arthur froze in place and remained there until the panic returned to a manageable level. He was a nervous wreck, but a functioning one. This imposing tower could never terrify him like his father did. That knowledge gave him the courage to carry on. The determination came from his abject need to please Warren.

The staircase took a final turn and, coming around it, he saw a small wooden gate that signaled, after five more steps, he'd reach the top. Still on his hands and now sore knees, he scaled the final steps. His plan was to rest a bit and refortify his nerves inside the booth before dealing with the task of going back down. Ah, the booth! A sanctuary with its wraparound walkway, all enclosed by a five-foot-high wooden barrier.

Reaching the top step, he cautiously stood up and prepared to open the gate. It was padlocked! There he was, ninety feet above ground, a stupid gate standing between him and the safety of the booth. Arthur stared at the wooden enclosure, an oasis he'd never be able to reach. Instead, he was stuck on the tower's highest step, gripping on to the gate for dear life. He didn't dare look down below, terrified by the near-impenetrable darkness that now enveloped him and hid what he knew awaited below if he fell.

"Warren."

"Are you up there yet?" Even though it was now too dark for the boys to see each other, Warren insisted, "Let me see your hand over the wall."

"I can't get in. There's a door. It's locked."

"Don't be chicken. Climb over it."

"I can't do it. I can't. It's too high for me."

"Chicken."

"Stop it!"

Warren misspelled his taunt out loud. "C-h-i-k-i-n."

Arthur could see over the trees all the way down to the village and the harbor. With nightfall, lights were now sporadically coming on in different parts of the town. He had never been this high up in his entire life. Having finally gotten what he had longed for, Arthur was in no mood to celebrate. Fear tends to put a damper on things.

Even if he'd had the stomach to enjoy the view, there was no time for that anyway. He had to get off this wooden monster and fast! It was getting darker by the second and he pictured his parents at home—his mom fretting, his father fuming. As tough a choice as it was to make, he decided he'd rather deal with Warren Howell's ridicule than with his own father's ire.

Though wanting so badly to cry, he forced himself not to, afraid he'd lose his balance and fall if he did. Arthur was having second thoughts. He was terrified he would never be able to descend the tower on his own. Perhaps putting himself in this perilous predicament was worse than dealing with his father. If he couldn't get down by himself, would anyone come up the tower to rescue him? What if the police were called? What awaited him if he survived? Whoever saved him would tell his parents for sure. Why did he ever do this?

The only way possible to be held unaccountable for this stunt? Get back down unassisted and then concoct a story his parents would buy, both daunting tasks indeed.

His dream of reaching the booth shattered, Arthur readied himself for the descent. Picturing what would happen if his dad found out about this adventure gave him all the incentive he needed to do what he had to do to get out of this quandary. But that didn't make the job at hand any easier.

"I'm coming down."

"Chicken."

So much for encouragement from his sidekick.

Taking a deep breath, Arthur forced himself to turn around and sit on the top step. After summoning up sufficient courage, he got back on his feet and began his descent, taking each step ever so slowly. To make it all the more perilous, he was wearing hard-soled, loose-fitting, hand-me-down shoes, not the recommended footwear for illegal tower climbing.

In a fruitless attempt to avoid seeing what lay waiting below should he fall, Arthur squinted his eyes, leaving them open just enough to watch his own footwork. After negotiating the first few steps, Arthur sat down on one. As frightening as scaling the tower had been, coming down it turned out to be even worse. Too fear-stricken to take another step, he burst out in tears.

Warren heard him. "Chicken."

Out of the darkness above came a sobbing, "Shut up."

Warren did his poor imitation of a chicken one more time.

It was now past six o'clock. Things were beginning to rapidly darken all around Arthur. Ironically, he found his precarious perch a bit less frightening, because the ground below had faded into obscurity, helping him lose sense of exactly how high up he was.

He called to his friend, "Warren."

No answer.

"Warren. Warren!"

No response. Was his pal gone or just playing a prank?

"Warren!" Every time Arthur called, the only feedback he got was more whining and barking from Rex.

After negotiating some more steps, he sat down again, pondering his fate while recharging his mind's "courage batteries."

So much adrenaline had pumped through his system that he felt an exhausted kind of calm, like that after a storm, although this storm was not over. He came up with a less frightening way to resume his descent. Rather than standing up, he'd bounce from step to step on his butt, using his hands as support to cushion the landing on each step.

Downward he went. Forty steps to go, then thirty-five, thirty, twenty-five. Along the way he occasionally yelled to Rex, finding comfort in his dog's responses. When he reached the final fifteen steps, he regained the nerve to look at the now visible ground—seeing it as a welcoming friend rather than the life-threatening enemy it had been only moments ago.

Feeling much more confident, Arthur stood up and handled the last fifteen steps like a pro. A strong, gusty wind kicked up, considerately having delayed its arrival until the youngster neared the end of his perilous mission. Had it arrived just a few minutes earlier, Arthur's scary situation up above would have been that much scarier. When he came to the bottom five steps, he could see Rex waiting, dancing in anticipation. Arthur jumped off the last step, rejoicing when his feet hit the ground. Rex ran to him, jumped up, and slobbered all over his face. Now the dog's whining was out of pure joy.

As for Warren, he was nowhere to be seen.

Having just escaped one dilemma, Arthur faced another. He knew he'd be getting home very late and would have to face the consequences. He began a reluctant walk back to his house, searching for an alibi on the way. It should have been creepy walking through the neighborhood in the dark, but Arthur was too busy drumming up an alibi to notice. Besides, walking with Rex on paved streets in Suassa Park at night was literally child's play compared to trekking alone through the woods after sunset, something Arthur had occasionally done when things at home were just too unbearable.

Arthur turned onto Lowell Place and walked up to his house. The thought struck him that, for his part, Rex didn't have to explain anything. What a lucky dog!

What kind of mood would his father be in? There was nothing to do but face the music. Hand trembling, Arthur took a deep breath, opened the front door and went inside, resigned to his fate. He found both his parents sitting at the dining room table.

Marguerite's weary eyes betrayed the fact she had been crying. They again began to water. "Arthur, where were you? I called Warren's mother. Warren didn't even know where you were."

August expressed his concern less warmly. "Where the hell were you?"

The young boy had his alibi ready. "Rex got away. I had to hunt for him."

"Well, for Chrissake, keep a better eye on him, dammit."

That was it. Sometimes, Arthur caught a break. He had dodged two bullets—one manmade, the other a man—in the same day.

# Chapter 13

ALTHOUGH WARREN HAD LEFT Arthur to fend for himself on the tower, the younger boy accepted that betrayal and the two continued to hang out together. On Halloween, they trick-or-treat-ed together, like big brother, little brother.

Then, one day, Warren crossed a line. Friend or no friend, he did something that Arthur just couldn't abide by.

The two were sitting in the Howells' backyard, hanging out the way they often did, having no plan of action and bored to the max. After being let out of the Berndt house, Rex quickly tracked down his young master. Tail wagging, he happily ambled onto the Howell property and joined the two youngsters.

Warren got up and began collecting a few loose stones.

"Whatta ya doing?"

"I know. Let's throw rocks at your dog and see what he does."

Not waiting for Arthur's response, the older boy hurled a stone that hit the dog squarely on his head. Whimpering in pain, Rex quickly separated himself from the boys. Rattled by the sneak attack, the dog ignored Arthur's command to come to him. Instead, from a distance he eyed the two youths warily.

"Hey, what didchya do that for?"

Ignoring the younger boy's question, Warren reached into his pocket and pulled out another rock. He began inching his way towards the dog, preparing to launch a second missile at his four-legged target. Arthur leapt to his feet, charged at Warren, and tackled him from behind, both boys falling to the ground. Caught off guard, Warren dropped his ammunition. He easily escaped from the younger boy's grasp and both scrambled to their feet. Arthur began swinging his arms like windmills, blindly throwing punches, very few landing. Having a few more pounds and inches than his opponent, Warren soon took control of the scuffle. He threw Arthur back on the ground and sat on top of him, pinning his arms to the ground. Rex rushed over and began nipping and pulling at Warren's shirtsleeve. One of the nips hit home and Warren let out an "Ow!" Rex continued lunging at the older boy, forcing him to release his hold on Arthur so he could use his arms to fend off the aggressive canine.

"Stop him! Stop that mutt! Get that darn dog offa me."

"Ya gotta let me up."

Warren didn't need further persuading. He got up wailing "Mommy!" and hightailed it for his house, Rex staying behind with his young owner.

After conducting a medical exam of his dog to the best of a seven-year-old's abilities, Arthur happily declared his patient unharmed. The youngster gave his dog a couple of pats on the rump and an enthusiastic "Good boy!"

Dolores Howell came outside. This was the first time the young boy had ever seen her wearing a frown. "Arthur, what happened here?"

"Nothing."

"No, it wasn't 'Nothing.' Your dog went after my son. Why?"

"I don't know. Well, Warren thr—"

"Arthur, you can't bring your dog over here with you anymore. He bit Warren. It's not too bad, but just the same... You're welcome here, but not that dog. He can't be trusted."

Arthur silently refused the standing invitation. He had already made up his mind. Neither he nor his dog would be setting foot on the Howell property again. As far as Arthur was concerned, Warren had done something unpardonable. Rex wasn't a person, but, to Arthur, he wasn't "just" a dog either. In his young master's eyes, Rex stood in a class all by himself.

# Chapter 14

"RAUS! RAUS! GET OUT of bed!"

Arthur was jolted out of a deep sleep at two in the morning, first by his father's screaming and then by his father's hard calloused hands. They were wrapped tightly around the young boy's neck, so tightly that Arthur began gagging. Not relaxing his grip, August pulled his son out of bed and threw him on the floor.

"You goddamn pig. You did it again! Get into the bathroom!"

Arthur, bursting into tears, quickly got to his feet and ran for his life into the bathroom, his father kicking at him from behind.

Arthur knew the drill. He had committed the crime and must face the punishment. He turned on the only faucet he was allowed to, the one marked "hot".

"You stop pissing on yourself, then there'll be no more baths."

Arthur watched in terror as the bathtub filled with steamy water. Reluctantly, he stripped off his urine-soaked pajamas. He knew what awaited him—excruciating searing pain—but his father was watching and would not tolerate any delay.

Arthur had already gone through this so many times that, in some sick way, it had become routine. He couldn't count on his mother to rescue him; she stayed in bed throughout her son's ordeal. The young boy knew better than to ask for mercy. Would more crying help? No. Besides, he had already run out of tears on the way to the bathroom.

He inched his way into the tub, stepping into water that reached just below his knees. His body trembled at the thought of sitting down, but he knew his father wouldn't leave the bathroom until he did. Slowly he sunk into the boiling pit, hearing "Chickenshit!" and "Bedwetter!" screamed into his ears. The combination of hot water and skin already irritated by urine produced a burning stinging sensation—one that had Arthur gasping for breath.

His father left the bathroom. Mercifully, Arthur was alone. In his world, solitude had its benefits.

Early in his life, Arthur had discovered that rapidly opening and then closing his legs together in near-scalding water produced the illusion that the water wasn't so unbearably hot. He did that now while the water slowly cooled. Then Arthur soaped himself, rinsed, and dried off.

The rest of the ritual was always the same. After putting on clean pajamas, he stripped his bed and, taking the soiled sheets and pajamas in hand, he went downstairs. On the way to the cellar, he met his dog in the kitchen. Rex got up, yawned, stretched, and greeted Arthur with a wagging tail. Together they descended the steps into the basement. Arthur filled up the large washbasin with water, added soap, and washed the sheets by hand. The washing machine could not be used. That was part of the punishment.

On to the next step. Arthur went outside with his dog and a basket of wet laundry. At least at this early hour, there were no prying neighbors to add to the youngster's shame, as they did on so many other occasions when he was forced to broadcast his crime in broad daylight. While he labored to hang up the heavy water-soaked sheets on a clothesline he could barely reach, his dog frolicked in the backyard. Only Rex thought they were having fun.

Chore done, back inside Arthur and his dog went. Arthur gave Rex a gentle pat on the head and left him in the kitchen. He stumbled through the darkened house until he got upstairs to his bedroom. Using clean sheets obtained from the linen closet, he made his bed in the haphazard manner of a seven-year-old. Finally, all work done, he lay down to go back to sleep. This ritual had been going on for several years and there was no end in sight.

The only thing that could make a night like this even worse? Wetting the bed a second time.

# # #

Bed-wetting. It was Arthur's cross to bear.

His parents tried various stratagems to "cure" their son. Forbidding him to eat or drink after mid-afternoon produced unsatisfactory results. Enemas likewise. At times, Arthur attempted to force himself to stay awake through the entire night. Such attempts always failed. Before going to bed, on his knees the youngster also desperately prayed to God for help in staying dry, with very mixed results.

The most utilized intervention was conducted by Arthur's father. He'd set the alarm clock to ring at 2 A.M., get up, and check on his son. If he was dry, he'd be marched into the bathroom with orders to urinate. If he was wet, all hell broke loose. Wetting his bed up to five nights a week guaranteed up to five fearsome middle-of-the-night visits from his father every week—complete with torturous baths. Hanging out the bed sheets (sometimes in full view of the neighbors), occasionally going to school still smelling of urine, not being able to attend overnight functions for fear of wetting a bed, and having more people discover his dirty secret—all became constant humiliations.

This ritual had been going on for as long as the young boy could remember, and there was no end to it in sight. Those nights his father found him dry were miraculous reprieves for the young boy, sporadic pardons from punishment—pardons he had no idea how to make permanent.

# # #

One morning, Arthur woke up soaked and decided he just couldn't face the music. Even though he knew he was only postponing the inevitable, he lingered in bed instead of rising. Everyone else, except Liz (away at college), was already downstairs eating breakfast. Arthur remained upstairs, a prisoner trapped in his own smelly bed.

It became obvious to his family why he was still in bed. The sarcastic comments started floating up from the kitchen. Finally, August and Ruth came upstairs, stuck their heads into Arthur's bedroom, and taunted him. One particularly creative phrase uttered by his sister: "Wet-bedded woodpecker". For the two mockers, it would be a favorite for years to come.

# Chapter 15

WHILE HIS FRIENDSHIP WITH Warren had ended in late autumn of 1951, earlier that fall Arthur had also initiated a relationship with an older married woman—Joyce Goward, his second-grade teacher. The two hit it off immediately. The first day of school Arthur grabbed the front seat directly in front of her desk. He quickly got into the habit of raising his hand in response to all the teacher's questions, whether he knew the answers or not. In fact, his hand often went up so he could pose questions of his own. "Are we having a spelling test today?" "Can I clean the blackboard?" "What's for lunch today?" A small kid making small talk.

Arthur would do anything to keep this teacher's attention. He got in the habit of straightening up her desk every morning before class started. One day, in a classic show of generosity and affection, Arthur came back from the cafeteria and put the apple that had come with his lunch on his teacher's desk when she wasn't looking. He wanted her to have it but didn't want her to know he had placed it there; that would be too embarrassing. When she spotted the apple, Mrs. Goward exclaimed, "Oh, who was so thoughtful?" Several students pointed at Arthur. The young boy didn't have to say a word; the answer was written all over his beet red face.

# # #

# Chapter 15

Arthur could not rein in his antisocial tendencies, even when it meant risking the good standing he enjoyed with his teacher.

Arriving at school early one morning, Arthur was hanging his jacket up in the cloakroom that adjoined the classroom, when he spotted the end of a candy bar sticking out of the pocket of another kid's coat. His first instinct was to take it; thinking that too risky, he fought off the urge and went back into the classroom. For the rest of the school day the candy bar kept popping up in his imagination.

When the bell rang at 2:15 p.m., Mrs. Goward conducted an orderly dismissal of her students. By now, everyone in the classroom knew the drill. While children that were in walking distance of school impatiently waited, children that took a bus got their jackets first, based on the destination of the school buses lined up outside. The first bus went to Shoreham, next was Wading River, then Coram, etc. The teacher had each child go into the cloakroom separately to avoid a stampede. Until today, only Johnny Archibald had gotten onto the Shoreham bus. Now, when Mrs. Goward told Johnny he could get his coat, Arthur raised his hand.

"Yes, Arthur?"

"I go on that bus, too."

"Since when? I thought you lived in Suassa Park."

"We moved."

"Oh, all right. You can get your coat as soon as Johnny comes out. Do you like your new home?"

"It's okay."

When Johnny, busily putting on his coat, exited the cloakroom, Arthur went into it. He took both his jacket and the candy bar he had coveted all day. It didn't fit completely into any of his pockets, so he dropped it down the open top of his shirt and buttoned up his jacket. Then he headed out of the cloak room, out the classroom, out the building and out of sight, stopping himself behind a huge oak tree on High Street, beyond the range of any potential roving eyes. He reached down the front of his shirt, and pulled out his prize. It was an Oh Henry! candy bar, one of his favorites. He devoured it and headed home.

This all had happened on a Friday. The following Monday, Mrs. Goward made an announcement to the class. "Billy told me that he had a candy bar in his coat pocket that went missing Friday. Does anyone have anything to say about that? Anyone have anything to do with its disappearance? As I always tell you, honesty is the best way to repair something you've done that you shouldn't have."

Arthur weighed his options. If he admitted being the culprit, he might impress Mrs. Goward with his courageous confession and get some of that positive attention he thirsted for. If it were to come from the teacher he worshipped, that would be all the better. But, after turning himself in, he was sure she would tell his parents what he had done, and that would lead to a whole lot of negative attention. The deciding factor? If he kept his mouth shut, Arthur envisioned reaping a harvest of goodies that, every school day, would be there for the taking in the cloakroom. Who knows what he might find in his classmates' jackets? The anticipated thrill of such a treasure hunt convinced Arthur to keep his lips zipped.

A few days later Arthur was alone in the coatroom getting his jacket before supposedly getting on the bus to Shoreham. He spotted a bulge in Richard's jacket and found a Three Musketeers poorly hidden in an inside jacket pocket. Grabbing it, Arthur then walked along the entire row of jackets, feverishly searching as many pockets as he could, looking for more valuables. He got some gum and a girl's comb for his efforts, and then a bonanza—two boxes of Smith Brothers Wild Cherry cough drops, way better than Luden's in Arthur's opinion. He hurried out of the cloakroom just in time to hear his teacher ask, "What took you so long?" His less-than-honest reply: "I don't know." Arthur then left the classroom, allegedly heading for the Shoreham bus.

The perpetrator kept perpetrating; he couldn't stop himself. During the next few days, the spree netted Arthur more candy, some marbles, and a few coins.

The complaints started coming in at a fast and furious pace. Arthur sensed his classmates' suspicion and with good reason. He had a lengthy history of taking anything that wasn't nailed down, sometimes in broad daylight, all the while protesting his innocence. His teacher had lectured the young boy more than once about the evils of stealing. In an attempt to distance himself from the current cloakroom crimes, Arthur claimed he'd had some baseball cards stolen, feigning outrage and adding his name to the class-action suit against the not-yet-officially-named defendant. His schoolmates were unimpressed by Arthur's tale of woe.

The heat was on, so he reluctantly forced himself to stop the pilfering. Making his task mandatory, though no less uncomfortable, Mrs. Goward temporarily allowed her students to keep any valuables, especially of the edible variety, inside their desks. Arthur had to spend all day in class surrounded by tempting gifts ironically both within and yet out of his reach. This system proved impractical, as the kids spent much of the school day opening and closing their desktops just so they could periodically feast their eyes on the sweet treats that lay inches from their grasp.

The teacher switched gears. The students once again were to leave treats and other personal items in their jackets or coats during the school day, but now their teacher had a student monitor each student's activity inside the coat room at dismissal. This led to far less distraction during the school day, while also keeping a young kleptomaniac at bay.

After several weeks of having to lie low, Arthur's addiction got the best of him. One day Mrs. Goward stepped out of the classroom, giving students a reading assignment to complete in silence. As soon as she exited, Arthur went into the coatroom, in full view of his fellow students, announcing, "I have to get a pencil."

Several classmates chimed in. "You don't need a pencil to read."

"You're not supposed to leave your seat. I'm telling."

"Better not take my stuff."

Undaunted, Arthur proceeded to make a particularly impressive haul from various jackets: a Hershey's bar, an oversized rubber eraser, some wallet-sized photos of people he didn't know and fourteen cents. He headed back into the classroom, only to find his teacher already there. She summoned the young boy up to her desk and asked, "Arthur, do you have anything in your pockets that doesn't belong to you?"

"No, Mrs. Goward."

"Can I ask you to empty your pockets please?"

Arthur wanted to say "No!" again, but sensed that would further complicate things. Better to lie his way out of things. He pulled out the chocolate bar. That got a quick response from his classmate Andy. "Hey, that's mine."

Arthur stood his larcenous ground. "No it isn't. It's mine. I bought it."

Then out came the fourteen cents and the eraser.

Phillip cried out, "He has my eraser." George ran up from the back of the class. "That's my money. That's what I brought, two nickels and four pennies."

Arthur stuck to his guns, insisting everyone else was lying. Why couldn't a candy bar, an eraser and some change be his? In his book, if he couldn't be proven guilty, that made him innocent.

"Anything else, Arthur? What's that?" she asked, pointing to what she had spotted sticking out of his shirt pocket.

"Oh, I was going to give them to you. I found them on the floor." He pulled out the purloined photos and gave them to the teacher. She looked at one and described it to the class.

"This is a photograph of a young man in military gear."

"Is he waving?" asked Allison.

"Yes, he is."

"That's my dad!" Allison shouted.

Addressing the victims of the class's seven-year-old bandit, Mrs. Goward said, "All right. Come up to the desk—in an orderly fashion—and take what belongs to you. Only what's yours."

As students retrieved their pilfered possessions, the teacher, a mixture of disappointment and disapproval on her face, turned to Arthur and said, "I think you have some explaining to do."

The dismissal bell rang, but Arthur wouldn't be saved by it. As his classmates began an enthusiastic departure, Arthur remained at his desk per his teacher's request. Mrs. Goward walked over to one of the large classroom windows, opened it, and called out to the driver sitting in the lead bus. "Sir, Arthur Berndt will be out in a minute. I have to talk to him."

"Arthur who?"

"Berndt. He goes with John on your bus."

"Since when? He's not on my list. Just the Archibald kid. Hasn't been anyone else from the second grade all year."

"Are you sure?"

"How do you spell it?"

"B-e-r-n-d-t."

"Nothing here on the list. Ask him what street he lives on."

Mrs. Goward turned to Arthur and did just that. He had no answer. The young boy was crying. Turning back to the open window, she asked the driver, "So, you're sure Arthur doesn't take your bus?"

"He hasn't up to now."

"Okay. He won't be today either."

As a punishment for misbehavior, Mrs. Goward usually dished out a written assignment of a single sentence to be written fifty times—100 hundred times, if dealing with a really serious infraction. Arthur had to write I will not steal or lie 150 times, his crime having risen to the level of a felony. A grueling chore indeed, but nothing compared to the kind of discipline his father would administer if he ever found out what his son had done.

That night Arthur was careful to complete the assignment in his bedroom, far from his parents' prying eyes. He was determined to make sure this entire incident flew under their radar.

For the remainder of the school year, Mrs. Goward had a student stand inside the cloakroom as a monitor both before class began and when it ended. On the rare occasion she left the classroom during the school day, a student was given the duty of reporting anyone leaving their seat in her absence. No more thievery. Arthur's crime spree had been stopped in its tracks. The youngster took consolation in the fact his parents hadn't found out. Short-lived consolation, as it turned out.

# # #

A month after Arthur's cloakroom capers had been foiled, the marking period ended, and report cards were issued a few days later. Mrs. Goward handed them out to her students to take home and have signed by a parent or guardian.

Port Jefferson Elementary School student reports opened like greeting cards. On the left side were the student's academic grades and on the right side, an area to evaluate a student's social skills. Arthur took a peek at his report card. The youngster's grades were more than acceptable, even by his parents' demanding standards. The other side of the card listed various criteria that measured a child's capacity to socialize. On Arthur's card one of the criterion, respects the rights of others, had been underlined in red ink followed by the words "fails to," also in red ink and handwritten by the teacher. Arthur wasn't exactly sure what the words meant, but the fact that there was a lot of red ink left him convinced he was in trouble. How could the teacher he idolized turn on him like this? He needed to come up with an explanation and quickly.

Walking home from school, the youngster concocted alibis:

*It was supposed to be on another kid's report card. That's what the teacher told me. She couldn't take it off because it was in ink*

*I got in a fight with Roger Davis. He started it. I got the blame.*

*I cut ahead of two kids on the lunch line and a teacher saw me.*

Lame excuses. Arthur had no confidence that any of them would hold up.

When he got home, Arthur gave the report card to his mom, clinging to the hope she'd sign it, give it back to him, and let the whole thing slide. She didn't.

"Oh, what's this rights of others all about?"

"I don't know, Mom."

"Didn't Mrs. Goward explain it to you?"

"No."

"Well, I certainly need to know."

Later that day, August tried to shake an answer out of his son, but Arthur stuck to his claim of ignorance. Marguerite signed the report card and Arthur gave it to his teacher the next day. Case closed? Not quite.

One day during the following week, Arthur arrived home from school to find his mom on the phone, a disappointed look on her face. She was talking to his teacher and getting the whole story. After hanging up the phone, Marguerite turned to her son.

"How could you do such a thing?"

"What, Mom?"

"You know very well what! I just got off the phone with Mrs. Goward. She thinks you've been taking other people's things all year. At least until you got caught."

Short on alibis, Arthur instead pleaded for mercy. "Please Mom, don't tell dad, please?"

"Well, he's your father. Don't you think he has a right to know?"

"I promise I won't do it again. I really promise. I really mean it."

"Whatever will it take to get you to stop stealing? Why on earth do you keep doing it?"

"I don't know. But I won't do it anymore. I really mean it this time. Just please don't tell dad. I'll do the dishes—wash 'em and dry 'em—the rest of this week...and next week too. For free!"

"And how would you explain that to your father? You hate doing the dishes. I don't know...Don't go anywhere. Your dad'll be home in a bit. We're going to eat in about a half an hour."

"Please, Mom."

"I'll have to think about it."

The young boy went upstairs. He fiddled with a model ship he was building but didn't really have his heart in it. He lay down on his bed, staring at the ceiling. He'd have given anything at that moment to be in the shoes of any other kid in the world. Then, his mind began singing a more optimistic song. Every once in a while his mother covered for him; maybe this would be one of those whiles.

Arthur cringed when he heard the family car pull into the driveway. His pulse sped up, his hands got clammy, and his mind raced, fear and hope battling each other to control the young boy's thoughts. He got up and sat on the edge of his bed, straining to hear the conversation about to begin downstairs, all the while praying his mother would have pity on him. Mrs. Goward hadn't. As the only person he'd ever completely trusted, she had proven to be untrustworthy.

"What a day, what a day. I am the only son of a bitch that wants to work in that place. Americans are a bunch of loafers."

"Well, you know the way you work...You can't expect everyone to work that hard."

"Yeah, well a lot of people are making a lot more money than I do, and doing nothing for it."

"Well anyway, we're having something for dinner you'll like. Baked chicken."

"So where's everybody?"

"Ruth's visiting over at the Regalmutos' house. Arthur's upstairs...Oh, by the way, I spoke to Art's teacher today (upstairs, the bottom dropped out of Arthur's stomach). She's a very nice lady. About that comment she made on Art's report card...Now, I don't want you to get upset. Arthur had a little problem—"

"Let me hear it. What kind of problem? What's he done now, dammit?"

Marguerite proceeded to give her son cover. "Well he says he mistakenly took another boy's jacket—it looked just like his—and put it on at the end of school. He insists he didn't know there was candy and money in the jacket. It only happened that one time, but Mrs. Goward was concerned enough to note it on his report card."

"So, what did she do about it? That little sneak. There's no way he did that by mistake. What did she do?"

"Well, she had a long talk with him. She had him do a writing assignment. And she mentioned there was a problem on the report card."

"And that's it? She's too easy on him, just like you. You women are naïve. What did he tell you? That little shit's going to wind up in reform school. I'll bet that's where his pal O'Brien wound up."

"He swore it was an accident and wouldn't happen again."

"I'll say it won't happen again."

August slammed his lunchbox on the dining room table and, without taking off his coat, started walking upstairs.

Arthur still sitting on the edge of his bed, feet not quite reaching the floor, awaited his fate.

# Chapter 16

FOLLOWING HIS BRAZEN CLASSROOM stealing spree and ultimate capture, Arthur lost the blind faith he'd had in Mrs. Goward forever. She'd betrayed his trust by ratting to his parents. Arthur's already sketchy view of grownups became sketchier.

Deciding to seek friendship from among his peers, he found Walter Ostrowski, a student that had joined Mrs. Goward's class several months into the school year. Maybe Arthur was the most troublesome child in his classroom, but he had to share the title of most troubled with Walter. Walter had a moon-shaped face with slanted eyes and puffy cheeks, was on the short side, and quite chubby. Because of his features, a few of his classmates called him Chinaman. During recreation his lack of coordination was a source of amusement for his classmates. He didn't talk like the other students. Although at times he could be understood, often he stuttered or uttered nonsense syllables. He wore a contraption in one ear that no one else in the class did. When something struck the class as funny, Walter often sat impassively at his desk, unmoved by all the hilarity around him. Sometimes, trying hard to fit in, he'd eventually force an inappropriate cackle, long after the rest of the class had stopped laughing. Because of his difficulty communicating, the other students often excluded him from their activities. Due to his near dwarfish stature, his classmates had given him another derisive nickname: Little Walty.

Riddled with shame and the compulsive need to keep his family life a secret, Arthur found it difficult to socialize in a healthy way with those his own age (or any age, for that matter). He was convinced that all the kids in his class were normal—except for himself and Walter. Both were low on the classroom popularity totem pole, one for being a lying thief, the other for being odd. Sensing that Walter sat at the very bottom of that totem pole provided Arthur's fragile ego with a tiny measure of cold comfort. He knew what it felt like to be shunned and, out of a twisted feeling of superiority and comradeship, Arthur gravitated to this fellow misfit. The two boys forged a friendship.

# # #

Walter Ostrowski had difficulty with all schoolwork. One day in class Arthur's hand shot up.

"Mrs. Goward, can I help Walter?"

"What do you mean?"

"Well, if I get my stuff done, I could sit with him and help him do his."

"Hmm...I suppose so. But the two of you have to behave. And you have to be sure you finish all your work. Besides that, I don't want Walter copying your work. He'll never learn that way."

With Arthur's coaching, Walter's math skills soon began to show some improvement, but his reading remained as abysmal as ever. Early in their partnership, Arthur pretended to understand Walter when he spoke gibberish, figuring that would make his pal feel better. As time went by, he began to grasp his friend's mumbling to such a degree he could translate it for the teacher. Arthur filled dual roles as Walter's tutor and interpreter.

Once they became friends, Arthur started hanging out with Walter during noon recess. Because of his lack of physical coordination, Walter did not participate in any games his classmates played. Instead, the two boys sat on the sidelines watching others play. This was a huge sacrifice for Arthur because he loved sports activities. Occasionally Arthur entreated his companion to join whatever activity was ongoing. His pleas always fell on (partially) deaf ears.

# Chapter 17

DURING THE FIRST WEEK of the school year, Mrs. Goward had proised her class they'd be going to New York City around Christmastime to see the Ringling Bros. and Barnum & Bailey Circus show. Back then the month of December had seemed light years away to the youngsters, and the teacher's announcemet ws quickly forgotten. However, by late fall, after their teacher reminded the children of her promise, the circus became a daily topic of conversation among the students, Arthur being no exception. He had never been to a circus and now he would be going to the biggest and best in the country.

On a mid-December school day, immediately after morning attendance was taken, Mrs. Goward's students happily filed outside and onto a waiting bus. This was no ordinary school bus, but a posh charter coach with upholstered seats and even a bathroom. After a final headcount, the teacher introduced Al, the bus driver, and Miss Terry, a monitor, to the children. After reciting the code of conduct she expected every student to live up to, the teacher nodded to Al and he pulled the bus out of the school parking lot onto Tuthill Street. After reaching Main Street and chugging up the steep hill to Port Jefferson Station, the bus headed towards Route 347 to begin the long drive west to Manhattan. Along the way, the kids maintained a steady, headache-producing din that the bus driver, due to years of experience, was immune to. The teacher and the monitor weren't so lucky.

For most of the children, this would be the farthest they had ever traveled from home. Along the way, the kids took turns gazing out windows at all they passed by—the many cars, buildings, pedestrians, etc.—that easily impressed their youthful lack of worldliness. Sitting together, the class's odd couple, Arthur and Walter, were no exceptions. They chatted about all the marvelous sights, Arthur in English, Walter in a language secret to all but his sidekick.

Halfway to their destination, Walter got up, wended his way back to the bathroom, and entered it. After several minutes, another student got up to use the bathroom. He waited a bit and then began to pound on the bathroom door.

"Hey, Little Walty, you can come out now. You better come out. I have to go."

A few of the other students chimed in unison, "Oh Little Walty, come out, come out, wherever you are."

Mrs. Goward shushed the class, warning them the bus would turn around if they didn't behave. She walked back to the bathroom and asked through the door if everything was okay. From inside, Walter blurted out something indecipherable to the teacher. She asked him to repeat himself. He mumbled something that sounded like "I can't tell you."

Mrs. Goward called on Walter's confidante. "Arthur, come here please." Arthur got up and walked back to where his teacher was standing. "Please ask Walter what happened."

"Hey, Walter. What did you do?"

From behind the bathroom door, Walter uttered something. Arthur turned to his teacher: "He says he did doo-doo in his pants. He can't come out. Turning back to the door, Arthur shouted to his friend, "Hey, what happened, did you make a mess with poopies?"

"Yes."

Walter had soiled himself before in class. Sometimes the foul odor tipped off the other students that he'd had an accident, leading to merciless teasing by the usual cast of characters that Mrs. Goward was always quick to bring to a halt. After talking with Walter's mother, the teacher had packed a couple of diapers for this trip, figuring they might come in handy. She walked back to her seat, grabbed her pocket book, and returned to the rear of the bus. "Walter, I have something for you. Open the door and I'll help you."

The teacher wasn't fooling any of the passengers. One student declared with relish, "He did poopy in his pants." Another added mockingly, "I know what he's getting. He needs a diaper." Hearing that, several students stood up and craned their necks hoping to get a peek into the bathroom. Mrs. Goward turned around, flashing them a menacing look. They all immediately plopped back into their seats.

Walter opened the door, letting his teacher enter. After a few minutes, the two emerged from the bathroom, the teacher carrying a wrapped-up and foul-smelling diaper.

The word quickly scattered throughout the bus that Walter had just had his diaper changed. As he began walking up the aisle to his seat, Walter was serenaded with a chant. "Little Walty wears diapers. Little Walty wears diapers."

Mrs. Goward threatened her entire class. "Stop that this instant or we're going back home. How would all of you like that?" The only response was immediate dead silence.

The kids had quieted down, but when the teacher wasn't looking, Richard Blaskowitz "accidentally" stuck out a leg as Walter walked by him, tripping the youngster. Walter fell hard to the floor and, crying, took his seat. Arthur, seated next to him, had seen what happened and turned around to confront the instigator, sitting with a smug look in the seat directly behind him. "You tripped Walter on purpose."

Richard stood up and leaned forward in his seat. "So what are ya gonna do about it?"

"Plenty."

Richard Blaskowitz and Arthur Berndt had never gotten along. Richard took exception to the number of times he knew, but couldn't prove, Arthur had stolen stuff from him. Arthur didn't like the way Richard constantly picked on Walter. It was time to settle a score. Arthur, with his knees resting on his seat, leaned over the backrest and pushed Richard back into his seat. Richard leapt back up and, with a half-closed fist, clocked his opponent in the cheek. Arthur, used to far worse at home, shrugged off the punch. "You can't hurt me."

"Oh yeah? Bet I can."

"Yeah, try it."

Arthur stood up and, squeezing past Walter, got out into the aisle to get closer to his nemesis. Richard stood up, ready for a confrontation. Arthur rushed at him and got halfway into delivering an amateurish right cross. Halfway, because, before he could, Mrs. Goward grabbed his arm. "Arthur, you sit down right now!"

Down he sat, a bit relieved since, his bravado notwithstanding, he knew he was no match for Richard, who had a nearly ten-pound weight advantage.

"Arthur, you know how I feel about fighting."

"Richie started it."

"I don't care who started it. I'm stopping it. Richard, I want you to switch seats with Jimmy. You'll be sitting with Miss Terry the rest of the way. Arthur, I want you to turn around, go back to your seat, sit down and stay put for the rest of the ride. If you two don't behave, you'll be responsible for the whole class missing out on the circus. You understand?"

"Yes, Mrs. Goward," both boys said in unison.

The remainder of the trip into New York City was uneventful.

# # #

Manhattan. Thirty-fourth Street and 8th Avenue. Mrs. Goward pointed out Madison Square Garden to her class as they passed it. Twenty necks craned, twenty sets of eyes gaped and twenty mouths gasped in unison.

After the bus was parked in a nearby garage, the youngsters piled out and headed on foot for the circus, escorted by their three adult guardians. The skyscrapers, ultra-heavy traffic, and a seemingly seamless mob of people were all first experiences for Arthur and every single one of his classmates. But even these marvels couldn't distract the children very long. With every step the youngsters took closer to their ultimate destination, all they talked about was the circus.

Madison Square Garden—Arthur had never seen anything like it. He'd watched some events televised from the arena at home on a fourteen-inch television screen but in person everything became a hundred times more awe-inspiring. The building, the crowd, the noise—all were on a scale beyond anything Arthur's active mind had ever conjured up.

It wasn't long before the action began. Good thing, too, because Arthur's class was bursting at the seams with restless anticipation. Down below there were three huge rings, just as advertised. Kids' eyes darted back and forth, hoping not to miss one second of action in any of the ovals. There were acrobatic horseback riders, trapeze artists, more-than-one-trick ponies, knife throwers, trained elephants, sword swallowers, the list went on. More than enough to keep Mrs. Goward's charges enthralled.

Of course, there were clowns, acting as silly as...clowns. As part of their performance one jokester rolled out a cannon, daring another of his cohorts to get into it. After much coaxing, in he went. Boom! Out came a flying clown, landing safely in a net that, until that moment, had gone unnoticed by virtually everyone in the crowd. Most adults in the audience no doubt did notice the ever-so-thin wire attached to the "flying clown," but the children chalked the whole thing off as nothing less than pure magic.

Right after that initial firing of the cannon, some people clapped, other people laughed, and still others sat in stunned silence. Walter Ostrowski, however, let loose an unearthly scream and then burst out crying. Another clown got into the cannon, leading to a second hearty explosion. Tears streamed from Walter's eyes as he belatedly covered his ears with his hands. It looked like there would be more fireworks down on the circus floor so, after leaving Miss Terry and Al in charge of the rest of her group, Mrs. Goward stood up, took Walter by the hand, and hurriedly began heading towards the aisle to get out of the building. Arthur got up and joined them. His teacher turned to him. "Art, you don't have to miss the circus. I'm going to take Walter outside until things calm down."

"Why is he crying?"

"The noise is too much for him. He doesn't like loud noises. His mom warned me. The cannon took him by surprise. Kind of startled me, too. I think Walter and I are going to stay out of the building, just to be on the safe side."

"Can I go with you?"

"Well, Art, if you do, you're going to miss out on the rest of the show. I don't want to chance letting Walter back in here. We're going out to the bus." Walter pulled his teacher by the hand, desperate to escape the building.

"Okay. I'll go with you, Mrs. Goward."

"If you want to, but remember, if you leave this building, you can't change your mind."

"I won't, I promise."

Arthur heard someone behind him call out, "Hey, Smartie Artie, what's the matter? Can't take the noise?" He didn't have to look to know who was taunting him. He'd recognize Richard's voice anywhere. Ignoring his nemesis, Arthur kept walking and joined his teacher and Walter waiting for him out in the aisle.

The three headed down the escalator and out onto the street. After reaching the parking lot and boarding the bus, the trio tried to make themselves comfortable, unsuccessfully, because they were sitting in a parked, non-running vehicle surrounded by a nippy, mid-December chill. Their teacher decided they should go somewhere to warm up and grab a snack. She and her two students clambered out of the bus and headed up Eighth Avenue.

The teacher spotted a restaurant, and the three scurried to reach its doors to escape the cold. The second they entered the Horn and Hardart automat, the circus became a distant memory for the two boys. Neither had ever seen such a vast array of food all in one humongous room. The boys were awestruck. Way neater than the school cafeteria!

This was Mrs. Goward's treat. She gave each of the boys a quarter which they handed over to a female cashier who, in return, gave each youngster five nickels. The two made a beeline over to the rows of small glass doors behind which sat an unending variety of tasty treats. Picking only from the windows they were tall enough to peak into, Walter opted for macaroni and cheese, chocolate pudding, chicken noodle soup and a glass of milk while Arthur picked the hamburger steak, carrots, beets and strawberry shortcake. Their teacher selected the beef pot pie and a cup of coffee.

Arthur pictured the rest of his classmates enjoying the circus. Maybe he'd missed part of the big tent's activities, but so what? The other kids hadn't gone to an automat.

The eatery was teeming with people, forcing Mrs. Goward and Walter to sit at one table while Arthur had to take a seat at another. He was too far away from his teacher and Walter to chat with them. At his table, he was the only kid among a sea of adults, making him feel a bit like a grownup himself. There wasn't much conversation going on as people were eating in a rush, a table full of strangers thrown together for a few minutes before they went their separate ways. It reminded him of eating at home. There he always gobbled down his meal so that he could be excused from the table, putting distance as quickly as possible between himself and the fearsome stranger he called his father.

Upon leaving the eatery freshly nourished, the teacher and her two students were hit in the face by the frigid air they'd forgotten about. The three scooted back to the bus. Fortunately, it was only a brief wait before Al and Miss Terry returned from the circus, ushering the other students back onto the bus. The children were talking excitedly about the day's events. A few tried to stir up Arthur's well-known quick temper.

"Hey Artie, did you have fun with Little Walty?"

"I bet you didn't do anything. You missed the best stuff."

"Yeah, you should have seen the man doing flips on the horse."

"And this guy was throwing around and catching these big wood things that were on fire. Al says he's called a juggler."

Richard offered the unkindest cut. "While you were with Little Walty, guess who I saw—Hopalong Cassidy, the real Hopalong Cassidy. He had his white horse, too."

Another student chimed in, "Yeah, you know, Silver."

Richard mocked that comment. "No, his horse isn't called Silver. It's Topper. Silver is the Long (sic) Ranger's horse, stupid."

Arthur fought to stay cool. Luckily, it had only been Hopalong Cassidy. If he'd missed seeing Roy Rogers, his all-time favorite cowboy, Arthur would have been heartbroken.

Though keeping a lid on his anger, Arthur didn't take the taunts lying down. "Oh yeah. Well, we went to an automat, so there."

"What's an automat?"

"It's the best place in the world. I bet you've never been there."

"Ah, so what? I don't care. "

The verbal sparring petered out after Al started the bus. The kids settled down, ready for the long ride back home.

Arthur convinced himself that he did the right thing by sticking together with his pal Walter. Especially since he'd been rewarded for his good deed with a visit to a magical food emporium.

# Chapter 18

LATER THAT SCHOOL YEAR in February, Mrs. Goward made an announcement to her students.

"Class. I'm going to give you a special assignment. I want you to write a composition. It has to be at least seventy-five words long. You'll read your work in class. This is the topic..."

After the teacher wrote on the board *The most special person in my life and why I love that person,* she turned around towards the class and asked, "Can anyone of you tell me what the word love means?"

Hands in the classroom shot up.

Allison: "It means somebody is special."

Sal: "It means you like somebody because they do stuff for you."

Peter: "Somebody is extra special, more special than if you just liked them."

Nancy: "You love someone because they take care of you."

Arthur, usually eager to answer Mrs. Goward questions, didn't have his hand up for this one. Thanks to his father, the young boy had already heard a lot of four-letter words in his life, but love wasn't one of them. Certain he hadn't ever heard the word directed at him and uncertain of its meaning, the young boy tried to hide his ignorance by not participating in the class's conversation. Instead, Arthur silently squirmed in his uniqueness.

Mrs. Goward praised her class. "All very good answers. Anybody have someone in mind already?"

Several students were quick to respond.

"Oh, that's easy. My mom."

"I say my grandma. She lets me do anything"

"It's a tie. My dad and mom." That brought a protest from another student. "You can't do that. You can't pick two." Arthur couldn't pick one.

Mrs. Goward continued giving instructions. "Okay, class. Today is Monday. I want this assignment handed in on Friday. You have the rest of the week to work on it. This is to be done at home. When you get in the higher grades, you'll be getting homework on a regular basis. This is good practice for you."

That afternoon at his house Arthur looked up the word love in his parents' big dictionary and found the following: to feel great affection for, the strong affection felt by people in a romantic relationship, unselfish concern for another, affection based on admiration. Arthur was still clueless. He looked up affection, which seemed to be a key word. Definition: a feeling of liking or caring for someone or something; love. He was back to square one. The word love was just some obscure word in the dictionary, not an active part of his vocabulary.

Though the concept of love apparently was beyond his understanding, Arthur was determined to complete his teacher's assignment as if it weren't. He'd make himself fit in, even when he didn't.

Arthur thought long and hard about the people in his life. To whom might he profess his love? The first person that came to mind was Mrs. Goward. Though she could no longer be trusted to protect him from his parents, she was the warmest nonthreatening adult he knew, and that counted for a lot. Maybe, he thought, that was what other people called love. He started to write his composition but didn't get far. He quickly realized everyone in his class would laugh at him if he openly admitted his feelings for his teacher. He had to think of someone else to write about. Then it hit him—his soul mate, Rex. He began to write and the words came easily. Just like that the assignment was done, days before it was due.

At school the next day, a few of the students were talking about their special loved one.

"I put my mom because my dad died in Korea."

"My grandfather helped me to build a plane that really flies."

"I had to choose between my dad and mom. I chose my mom because she makes the best chocolate cake."

It was clear. No one else but Arthur had picked a dog to be his or her most beloved. If he read his report he knew he'd become the biggest joke in the class.

That day, after school, Arthur sat down and wrote an additional assignment continuing on the other side of the paper he had written about Rex. This set of sentences demanded all his creativity because, unlike the composition about his dog, it was a complete fabrication.

On Friday, every student got to read their written work. Arthur, usually eager to show off his English skills in front of his peers, let one after another classmate volunteer ahead of him. He paid little attention to his fellow classmates' presentations. He was too busy trying to stay afloat in a whirlpool of self-generated anxiety. Arthur offered to assist with Walter's reading ahead of his own, glad more than ever to help out his developmentally delayed buddy since it temporarily postponed his own moment of reckoning. He had now lost all confidence that his second composition would undo the embarrassment caused by the first.

After Allison read her work, it was Arthur's turn because all his classmates had taken theirs. From his seat, Arthur announced that he'd written two compositions. Richard immediately shouted out, "Teacher's pet!" After shushing him by putting her index finger in front of her mouth, Mrs. Goward turned to Arthur and said, "Go ahead, Art. I'm interested in hearing both of them." Voice trembling from nervousness, he began.

"The title is *My Pet*. My pet is a dog."

Snickers erupted throughout the room at the word "dog." Someone yelled out, "Hey, that wasn't what you were supposed to write about." Arthur's face reddened, but he read on.

"His name is Rex, but I call him Rexy a lot. When I come home from school he jumps on me. He is so playful. Wherever I go I take him. He likes it when I scratch and pet him. We had two cats and an owl. The owl died and one cat got run over. The other one we found, and the owners came to get him. Anyway Rex is so funny. We got a picture of Rex licking another dog. The picture looks funny. Once a friend of mine and I went down to a pond. There we were training Rex to swim, by mistake, he slip..."

Arthur looked up from his paper. "Mrs. Goward, I wrote 'slip' but I guess it should be 'slipped.'"

"You're right. I'm going to have everyone make any needed corrections after I look over the compositions. Please continue."

"...I mean he slipped and fell in the water and we were holding on because we were training him and we slipped with him and fell in the water too, but Rex could swim. *Dogs are lucky. They can get wet but they don't get in trouble.* Rex always begs for bones on his hind legs. I kiss my dog every night before I go to bed. I throw a stick and he goes after it. I love my pet very much. He is so frisky."

While reading, Arthur kept his eyes glued to his paper, trying his best to tune out the reaction of the other kids to his expression of love for his dog. Despite his best efforts, he couldn't help but hear the sporadic chuckles from members of his class, but halfway through the reading he'd sensed the students had begun to laugh with, not at, him. They were finding parts of his story quite amusing, more entertaining than any of their own compositions. When Arthur was done with the first part of his presentation, classmates chimed in.

Richard: "My dog Sparky is smarter. He learned to swim all by himself."

Allison: "I have a cat that comes when my dad whistles, just like a dog."

Sal: "Mrs. Goward, can I get extra credit if I write about Major? I bet he's the biggest dog in the world. He's a Russian wolfhound."

Before the teacher could answer, Arthur, now brimming with confidence, looked up from his paper and announced, "Mrs. Goward, that's the end of the first one. This is the second one."

"Go ahead, please."

"The title is *At the Lake.* One day Mother took us to the lake. We stood on the muddy shore. The sun was bright. 'I would like to row a boat,' I said. 'I'll go with you,' said Mother. We had a nice trip."

Arthur received an Excellent for the first composition and a Very Good for the second, though he'd had to work so much harder to write the latter.

Arthur couldn't shake his strong suspicion that something vital was lacking in his life. He took comfort in the fact he'd been able to hide that possibility from a roomful of people.

# Chapter 19

ARTHUR'S LIFE IN MRS. Goward's class would be relatively uneventful for the remainder of the school year. He suppressed his larcenous urges, thus preventing further bad reports from the teacher to his parents. Academically he proved himself to be as stellar a student as he had been in the first grade. Once gain only Kathryn Thomas earned better grades overall.

At home he continued enduring beatings on the all-too-frequent nights he wet his bed or for other infractions. The rest of the time, he dedicated himself to keeping a safe distance between his father and himself. One way he did that was to spend as much time out of the house as possible, with or without his dog. One day in late spring of 1952, Arthur was on such a jaunt, wandering aimlessly in the neighborhood. A voice stopped him in his tracks.

"Hey kid, ya out looking for trouble?"

Arthur turned and saw an older boy standing next to a car sitting at the far end of a driveway. "Hey, come here."

Arthur hesitated. "I can't. I'm not supposed to."

"Who the hell says so? Get your tail down here!"

Intimidated, Arthur obeyed and made the hike down the long driveway. There, with Peter Stanton, were three other teenage males.

"Let me guess, Pete. Is that your long lost son?"

"No, asshole. Guys, meet Arthur Berndt, the youngest hoodlum in the country. My old man told me people never used to lock their houses around here until Arthur came along. How old are you anyway?"

"Eight." Though the youngster didn't have a clue what "hoodlum" meant, he gladly let the word fill him to the brim with a sense of importance.

"Hey, you know your old man's nuts, don't you? He's one angry motherfucker, man. I wouldn't mess with him. I guess you're a chip off the old block, right?"

Arthur said nothing, uncertain how to answer.

"Hey, you wanna watch us work on a car, or were you on the way to rob a bank?" All four teenagers burst out in laughter.

Arthur, who often walked through the neighborhood searching for acceptance, jumped at this invitation to hang out, even though it came from an older intimidating group. The teens, all sporting greasy hands and clothes, had the hood up on a Ford Fairlane, tools scattered on its roof and around it on the ground.

While the four young men finished their cigarette break, Pete addressed the youngster in their midst. "Hey, Arthur. I almost forgot the introductions. My name's Pete. Meet my buddies. Richie, Scott and Four Eyes. Hey, Four Eyes, I don't even know your real name anymore."

"It's Dennis, dummy."

"So it is. Let's get back to work." Pete turned to Arthur. "You, try not to get in the way."

Prior to Arthur's arrival, the teens had been unsuccessful in diagnosing the Ford's problem. The engine would turn over, run briefly, and then conk out. The four mechanics resumed discussing the problem, talking in technical language totally beyond Arthur's grasp. The older boys tried several ways of correcting the problem, all to no avail. Arthur quickly got bored watching, but wasn't sure he'd get Pete's permission to leave. He stayed put, doing his best to look interested. After another hour of tinkering, the car's ailment had still not been diagnosed.

Richie wore a look of disgust. "This thing needs a new carb. Or at least the carb has to be rebuilt."

The bespectacled Dennis (aka Four Eyes) chimed in. "I still say it's dirt in the fuel line. It's probably clogged as shit."

Pete sneered at that comment. "Hey, Einstein, we already checked that out."

Richie looked at his watch. "That's it for me today, man. I gotta get to work."

Scott had a different agenda. "I'm going out with Julie. We're going to see *Bwana Devil,* man."

Four Eyes asked, "Isn't that in that 3-Dimension thing?"

"Sure as shit is! You gotta wear special glasses they give you."

Pete got in a dig. "Hey, for Dennis it'd be in 4-D."

Everyone laughed except Dennis, who got the joke, and Arthur, who didn't.

Pete, the apparent master of ceremonies, offered a suggestion with the air of a *fait accompli.* "So tomorrow, let's rebuild the carb and do something about those tires." The others all agreed on the plan.

Dennis began heading for his car. "Hey, Mister Arthur, you wanna ride home in my rod?"

"No."

"Suit yourself."

Arthur walked along the driveway, back out onto the street and headed home. Behind him, he heard the racket of three souped-up roadsters as they left the Stanton property.

On the trip back home, Arthur struggled to sort out his conflicted feelings. It had felt neat hanging out with these older kids, adult men in the youngster's eyes. But should he? He sensed this crew was a little rough around the edges. Were all teenagers like them? His big sister Liz was almost twenty and she didn't seem at all like them. Of course, she was a girl.

When Arthur got home, his mom asked, "Art, where did you go today? Rex was home all day long, waiting to go out with you."

"I went to David's house."

"David Blake?"

"Yup."

"Since when have you started to play with David?"

"Today."

"Well, I'm glad you picked him as a friend. He's your age. Not like that Buddy O'Brien. Or the Howell boy for that matter. Turned out he was older than you too."

To avoid any deeper interrogation, Arthur quickly changed the subject. "Ma, what's for supper?"

"One of your favorites, roast beef and mashed potatoes with—"

"With gravy?"

"Yes."

"Oh boy. When do we eat?"

"As soon as your father comes home."

Supper at the Berndt house was a mixed blessing. Arthur loved his mom's cooking, but always tensed up at the dinner table. Forced to sit within arm's length of his father, the young boy dreaded saying or doing something that would set off the person he most feared in the world. It didn't take much. This day, like any other, he could only hope nothing would happen to put a damper on his mother's tasty meal.

On this particular occasion, all went well and the young boy got to savor every delicious morsel his mom had prepared.

The following day, Arthur told his mom he was going to David's again because "we had fun yesterday." He rushed outside, walked down Lowell Place and onto Hawthorne Street. He passed right by the Blake residence and proceeded toward the Stantons', a block away. Nearing Pete's house, he slowed his pace a bit, thinking things over. It was exciting hanging out with older kids that drove hot rods. There was just this slender thread of a nagging doubt...he let the thread go.

# Chapter 19

When Arthur arrived, all four of his new "friends" were busy working on the Ford. They were so engrossed in their labor they ignored the youngster's arrival. Three of them were hunched over the front of the car, its hood up, putting the finishing touches on their repair work. Four Eyes, standing nearby, was the designated tool gofer.

Each of them had a can of beer near at hand. That worried Arthur. Would they get like his father did when he drank? Had making this return visit been a mistake?

Pete spotted Arthur. "Hey, you're back. I knew you had it in you. Help Four Eyes with the tools, he needs it. Dennis, teach the kid what a wrench looks like, and a screwdriver. Show him the sockets. We'll make a real mechanic out of him."

Four Eyes started pointing to and naming the different tools in the toolbox, way too fast for Arthur to absorb.

Richie chimed in, "Hey, I need a 9/16 wrench. Show the kid."

Four Eyes turned to Arthur and, brandishing a wrench, said, "It looks like this, but it's the one with the nine on the top of the sixteen. You know those numbers right?"

"Yup."

"Well, give it to Richie." After finding the requested tool, and with an air of accomplishment, Arthur handed the wrench to Richie. "Thanks, pal." In Arthur's world, any kind of compliment received went a long way. He took an instant liking to Richie.

The four older teens and their youthful assistant continued working. Instead of rebuilding the carburetor, they had decided to replace it, along with a brand-new fuel pump. After the parts were installed, Scott got in the car and started it up. The engine hummed and, when it didn't stall, the older boys congratulated themselves.

"Hey, why rebuild when you can get new parts, right?"

"Especially when those new parts are so cheap. Nothing like a 100% discount."

After a hearty round of laughter, all four teens finished off their beers in unison and cracked open new ones.

Scott invited their young guest to partake in the festivities. "Hey, Arthur. You did a good job today. Want to drink something real good?"

"Don't be stupid. He's way too young."

"Hell, I started when I was twelve, maybe eleven."

"Yeah Scott, and look what happened to you." The older boys laughed, including the target of the joke.

Pete offered his opinion. "Me, I wouldn't give that kid any. You should see how his old man is when he gets drunk. I wouldn't want to mess with him for nothing." He turned to Arthur. "I bet he kicks the shit out of you every once in a while, right?"

"Nope."

"Yeah, well—"

Richie butted in. "Hey, let's take this buggy for a ride."

The car's owner, Four Eyes, agreed. "Good idea. Pete, you drive."

They all piled into the car, except for Arthur. He stood alongside the car, not sure what to do next.

Pete craned his neck out of the driver's window. "Hey, get in the car. I'll give you a ride home."

Arthur hesitated. After the Buddy O'Brien fiasco, the youngster had been warned by his parents to stay away from older boys. He had lied to his parents about Warren Howell's age and his mother only found out Warren's real age after the two boys had stopped playing together. She kept her husband in the dark about that age discrepancy, but again warned her son even more forcefully he wouldn't be allowed to go outside by himself if he got caught with older boys one more time. The youngster knew he couldn't chance being dropped off in front of his house by this bunch. They were practically men! But he feared saying no to such an intimidating group. Four Eyes, after yelling "Get the hell in!" jumped out of the car and gave Arthur a shove in the direction of an opened car door. The youngster got the message and he clambered into the back seat. While getting in, he noticed an open case of beer sitting on the front seat between Pete and Richie.

After a couple of the boys lit up cigarettes, Peter pulled the car out onto the street and headed towards parts unknown, unknown at least to the youngest passenger. Arthur sat squished between Four Eyes and Scott. Four Eyes blew a cloud of smoke into Arthur's face. Taken by surprise, the youngster breathed it in and coughed. Scott flicked the ashes of his cigarette out the window and asked Arthur, "You want a drag?"

Pete protested from the front seat. "Hey! Don't teach the kid how to smoke. It's a bad habit."

"Bullshit. Arthur, you want to take a puff? Go ahead. It won't kill you. You're gonna do it someday anyway. Every hoodlum smokes." All four teens broke out in laughter.

Scott handed his cigarette to Arthur. The youngster had seen his father and older sister smoke. His mother hardly ever did, but she could make smoke rings. He decided he'd give it a try, especially since, by doing so, he was sure to impress his audience.

Arthur put the cigarette in his mouth. He blew on it. Scott grabbed the cigarette from the young boy's mouth and said, "That's not how you smoke. Let me show you." After inhaling with all his might, he let the smoke shoot out of his nose and mouth.

"That's how you do it." He started to hand the cigarette back to the young boy but stopped. "This one's too short now. You'll get burned." Scott flung the cigarette out the window.

Suddenly, the car swerved. Pete, driving erratically, had been straddling both lanes and eventually drifted completely into the oncoming lane, almost hitting a car head on. He was able to yank his vehicle back into the proper lane just in time.

From the back seat, Four Eyes shouted, "Christ, Pete, look the hell where you're going. Are you drunk or something?"

"No. I can hold my liquor better than you any day."

"Just be careful, for Christ's sake. I'm too young to die. And this little kid's for shit way too young."

Scott took a fresh Chesterfield out of his pack, lit it, and handed it to Arthur. "Okay, where were we?" He handed the cigarette to Arthur. "Here you go, kid. Suck on it. Hold your breath as long as you can and then let the smoke out slowly. Keep your mouth closed. The smoke will come out of your nose. I wanna see you do that."

The youngster did as he was told. The teens had the time of their life watching the young boy fight to hold the smoke in. Finally, he let it out, at first through his nose as instructed. Then he lost control and coughed the rest out from his mouth.

"Hey, the kid's a real smoker. I knew he had it in him."

"Yeah. He beat me by a mile. I think I was thirteen when I started."

Arthur was in no condition to enjoy the compliment. His head swirled; his stomach, a sickened pit of nausea, threatened to hurl up its contents at any moment. He was seasick on dry land.

Four Eyes challenged the youngster. "I bet you couldn't do that again. Go ahead, take another drag"

Though he shouldn't have done it the first time, Arthur knew he'd really impress his new gang of friends if he inhaled again. So he did. This time he got even sicker than before. He dropped the cigarette on the floor.

Four Eyes stomped it out. "Hey, kid. Be careful, goddammit. I paid good money for this car." That comment elicited laughter from the other three teens.

"Yeah, like how much?" Pete asked. "Your old man practically gave it to you."

Four Eyes had to agree. "Yeah, he did. Anything to get me out of the house. The old fart."

"Whadda ya expect?" replied Pete. "You're a goddamn juvenile delinquent, just like Arthur's going to be. Or, maybe he is right now."

Dennis entered the conversation. "So what does this kid do that's so bad, anyway?"

Pete answered. "You didn't hear about the Cohens? He practically leveled their house with some other kid. Cops and everything." He peered at Arthur in the rearview mirror. "How old were you?"

Arthur said nothing.

"Well, tell me again. How old are you now?"

"Eight."

"Shit, I'm guessing that happened a couple of years ago. The kid was six, maybe even five, man."

"Christ!" Dennis exclaimed.

Pete wasn't finished. "Then he broke into the Harrisons' house, by himself. He busted their TV and stuff."

"How'd he get caught?" asked Dennis.

"Their house is right across from his. His dog was whining outside the house. His old man went to get the dog and investigated. Caught his own son in the act. I bet he beat the hell out of you for that one, right Mr. Artie?"

"Uh, uh," Arthur answered defensively.

"Yeah, sure."

"So, Pete, how do you know all this?" Four Eyes asked.

"Christ, you know my old man is the unofficial mayor. He gets all the complaint calls in Suassa Park. There's other stuff that happens around here and nobody gets caught. Cars get damaged—broken headlights, taillights. Betcha Arthur does it. He's good. I bet he does a lot of shit."

Scott gave Arthur a menacing look and warned, "Hey, kid. You better not touch my car."

Arthur remained silent. Partly, because the topic of conversation—his alleged crimes—was one that made him uneasy. Partly, because he was still recovering from the cigarette.

Richie had an idea. “Hey, you know what. He’s already such a big kid, getting into trouble...smoking.” (Turning to Arthur) “Maybe you should try a beer.”

Pete wasn’t in a generous mood. “He ain’t havin’ any of mine.”

“I’ve got two comin’ to me,” said Richie. “He can have one of mine. It’ll do more for him than me.”

Richie snapped open a can with a church key. He handed it to Arthur. Arthur recognized the can. Schaeffer. His father drank the same brand.

“Go ahead, kid. Bottoms up.”

Arthur was in an all-too-familiar, all-too-uncomfortable position. Does he do something he knows he probably shouldn’t, or does he surrender to his all-consuming need for approval?

All eyes were on the youngster, even Pete’s from the rearview mirror. The youngster surrendered to the pressure and took a sip. The drink’s bitterness immediately expressed itself all over his face. He heard the other passengers chuckling.

“That’s enough for you, kiddo. Anybody got any milk for the little baby?”

Determined to prove himself, Arthur insisted, “It tastes good.”

“Well, if it tastes so good, have some more.”

Author obliged. He took two more swigs and burped. More laughter.

“Betcha can’t finish the can.”

“Hey, don’t get the kid drunk.”

“Well, he said he likes it so...why the hell stop him?”

As much as he hated the taste, the youngster guzzled the can like a trooper. When he was done, Scott took the can from him and, after shaking it to be sure it was empty, turned the can upside down.

“Damn. What the fuck. He sucked it all out. What a lush.” That brought chuckles from Scott’s three associates.

Pete continued. “Don’t give him any more. I told you assholes. I don’t want him going home drunk. We’ll have his lunatic father coming after us." Pete decided to drive around while their young drinking partner sobered up. Then he drove the car back to his own house and parked in the driveway.

"Hey, Arthur, we got business to conduct. See you later."

Arthur got out. He had entertained his hosts and they showed their appreciation with some ribbing.

"From now on, I'll make sure to get a couple of extra cans just for you. Or would you prefer bottles?"

"And don't forget his cigarettes."

"You're gonna be a hell of a drinker someday, kid."

Pete told Arthur to walk over to the driver's window. The youngster did, and when he got there Pete grabbed him roughly by his arm, pulling him closer to the car. Then, while pinching Arthur's neck, the older boy gave him instructions. "Listen. Don't say anything to your parents. Nothing. You were someplace else today, got it?"

"Yes."

"Okay. So where did you go?"

"I was at David Blake's house."

"That's right. Perfect."

A rubber-legged Arthur wobbled off towards home. By the time he got there, he passed for sober.

The following day when Arthur woke up, the first thing he realized—his bed was dry! Such a magical uplifting feeling. However, this particular morning his elation at not having to face his father's ire and his family's barbs for being a bedwetter was tempered by his misgivings over the new friends he had made. Yes, they made him feel important, but he well knew there'd be hell to pay if his parents found out what he was up to. To complicate things, he was afraid to part ways face-to-face with Pete and his gang, fearful of how the older boys would react. Arthur decided to simply steer clear of the Stanton house altogether.

# Chapter 20

A FEW WEEKS LATER school ended. Summer had just begun. Arthur always greeted the end of a school year with mixed emotions. Like any child, he looked forward to the free time to do things. However, in his case, that often meant doing things alone, because he made it his business to stay out of his house as much as possible. Having decided to disentangle himself from the Stanton gang, he went back to hanging out with his dog in the nearby woods, entertaining himself there as best as a child his age could.

Family events were very rare in the Berndt household, but one day during that summer, Marguerite, ever the optimist, suggested that the entire family go to the beach. Getting her wish today would be especially difficult because her husband had started drinking late in the morning and made it clear he planned to keep drinking throughout the day, showing no interest in leaving the house. Downstairs in the living room, Marguerite pleaded her case to August. Upstairs, Arthur and his two sisters donned their bathing suits, silently hoping in unison that their mother would give up trying to convince their dad to accompany them. Why bring along a surly drunk for the sake of a family unity that didn't exist?

Negotiations between their parents always put the siblings on edge. Usually Marguerite deferred to her husband. Those rare times she dared stand her ground, she risked paying a physical price, especially if her husband was operating under the influence of alcohol. Following any such violence, everyone, Marguerite included, stayed isolated in their respective rooms upstairs while August spent the rest of the day downstairs, drinking and wandering aimlessly in a stupor from room to room. If he stayed conscious long enough, the rest of the Berndts could count on missing a meal or two. Better that than descending to the first floor and facing August's wrath. If he passed out on the sofa, and their hunger pangs grew bad enough, the other Berndts would cautiously come down, grab food out of the kitchen, and tiptoe back up to their temporary jail cells, careful not to awaken the sleeping monster in the living room. Would today be one of those days?

Marguerite called upstairs to her children, telling them to hurry changing into swimwear because they'd all be leaving soon. Moments later, with beach towels in hand, down the stairs and out to the automobile the three siblings went. Ruth and Arthur sat in the back while Liz, assuming they'd be going without their father, slipped into the front seat. All three children were cautiously optimistic they'd see the beach but, based on past experience, they were just as prepared to march back into the house if the argument resulted in their mother being assaulted.

From the car, the children could hear their parents squabbling inside the dining room. Since it was summer, the house windows were open, meaning neighbors might hear the domestic disturbance. Arthur checked the Sinclairs' driveway and saw no cars, so he figured no one was home there. On the other side of the Berndt residence was the Barney residence. No car there either. At least if the argument got out of hand, there wouldn't be any nonfamily witnesses. That counted for a lot in Arthur's world.

Then, things got quiet inside the house. Five minutes later, Marguerite came out the front door, dressed in her bathing suit and carrying bagged lunches and a blanket. Though not one of the children said a thing, they let out a silent collective sigh of relief that their father wasn't going along. Liz rushed to the garage and brought the beach umbrella to the car. It was too big for the trunk so, after Arthur and Ruth rolled their windows completely down, the umbrella was slid through the two openings. Ruth and Arthur were put in charge of holding on to it during the drive.

Marguerite got into the car, put the key in the ignition, and started the vehicle. At that moment, an obviously disgruntled August, in street clothes, bolted out the front door of the house, carrying a six-pack. He stumbled his way to the car and glared at Marguerite. "All right. Move over. I'll drive."

"Are you sure you can? You know...you've been drinking."

"Hell, I can drive in my sleep. Have I ever had an accident? The answer is no."

Resigned to the fact that her father was coming along, Liz got out of the car and crammed herself in the back seat with her two younger siblings. Now there were six hands to secure the umbrella.

Up front Marguerite slid over to the front passenger seat and August got in. He made sure his six-pack was close at hand, setting it between his wife and himself on the front seat.

When inside their house, the Berndts did all they could to keep their distance from each other. That wasn't so easy to do crammed together in the family car. The forced closeness sparked an instant tension. Sitting next to each other, Arthur and Ruth began jockeying for room on the backseat. Ruth was three years older and bigger, but Arthur was feistier.

"Mom, he keeps pushing me."

"She started it. I'll stop if she stops."

Marguerite turned around. "Look, I expect both of you to behave. You'll have to learn how to get along."

Arthur pleaded his case. "It's always my fault. It's not fair."

His mother begged to differ. "That's not true. When I say I want both of you to behave, I mean both."

August chimed in with a tipsy voice. "Look, I'm not going to put up with any nonsense. I'm going along, but I don't want to, and I'm not if you two are going to act like brats. In fact, none of you will go."

Liz took matters into her own hands. She rearranged the seating, placing herself between the two antagonists. Things immediately calmed down in the backseat.

With an open can of beer between his legs, August started up the car and backed out of the driveway, nearly hitting Ruth's bicycle. August stopped the car, turned around, and yelled at his daughter. "Dammit, watch where you park that thing, you—"

Marguerite interrupted. "Gus, the car's on the lawn. Are you sure you're okay to drive?"

"What is that supposed to mean?"

"Well, you've had quite a bit to drink."

"Yeah, so what? We're only going to Belle Terre. I could make that drive with my eyes closed."

August pulled out of the driveway and headed off, most of the car in the oncoming lane. His driving terrified Marguerite and Liz; Ruth and Arthur were still too young to fully appreciate the danger they were in.

August started sipping beer with one hand, while driving with the other. Hoping to minimize her husband's distracted driving, Marguerite offered to hold the beer can between sips. August let her, but continued to drive one-handed, out of spite.

Once reaching downtown Port Jefferson, August alternately strayed left towards the oncoming traffic and swerved right, coming dangerously close to parked vehicles.

Marguerite pleaded with her husband. "Gus, let me drive. You're going to get a ticket or hit something. Please let me drive."

From the backseat, Liz screamed, "I want to get out. I'll walk home. He's drunk again. I've seen films in school about what happens when drunks drive."

August slammed on the brakes in the middle of the street, whirled around, and slapped his daughter's face. "Don't you ever call me a drunk, you got it?"

Liz broke out into tears. "I can't wait to move out of this house for good. I can't wait!"

Several cars were stopped behind the Berndt car. From the rear another driver's horn sounded. August shouted at no one in particular, "Shut that horn the hell up or I'll shut it up for you!"

Marguerite turned off the car and pulled the key out of the ignition. "Enough of this. I'm driving."

She got out of the car and re-entered via the driver's side. Clutching the precious alcoholic cargo that sat on his lap, August slid over to the front passenger side. "Okay. You drive. So what? Who gives a damn?"

From the back of the car, Liz asked, "Mom, can you drive me home first?" Marguerite looked at her in the rearview mirror. "Liz, I'm driving now. I need you to come along. You're the best swimmer. Actually, you're the only real swimmer. You know Ruth is still afraid of the water and Art's just starting his first year of lessons next week. I'd feel much better with you there." Liz said nothing more and, for the rest of the drive, gazed despondently out the window.

The car arrived at the end of Belle Terre Road, a cul-de-sac sitting on a bluff overlooking the Long Island Sound. Nearby there was a private beach for the ultra-wealthy residents of Belle Terre. That wasn't the Berndts' destination. They headed for an unofficial public beach, without lifeguards or refreshment stand, accessed from an unofficial parking area on a cul-de-sac by way of a dirt path that worked its way down to the shoreline. Arthur loved this path as it went through thickly treed areas like those close to his home. Arthur had developed a fondness for the solitude and safety he found in woodlands.

## Chapter 20

The Berndts climbed out of their car. Liz carried the umbrella, Marguerite carried the lunches, and Ruth carried everyone's towels except Arthur's, who carried his own. August carried his beer.

The family reached the rocky shore in less than ten minutes, though it had felt like a much longer walk to the diminutive eight-year-old boy.

Today the Long Island Sound was especially rough due to a brisk and gusting wind. The water was extremely choppy, even sporting whitecaps. The Berndts had this beach all to themselves.

Liz planted the umbrella and then, with Ruth's help, opened up an old bed blanket on top of the sand, weighing down its four ends with heavy stones to combat the ever more powerful blasts of air nature was generating. That done, the two girls headed for the water. Liz jumped right in and swam away from shore. Ruth contented herself with lying on the shore and letting her feet and legs get wet from the incoming tide. Occasionally a crashing wave took her by surprise, soaking her up to her face, but she stayed put, enjoying the cat-and-mouse game she and the sneaky water were playing.

Arthur headed away from everyone, walking along the shoreline, occasionally attempting to skip a stone along the water's surface, a difficult task with the Sound being so turbulent.

Marguerite stretched out on the blanket and closed her eyes. August plopped down clumsily where he'd been standing and landed on a sharp rock. After cursing and then situating himself more comfortably on the blanket, he joked, "Gotta drink these beers quickly. Can't let 'em get warm."

Marguerite didn't relax for long. She sat up and began rummaging through her pocketbook. Not finding what she was looking for, she turned to her husband and asked, "Do you have the keys to the car? Did I give them to you?"

August fumbled in his pockets, but found nothing more than some small change. "Wait a minute. You were driving. Why would I have them?"

"I must've forgotten to take them out of the ignition. Gus, could you go check?"

"Why bother now? I'm enjoying myself. I don't wanna have to walk all the way back to the car until we go home." He let out a sarcastic laugh. "Besides, nobody in Belle Terre would steal our jalopy."

Marguerite wasn't satisfied. "Well, I'm uncomfortable not knowing where the keys are. I'm going to walk back to the car and check."

"Suit yourself."

Off Marguerite went.

Meantime, Arthur kept walking along the shore. Every once in a while he'd spot a flat stone, pick it up and try skimming it along the rough surface of the water. His best efforts yielded only two skips.

Along the way, the youngster stopped and glanced behind him. Off in the distance, he saw Ruth heading back to the blanket where their father sat. Seeing her father reach for another beer, Ruth had a change of heart, turned around, and began walking back to the water's edge. Arthur continued his visual survey and caught a glimpse of his mother disappearing onto the trail that headed back to the car. Then he looked out onto the churning water and spotted Liz swimming parallel to him, thirty yards offshore. While Arthur stood watching Liz, a surge of water briefly rushed over his feet up to his ankles and then retreated. As it did, the young boy eyed something being pulled away by the receding water. It was a horseshoe crab, an odd-looking creature the young boy had never seen before in his life. He rushed after it and bent down to grab it.

Smack! An incoming wave knocked him down. Taken by surprise, he scrambled back to his feet after swallowing a mouthful of saltwater. Undeterred, he resumed his hunt for the horseshoe crab. In short order, he found not one but two, attached to each other, crawling along the water's bottom. The young boy was excited. Now he could catch two of them! The hunt was on. Arthur stalked the crabs, but every time he was ready to reach into the water and grab them, he was stymied by the hyperactive water that kept pounding the shore with an endless succession of waves, making it hard for him to maintain his balance.

Arthur was filled with questions about the odd-looking crustaceans with their needle-like "noses." Were they friendly? Did they bite? What would happen if he picked them up? He thought of going back and getting more information on horseshoe crabs from his parents, but feared if he did that, he'd lose track of his prey. Besides, he'd probably be told to stop what he was doing. Arthur hated the word No, a word he heard often.

Not to be denied and determined to end the hunt successfully, he continued his reconnaissance in even deeper water, so deep it covered half his torso. The youngster hardly noticed, too preoccupied with his visual search into the water, where he alternately spotted and lost sight of his prey. Then, they disappeared for several minutes. Had they given him the slip? Just as Arthur was about to admit defeat, he eyed the two crabs heading towards him. Though they were dangerous looking, the youngster summoned up all his courage and seized the chance to capture them. He bent over, reached as far as he could to the bottom and—!

A huge wave swept over Arthur, pulling him away from the shore and out of sight. Completely submerged and at the water's mercy, the young boy looked up through the filmy liquid that had engulfed him. He could see the quickly dimming light of the sun, barely visible from underneath the water's surface, a surface he had been sucked below and was sinking further and further away from. He gasped for air but only salty liquid rushed into his body. Drowning was dreamlike, surreal—not pleasant, yet not totally unpleasant.

Just as he was losing consciousness, something yanked him to the surface—a pair of hands. Arthur coughed out water as Liz pulled him out of his would-be watery grave and carried him onto shore, where she lay him down. Flat on his back, the young boy opened his eyes and viewed the world he had been this close to leaving forever. Liz was the first to greet him back into it. "You better learn how to swim better!" Standing silently next to her was Ruth, looking quizzically at her brother.

Arthur slowly got back on his feet and the three siblings started walking back towards their father, who was still sitting on the blanket, polishing off his last beer. Ruth turned to Arthur and said, "You're going to get in trouble."

"Am not."

"Are too."

"Why? I didn't do anything."

"Yes, you did. You're not supposed to go in the water."

"I didn't. Something happened."

Liz chimed in. "What were you doing anyway?"

"I was chasing these things. They're brown and have a long needle sticking out of them. And they move pretty fast."

"Oh, horseshoe crabs. There's a ton of them today. Well, your curiosity almost got you killed. But we have to think of something to tell Dad."

Arthur said hopefully, "Maybe he didn't see it happen."

"Yeah, but that doesn't matter. You're soaked, how do we explain that?"

Ruth had an idea. "Let's say he tripped over a rock and fell in. Then a big wave came—"

Liz interrupted. "That'll never work. Dad would say (sarcastically mimicking her father), 'Yeah, he didn't see the damn rock because it was in the damn water he wasn't supposed to be in in the first place, dammit.'"

She gave it some more thought. "Alright. Let's blame the horseshoe crabs. You were walking along the shoreline, and a wave washed up the horsesh..." She turned to her brother and asked, "How many were there?"

"Two."

"Well, let's say there were five. That makes it better. They came from behind you and you got scared and backed up into deeper water. Then a wave hit you. I don't think Dad saw me pull you out, so we won't have to get into that at all. Anyway, he might be so drunk he won't even care you're wet."

Armed with their story, the trio headed back. On the way, Liz had another idea. "Ruth, start running back to the blanket. When you get there, start talking to Dad. You know...about anything. I know. Talk to him about Beethoven. That'll keep his attention."

"But I don't know what to say about Beethoven."

"Ask him to tell you about Beethoven's life. You know, he went deaf."

Ruth had her doubts. "Dad's scary when he's drinking."

"Yeah, well he's scary when he's not drinking. Just talk to him. You're his favorite, anyway."

"Why do I have to?" Ruth asked.

"You keep him busy so I can dry off Arthur behind Dad's back. Maybe it'll be as simple as that."

Ruth turned toward Arthur. "You and your stupid horseshoe things."

Reluctantly, Ruth sprinted ahead while her sister and brother veered in a direction that would let them reach the blanket from behind August, out of his sight.

Walking up to the spot where her father sat, Ruth struck up a conversation. "Dad, why don't you ever go swimming?"

"Not interested. It's pointless. You go somewhere and then just come back to where you started. Why not stay where you were in the first place?"

"Well, my teacher says it's good for you."

"Yeah, well teachers say a lot of things."

"They might build a pool at the high school."

"I heard about that. Just another chance to milk the taxpayer. This damn town is surrounded by water and they want to build a goddamn pool. Nonsense. Typical."

While this conversation was going on, Liz and Arthur cautiously walked up from behind and reached the blanket.

Ruth brought up Beethoven. Her father began to wax philosophically and enthusiastically about his favorite composer. While the two talked, Liz stood behind them feverishly drying off her brother, praying their father wouldn't turn around.

August tilted his last can of beer and let the last remaining drops dribble into his wide open mouth.

"Dammit. Out of beer. Time to go home." He turned around to see his wife just coming out onto the beach from the trail. He also saw Liz and Arthur standing behind him, the drying mission completed just seconds earlier. The young boy's swim trunks were white, helping conceal their wetness.

"Start picking up everything. We're leaving."

"But Dad," Ruth protested, "we haven't had lunch. I'm hungry."

"Well, you can eat at home. Look at the sky. Rain's coming. We're getting the hell out of here."

Dark clouds had rolled in, and the wind was kicking up swirls of sand that stung the beachgoers' skin.

Marguerite, clutching the car key in her hand, reached the family just in time to do an about-face with them and head back to the car. A day of fun at the beach was over.

# # #

The following Monday Arthur had his first swimming lesson of the summer. After it was over, he came home bursting with excitement, hardly able to wait for the next day's class. The youngster had no fear of water despite having almost drowned just days earlier. In Arthur's mind, that near-death experience paled in comparison to the disciplining he received at home. At his age, death was still a relatively abstract concept, his father's beatings weren't.

Arthur made rapid progress as a swimmer, quickly learning the crawl, sidestroke, and backstroke. He reveled in the sense of freedom—and safety—mastering the water gave him. His enthusiasm was such that he often ignored the teacher's whistle, a signal for the group to stop swimming and stand up in the water. Arthur would continue on, stopping only by special invitation—*"Arthur, that means you too!"* On one occasion Mr. Blaine, the instructor, grabbed him in midstream and remarked, "Whoa, young man! You look like a shark is chasing you!" With a brash confidence bolstered by the knowledge his father couldn't swim, Arthur defiantly responded, "In the water, no one can catch me."

# Chapter 21

FIVE WEEKS OF SWIMMING lessons later, on the day of the final class, Arthur was at home alone, anxiously waiting for his mother to come back from her part-time job selling burial plots so she could take him to the beach. The phone rang.

"Hello."

It was his mother. "Art, I'm going to be late. I'm in the middle of a discussion with a nice couple. I called Louise Harmon. She can take you with her. You know, her son Robert is in your swimming group. She'll be at the house around eleven, eleven-thirty. Are you ready?"

"Nope."

"Well, put your trunks on and wear some shorts over them. Wear a clean T-shirt. Oh, and wear your sandals. Those sneakers just get loaded with sand."

"Okay."

"Now, I want you to behave yourself. Be polite. You promise?"

"Yup."

"Okay. Have fun."

Arthur hung up the phone and rushed upstairs to dress. Then he flew back downstairs and went out onto the front stoop to wait for the Harmons' car. He hadn't sat long before Rex, nose pressed up against the screen door, started whining to come join him. Out the dog came, and the two killed some time, Arthur throwing sticks for his canine pal to retrieve. Arthur knew he wasn't supposed to play with his dog on the lawn, his father's pride and joy. But August was at work so boy and dog merrily trampled on "sacred ground." Done playing, the two sat down side-by-side on the stoop and waited. And waited. And waited some more.

Getting antsy, Arthur went back into the house and checked the kitchen clock. The little hand was on the eleven, the big hand on the five. The young boy panicked. He did not want to miss the final day of swimming lessons for anything. Ribbons were going to be given out for everyone who had participated. Plus, the instructor had said something about having additional classes for the more advanced swimmers, of which Arthur was one. Based on a child's impatience and not on any objective evidence, Arthur decided Mrs. Harmon was going to be late.

The young boy decided to take action. After calling Rex into the house, he stepped back outside, with beach towel in hand, and, closing the front door behind him, set out for the Harmons' residence. Arthur had been to Robert Harmon's house once before and had a good idea of how to get there. He walked down Lowell Place, turned left onto Hawthorne Street and walked a little bit before making a right turn onto Owasco Drive. Reaching the end of Owasco, he took a left onto Emerson Street. He was pretty sure this was the road that Robert Harmon lived on.

Throughout the walk, he passed the scenes of former crimes: the Harrisons' property, the Cohens', and the vacant lot from which he had stoned cars. Arthur was a lawbreaker who continued to live among those he'd victimized. After all, there was no place to send such a young perpetrator. Or was there? Every so often his father threatened to send him to a reform school, where they "knew how to straighten out troublemakers" like Arthur.

The young boy kept walking along Emerson Street, now more confident than ever that the Harmons' house sat at the very end of that road, two houses past the Stanton residence. He felt a sense of pride at not having gotten lost. As he passed the Stanton residence, he knew there were just two houses to go.

"Hey, Art! Get the hell over here!"

The youngster turned to see Peter Stanton, head sticking out of the driver-side window of his car, which sat idling in the Stantons' driveway. The older boy motioned with his hand for the youngster to come over to him.

"I can't. I have to go swimming."

"Swimming, schwimming. The water ain't goin' nowhere. Get over here."

Dutifully, Arthur took that long walk down the Stantons' driveway for the third time in his life. He shouldn't have.

Four Eyes greeted the young boy. "Hey kid, where you been? Did we scare you off?"

"Nope."

"Well, whatcha been doing? Rob any houses lately?"

"No, I don't rob houses."

"Do you even know what rob means?"

"Yup, it means when you take stuff."

"Yeah, mainly when you take stuff that isn't yours—at least not until you take it." Scott, in the front passenger seat, and Four Eyes in the back, both chuckled at the latter's deviant definition of delinquency.

While his cohorts laughed, Pete continued the conversation. "Hey, so hop in. We're going for a little spin. No booze today, but we've got cigs."

"I can't. I have to go to a swimming lesson."

"Yeah, so you said. Where at?"

"A beach. It's called West Meadow something."

"Oh, near Setauket. Get in. I'll take you there." Pete looked at the other two teenagers and winked. "We were heading that way."

"I'm supposed to go with Mrs. Harmon."

"So what? We'll get you there a lot faster."

"But will you take me back home too?"

"Of course."

"Am I going to get in trouble?"

"Why would you?"

"I don't know..."

"Look, get in. We'll check on old lady Harmon. If she's there, I'll drop you off. If she isn't, I'll take you. Either way you get to the damn beach. But you'll get there a lot faster with me. Deal?"

All Arthur wanted to do was attend his last lesson and get his ribbon. He didn't really care how he got to the beach, but he sensed that, in his parents' world, Mrs. Harmon was an approved ride and Peter Stanton wasn't. At the same time, he was feeling that same pressure to comply he felt that very first day he met these older kids. A need to please mixed with a heavy dose of intimidation.

"C'mon. Scott, man, hop in the back seat." Turning back to Arthur, Pete continued. "As a special treat, I'm going to let you ride shotgun. Now, get in."

That sounded more like a command then an offer to the young boy, so Arthur did as he was told. He circled around the front of the car, Pete reached over to open the passenger door, and the youngster reluctantly climbed in. He looked at Pete and the other boys in the back seat. The thought briefly crossed Arthur's mind that as scary as these big kids could at times be, there was something even more frightening about his father. That gave him an odd fleeting sense of twisted comfort.

Pete pulled his car out of the driveway and onto the street. He proceeded past the Harmon residence. No cars in the driveway, garage door open and garage empty.

"Well, Art. See, you can't count on that old bag, but you can always count on me. Hang on for the ride of your life."

Seconds later the speeding car was on Old Post Road, heading west.

Pete grabbed a new pack of cigarettes out of the glove compartment and handed it to Arthur. "Here. Make yourself useful. Open up a pack of cigarettes for the first time in your life. I'm sure it won't be the last."

Arthur fumbled with the pack but couldn't figure out how to open it. Scott's hand shot out of the back seat and grabbed the pack out of the young boy's hands. "Here, gimmee that. I might as well quit smoking if I have to wait for you to open the damn thing."

After the two boys in the back lit up, Four Eyes fired up a third cigarette and handed it to Pete. After a couple quick drags, Pete offered his to the car's youngest passenger.

"You remember what to do with it, right?"

"Yes, sir. But I'm not—"

"So, I'm a sir." Pete looked into the rearview mirror. "Hear that guys? I want you two in the back to start treating me with more respect."

Four Eyes answered mockingly. "Yes, sir. We dun heard, massah."

Pete turned his attention back to Arthur, handing him the cigarette. "Here, take it."

The youngster did. He put the cigarette to his mouth and drew on it hard enough so that the lit end glowed a bright red. Arthur forgot what he was supposed to do with the smoke in his mouth, so he swallowed it, forcing him to belch out some of the cigarette vapors accompanied with an unearthly mix of coughing and burping. The three older boys broke out in laughter.

Four Eyes chimed in. "With a sucker like that, you're going to make the girls happy." The three older boys laughed again.

Pete grabbed the cigarette out of Arthur's hand. "That's enough for you, sonny. Anyway, you need your lungs for swimming today. And maybe for running, too. Right guys?" Pete gave a knowing look in the rearview mirror that elicited sinister chuckles from his sidekicks in the backseat, even though they didn't yet know exactly what Pete had in store for their youthful passenger.

Pete continued. "Hey, Art. You know what? You're a real lifesaver. You came along at just the right time." The car came to a stop and Pete extended his hand. "Put it there, pal." The youngster didn't know what to do next, so Pete grabbed Arthur's hand and shook it.

The car again proceeded west, passing through Setauket and past a sign that read West Meadow Beach with an arrow indicating a right turn. Arthur recognized the sign and spoke up. "Hey, that's the way my mom takes me." Pete had an answer ready. "We're going the secret way." Scott joked, "I'll sure-as-shit say."

Although it rarely helped him, just like any child his age might, Arthur began crying. "I wanna go to the beach."

Pete lost his temper. "Okay, you little shit. We'll go to the beach. You know, you can be a real pain in the ass." He cut the steering wheel sharply and pulled a U-turn across a double yellow line, causing several other cars in both lanes to brake and swerve, and throwing his own passengers around inside his car.

Four Eyes shouted from the backseat. "Jesus Christ, Pete, what the hell ya doing?"

"I'm taking this brat to the damn beach. What does it look like?"

"Yeah, why? I thought we were—"

"Shut the fuck up. I know what I'm doing. We'll just have to wait a little longer. Gotta keep this kid happy."

Pete turned onto the road leading to the beach and shot a look at Arthur. "There. Ya happy?" The young boy nodded his head while rubbing his eyes dry with the backs of his hands.

Minutes later, the car pulled to a stop in the West Meadow Beach parking lot. Arthur, clutching his towel, immediately leapt out of the car and started to run out onto the sandy beach, heading for the spot where his class always met. Before getting far, he stopped in his tracks, turned around, and shouted back to Pete, "Will you be here when I'm done?"

"Sure thing, kid. You and me have business to conduct."

Reassured, Arthur again took off for his class. He found his classmates already standing in shallow water, taking turns practicing the swimming strokes they had learned under the watchful eye of Mr. Blaine. Arthur quickly shed his T-shirt, shorts, and sandals and waded into the water to join them. The instructor spotted him and asked, "Art, wherever have you been?"

"I don't know. My mom couldn't take me."

"So, how did you get here?"

"My friends brought me."

Robert Harmon joined the conversation. "My mom was supposed to take you."

"Well, she didn't."

"That's because you weren't there at your house."

"Was so."

"No, you weren't."

Mr. Blaine cut off the two boys' blossoming spat. "Okay, okay, boys. It doesn't matter. Art, do you have a ride home?"

"Yup."

"Good, now get behind Mickey. Robert, get back in your place on the line. We're doing the sidestroke next."

Arthur eagerly did as told and participated in what was left of the swimming session. Completing the day's final exercise, Arthur performed a skillful backstroke. That brought the group's swimming lessons for that summer to an end. Before the students were sent home, ribbons of participation were handed out. Then Mr. Blaine announced that the children would be getting a letter in a few days letting them know if they had qualified for a more advanced class that would begin the following month. Those that didn't qualify would be invited to repeat the beginners' class the following summer.

The class was dismissed and Arthur quickly toweled off, dressed himself, and scooted back to the parking lot, relieved to see Pete's car still parked there. Pete warmly greeted him through the window. "Well, I guess you didn't drown."

"I almost did once. Way back at the beginning of summer. My sister pulled—"

"Okay. Okay. Get in. No time for sob stories. We've got something to do before I take you home."

"Remember to take me to your house. You can't take me to my house because—"

"Yeah, I know. Your old man. Hey, believe me. I'd just as soon avoid him anyway."

The car pulled out of West Meadow Beach and headed back towards Route 25A, the road that, going east, led to Port Jefferson and Arthur's home. When Pete reached 25A he made a right turn and headed further west. His youthful passenger wasn't sure at first, but then realized something was wrong. "Hey, this isn't the right way."

Four Eyes chimed in from the back. "It is for us."

"I wanna go home."

Pete tried to calm the youngster down. "Look, don't start crying on me again. We just have to pick something up around here. It'll take a couple minutes. I'll get you back in plenty of time. Have I ever let you down?"

Four Eyes leaned forward from the backseat. "Hey, man. Are you sure he's gone?"

"Sure as shit am. My cousin lives on the street behind his store. He said Juska went to Canada somewhere."

"It sounds too easy."

Four Eyes chimed in. "Well, we haven't got caught yet. But this is the daytime, man."

Pete had an answer. "Yeah, it's the daytime. Look, I just found out about this. We can only do it today. I told my old man the band has a gig tonight, and tomorrow you guys have to work, right? The owner's supposed to be getting back sometime tomorrow, anyway. So it's fuckin' now or never. This is way too good to pass up."

Four Eyes had his doubts. "Shit, I guess so."

Pete kept arguing the point. "Think about it. We'll have a field day. Tires, oil, wiper blades, tools, you name it."

Scott agreed. "Yeah, the way my cars been eatin' up oil, I might keep a couple cases for myself."

Four Eyes mocked his buddy. "If you weren't such a lazy son of a bitch, you'd do a ring job on that crate and get it over with."

"Shut up. I got a lot of other things to do."

Pete agreed. "Yeah, like knocking over gas stations."

All three boys laughed.

Arthur sat quietly in the front passenger seat, oblivious to the teens' plans. It was getting late and he just wanted to get home to avoid trouble of his own.

The car kept heading deeper into territory Arthur had never before entered. He stared out the window, his curiosity at the unfamiliar scenery mixed with the gnawing fear he was in a bad place—Peter Stanton's car. It seemed that no matter where the youngster was, he was in a bad place.

"Hey, Pete. Where is this store again? Stony Brook or St. James?"

"Scott, did you leave your fuckin' brains at home? Where does my cousin live?"

"St. James."

"Where does he work?"

"St. James."

"So, where are we going?"

"Okay, I got it."

Four Eyes jumped into the conversation. "Let me ask you something, Pete. Your cousin Doug—you trust 'im?"

"Damn right I do. He's helped me out of some shit before. And every time I lend him money, he pays me back. That's more than I can say for you."

Four Eyes defended himself. "Hey, I've always paid you back up to now."

"Yeah, up to now. I've been waiting for those twenty bucks for weeks."

Scott nudged Four Eyes with his elbow. "Hey, you can pay Pete back after this little maneuver. Twenty bucks. That's like a couple of stinkin' cases of oil."

"Are you kidding? More like five or maybe even six. Remember, I'll be selling them wholesale."

The three teens chuckled. Their young passenger didn't. He was too busy glumly gazing out the window.

Arthur still hadn't grasped the significance of the older boys' conversation. He just hoped whatever was going on would end soon. He didn't know where he was or how far from home he was. He did know he was probably already in line for a beating.

The young boy felt an urge to cry again but fought it off. His gut told him tears would get him nowhere; these teenagers were on a mission that no child Arthur's age could derail. Little did he know he would be a major player, critical to the operation's success.

Reaching Main Street in St. James, Pete brought the car to a stop at the traffic light in the middle of town. St. James, a small hamlet, featured a post office, grocery store, a Rexall pharmacy, local butcher, barbershop, and, of course, the requisite bar. It also was the home of Juska's Auto and Marine Supply.

Glancing at their target, Scott commented, "There it is. Ripe for the pickin'."

Four Eyes looked troubled. "You know, I feel kind of bad. Old man Juska gave me a real good deal on tires once."

Pete replied, "Oh yeah? Well, he's gonna give you a way better deal this time, only he won't know it." Scott and Pete had a laugh while Four Eyes continued to battle with his conscience, a fight his conscience quickly lost.

Pete turned off Main Street, drove one block, and made a right onto the first cross street. He pulled to a stop in front of a yellow cape cod. "I'll be out in a second. Just have to check with Doug." He hopped out of the car and headed for the house. The other three passengers sat and waited his return.

Scott turned to Four Eyes. "You know, Pete's okay, but I sometimes wonder...His old man practically owns Suassa Park. Pete doesn't really work. You know, not like you and me and Richie. He's in a band. He makes in one night what I make in a friggin' week. I know why you and me steal. I'm not sure why Pete does. He could just ask his dad for dough."

"You think so, huh? Didn't he ever tell you? He hates his old man."

"Why the hell—?"

Four Eyes interrupted. "One of the guys in his band told Pete he saw his father in a bar somewhere in Smithtown—I think it was the Broadhollow, a real shithole—drinking with some woman. They were getting real lovey-dovey. When he asked his old man about it, he gave him some bullshit. Then, one time he was helping himself, on the sly of course, to some of his old man's money and he found a phone number in his wallet. Just a chick's first name. Pete called it, pretending to be his old man. He got quite the answer. 'Harry, is that you sweetheart? Doesn't sound like you.' Some shit like that. Pete got real pissed off, man. He said he was only going to steal ten bucks but decided to take a fifty or something. I think his old man found out about that phone call—and the fifty bucks. They almost came to blows, man. Pete and his dad hardly ever talk to each other anymore."

"And I bet his old man doesn't leave his wallet layin' around anymore, either."

"Yeah, you're probably right."

Scott continued. "Oh shit! I see what you're saying. So he can't hit up his old man for money anymore. And he probably can't steal it anymore, either. He's poor just like you and me. Well, almost. He still makes more playing drums than I do fixing cars."

"Maybe, but sometimes it's a long wait between gigs. That's why he's got this 'second job' like we do."

"Yeah, I guess so."

Arthur interrupted the conversation. "Can I go home now? I have to—"

Four Eyes attempted to console the youngster. "Hang in there, kid. I'm still not exactly sure why, but Pete says you're vital to this operation. Don't worry. There'll be something in it for you. Hey, whadda ya want—lollipops or ice cream?"

"I just wanna go home."

"Oh, you'll get home all right. As soon as we make ourselves rich."

The car door opened and Pete hopped back into the driver's seat. "We're all set. Doug got a call from his boss. Juska will be back to open the store tomorrow morning. Eight o'clock. And it's just like he said. The butcher is right next door. It's got like about a foot of space—maybe not even—between the two buildings. You know who can fit in there..."

As if on cue, the three teens all looked at Arthur.

Pete continued. "We were sittin' in the driveway and I'm trying to figure out what to do and along comes Arthur. Remember, I told you we caught a break bumping into this kid. I knew we could put him to use. We'd be jackasses to pass up this chance."

Four Eyes had his doubts. "You sure about this, Pete? I mean, you trust a little kid?" Pete was quick with an answer. "You want to try to squeeze your fat ass in there?" Four Eyes stayed mum. "I didn't think so." Scott had his own doubts. "Shouldn't we bring him here at night, when it's dark?" Pete scoffed. "Yeah, like his parents would let him out at night. Christ, use your brains—for once. "

Pete turned to Arthur. "Well, are you ready to have some fun? I know you've done this kind of shit before."

"I have to be home or I'm gonna get it."

"Don't worry. We're not gonna waste another minute."

Pete started his car and drove back toward Main Street. On the way he asked Arthur, "Hey kid, what do you want more than anything else in the world?"

"I wanna go home."

"Forget that. Besides that, what kind of prize do you want?"

The youngster didn't have to think very long. "A Roy Rogers cap gun."

"Oh yeah? Well, I'll get you one."

Arthur's eyes lit up. "Really? Promise?"

"Damn right. Just do what I tell ya to do and it's yours."

"What do I have to do?"

"It's easy. I'm gonna show you real soon."

It was nearly five o'clock; the day still basked in sunlight. Pete parked his car behind the supermarket that sat directly across the street from Juska's. He looked in the rearview mirror and ordered, "You guys wait in the car." Then he turned and looked at Arthur. "Okay, Artie boy. You and I are going for a little walk. Come on."

The youngster did as told. The two exited the car, walked past the back of the grocery store and out onto the sidewalk. They could see Juska's facing them directly across the street.

"All right, kid. Here's what—"

Arthur interrupted. "I have to go home. Right now! I mean it! I'm gonna get in trouble if I don't."

"Yeah, I know. We're going home soon. I just need you to do me a favor. You see that big store?"

"You mean with the boat in the window?"

"Yeah. You see the meat market next to it. Over there to the right?"

"Yup."

"Okay. I want you to walk across the street —"

"By myself?"

"Yeah, by yourself. Shit. Then you walk along the sidewalk to the back of Juska's, you know, the boat store."

"I don't wanna."

"Christ, and I thought you were some kind of little tough guy."

"I'm gonna get in trouble."

"No, you won't. Not if you do what I say. We're just helping the owner. He locked himself out and lost his keys. You're doing a good deed. That's why you're gettin' the gun. You—ah, shit. Let's get going. What the hell am I explaining this to you for? You're a freakin' little kid. Follow me."

Yanking Arthur by the arm, Pete marched his reluctant protégé across the street, up onto the sidewalk and towards the back of the targeted building. Except for the rear entrance, the rest of the backyard was enclosed by a chain-link fence.

Pete barked instructions to his youthful cohort. "I'm going to climb the fence. After I do, I want you to do the same thing."

"But, I'm not big enough."

"Don't worry. I'll grab you and lift you over."

"I don't wanna."

"Well, you're gonna. Don't fuck around. You want that gun, right?"

"Roy Rogers?"

"Yeah, Roy Rogers."

Pete looked around. The coast was clear. He quickly scaled the fence, vaulting over the top and nimbly landing on the other side. Eyeing Arthur, the older boy gave the order. "All right, now it's your turn. And hurry!"

Arthur awkwardly struggled to start climbing the fence from his side. He'd barely begun when he got cold feet. "I can't. I'm not big enough." Pete quickly scaled back up the fence to its top. After once more scanning the surroundings to assure himself there were no spectators, Pete leaned over the top of the fence, reached down, and grabbed the young boy under his armpits. Arthur felt the older boy's strong arms jerk him upward. With all his strength, Pete flipped the youngster straight up in the air, caught him one-handed around his torso on the fly, let go of his own hold on the fence, jumped, and safely landed onto the forbidden turf with his prize catch.

There were boats of all sizes in the huge back yard, some for sale, some being stored, and some being repaired. Pete ducked behind a cabin cruiser, yanking Arthur with him.

"Follow me, stay low and stay behind the boats. And keep quiet! Don't open your trap!"

Arthur dutifully played follow the leader as the two wended their way up to the rear of the building.

Pete turned to his young unwitting cohort. "This is where you come in." He guided the boy over to the side of the building that faced the butcher shop next door. There was barely a foot-and-a-half of width between the two buildings, a bit too tight for a teenager, but just wide enough for a child Arthur's age to negotiate.

Pointing to the dark narrow opening, Pete ordered Arthur into action. "You get in there and keep going until you get to a door. It's already unlocked. So open it, and go inside and stay in there. Duck your ass down and wait until I knock on the back door. Got it?"

"I'm not sure —"

"Well, I am. Don't fuck this up. Remember, the cap gun."

"But it's gotta be Roy Rogers. Promise?"

"You got it. I'll even throw in the caps. So go ahead."

"But I have to be home now. I'm gonna get in trouble."

"Will you quit fartin' around?"

"Promise you'll take me right home after—"

"Promise, for chrissakes!"

"But, I'm in trouble. Why can't that man, Mr. Juice-cup, open his own door? "

"You ever see him?"

"No."

"He's as fat as a cow. Now get back to work."

"But what am I going to tell my father? He's going to be real mad. I know it."

"Don't worry, we'll think something up. The sooner we get this done, the sooner you get home. So get movin'. And remember, when you get inside wait for me to knock on the door, that door near the back of the store. The one we walked by just before. Do not go to the front of the damn store, understand?"

"Y...y...yes."

"When you hear me knock, sneak—you gotta keep low—sneak up front and open the door. You got all that?"

Arthur nodded. Yielding to the older boy's pressure, he turned sideways, and, entering the space between the buildings, inched his way forward, sliding his back and butt against the butcher shop's exterior as he advanced.

"It's dark in here. How far do I have to go?"

Pete answered in a whisper. "I already told you. Until you get to the door. You should be near it by now. And for chrissakes, keep quiet! Don't make any friggin' noise."

"But I'm not making a lot of noise," Arthur answered defensively, still sniffling from his latest crying spell.

"The hell you aren't! If you don't want to get caug—! Aw, forget it. Just shut up and stay shut up!"

Moments later Arthur had squirmed and sidestepped his way up to a door. He turned the knob and opened it. After stepping inside, he carefully and quietly closed the door behind him, though there was not a living soul in the store that could have heard him. He took a seat on the floor, waiting in dead silence for Pete's signal from outside.

It wasn't long before he heard a knock! knock! on the back door. Arthur got on his hands and knees and crawled down one of the aisles to the rear of the store.

"Is that you, Pete?"

"No, it's the man in the moon. Open the goddamn door!"

Arthur looked but there was no doorknob. "I can't. There's nothing to turn."

"Push down on that long bar on the door."

Arthur did, and the door opened. Pete rushed in, with Four Eyes right behind him.

"Hey, Art. Look who's here. Your pal. He couldn't stay put in the car." He scowled at Four Eyes. "I just hope to hell no one saw you."

"Aw, nobody did."

"Just remember, not everybody's blind as a bat like you."

The two older boys declared a truce and took a moment to visually feast on their soon-to-be haul. One room contained all types of automobile merchandise—oil, transmission fluid, fan belts, gaskets, seat covers, etc.—that was neatly arranged on shelves and wall racks. There was a smaller adjacent room filled with new tires. Another large room featured boat accessories, but barely attracted their attention.

Impressed by the variety of goods around him, Four Eyes let out a whistle and declared, "Man, we're gonna fake Juska's ass out. When he comes in and all the shit's gone and all the doors are locked, no windows broken..." He whistled again. "Wait till Richie gets a load of this!"

Pete ended Four Eye's reverie. "Let's get the fuck outta here. We gotta get this kid home. He did his job."

Pete peeked out the door window. After waiting for a string of cars to pass by, he decided they should make a run for it. He grabbed Arthur by the hand and all three trespassers exited the building, using a can of oil to leave the rear door slightly propped open. Pete and Four Eyes pressed themselves against the door. Arthur followed suit, thinking it to be some game the older boys were playing. Pete peered around the corner of the building and gave the "All Clear!" signal with a thumbs-up. With Pete again pulling Arthur by the arm, all three popped out onto the sidewalk and began walking briskly as if with a purpose. They headed back to where the car was parked. Scott spotted them and leaned over the driver's seat to start the car. Within seconds, the foursome was on the road, headed back home.

It was now close to six o'clock. Though Arthur wasn't sure of the exact time, he was sure he would be late getting home. That could only mean trouble.

While driving, Pete began weaving an alibi. "Hey, Art. Here's the deal. You went to the Harmons'. No one was home. You started back home. I saw you. I gave you a ride. On the way home, my car broke down and— Shit... You know what? I'll call now. There's a friggin' pay phone. What's your phone number?"

"I'm not sure. I don't know."

"Yeah, I guess you wouldn't."

"But if you call, I'll get in trouble."

"No you won't...I have a great story."

Pete pulled over to the curb, got out of the car and, while searching his pockets for change, walked over to the phone booth. He rifled through the phonebook and then dialed.

"Hello."

"Yeah, is this Mr. Berndt?"

"Yes. What do you want?"

"This is Peter Stanton. Hey, your son is with me. He was walking by himself on my street. I asked him where he was going and he said something about old lady—uh, Mrs. Harmon was supposed to take him to some swimming class. I checked and she wasn't home, so I took him. He was crying about —"

"Yeah. So where are you now?"

"We're in Setauket. I'll be there at your house in about five minutes."

"Yeah, if you drive like a jackass!"

"Well —"

"Just get him here, you understand? I'll take care of this."

"Okay, Mr. Berndt."

Pete wasted no time getting off the phone. He hurried back to the car.

"Hey, Art. Your father got any firearms? You know, things you can shoot people with?"

"You mean like guns?"

"Yeah, like guns. Not cap pistols. I mean real guns, like the ones that kill people."

"I never saw any."

"That's good. He's pissed. Boy, is he pissed. Hey, I tried my best. He wouldn't even let me finish my story."

Arthur became quiet, fearful of going home, yet anxious to get his punishment over with. Pete could see the worry etched in his young passenger's face.

"Hey, well most of what I said was true. You have to tell your old man the rest—the made-up part." Arthur didn't respond.

"Tell him I took you to the beach, you had your lesson and, on the way home, the fan belt went on my car. Can you remember that? Say the fan belt broke."

Turning to Arthur, he barked an order. "Repeat after me. The fan belt broke."

"The fan belt broke."

"Perfect." Pete continued. "Okay. I had to wait for someone to...I know, Scott did it. Tell your old man I called Scott and he brought me this car from my house and then we took you home. Everybody knows I have a lot of different cars. Your old man doesn't know what car I was driving you in today. He'll buy it, so stop worrying."

Pete's encouragement fell on young deaf years. In Arthur's world, sometimes it was easier to face his father's wrath than other times. Usually Arthur preferred meeting his doom without having to wait too long for its arrival. At night, if his father angrily shook him out of his sleep in a urine-soiled bed, his punishment began immediately, sparing the youngster the stressful anticipation he suffered on other nights when his piss-soaked body forced him awake before his father came to check on him. In those instances, he'd lie in bed dreading the moment his father would burst into his bedroom, marking time in a state of growing terror, knowing there was no escaping his fate.

Today, he'd had several hours to feed his fear, raising his anxiety to a nearly unbearable level. When Pete turned onto Lowell Place, Arthur, now drenched in panic, got the urge to bolt from the car before it reached the house, just to temporarily postpone the inevitable. But if the young boy ran, Pete and his gang might see him getting chased by his father, which would be an utter embarrassment. Better to go right into the house. That way, his teenage pals would be long gone by the time Arthur's father got to work on him in the privacy of the Berndt residence.

The throaty roar of the oversized engine in Pete's car announced its arrival in front of the Berndt residence. Arthur jumped out of the car and hustled toward the house. He spotted his father standing unsteadily on the front stoop; he'd been drinking. The young boy slowed down to a walk, hoping Pete would drive away before he had a chance to witness Berndt family mayhem. No such luck. Oblivious to his son passing by him, August stumbled his way toward the car that had delivered his son, signaling Pete to stay put.

"Hey you, Stanton."

"Yeah?"

"You pull that shit again and you'll pay for it."

"What shit?"

"Kidnapping, that's what!"

"What are you talking about? Aw, come on—"

"Come on nothing. My wife got a call from the Harmon lady. She never picked him up. Then she's at the beach and spots him leaving there with you bums. And then you still don't get him home right away. Where the hell were you?"

"I told you. No, I didn't. My fan belt broke."

"Fan belt, my ass. You should've called here to tell us you had him."

Pete lied. "I did. No answer."

"Well, just get the hell out of here. Don't ever take my son anywhere, for anything. You got it?"

"Yeah. Sure thing, Mr. Berndt."

The older man stepped back and eyed Pete's hot rod with disdain. "Now, get that piece of shit out of here. You stay on your block, you understand?"

"Yeah. Whatever you say, Captain." Pete gave the Hitler salute with his left arm, accidentally poking August Berndt in the chest. Then he slammed his foot on the gas pedal, purposely fishtailing down the road and leaving behind tread marks that would remain on Lowell Place for months. Disgusted, August turned around and started walking back to his house, pointing at his son. "You, get in the house."

Marguerite, a concerned look on her face, greeted Arthur on the front stoop. "Art, what happened? Louise said she got here a bit after eleven thirty and you weren't home."

"I thought she forgot about me so I walked to her house."

August reached the front stoop and offered some advice. "When your mother tells you to wait for someone, you wait. Plus, you didn't close the door all the way and the damn dog got out. He must've been out looking for you, because he was all the way over on Washington Avenue." Arthur, by now an expert at reading facial expressions, especially those of his chief tormentor, sensed his father was looking for a reason to hit him, but was having trouble finding one. All the elder Berndt could come up with was, "I told you to get in the house."

All three went inside. Marguerite, trying to make peace, offered her son a plan for the future. "From now on, when you're home alone, I'm going to give you a phone number to call before you leave the house. I don't want you wandering off unannounced."

"Okay, Mom."

August brushed past his son and went to the kitchen. A few seconds later, the cap popped off another beer bottle.

Marguerite continued. "You had us worried silly. Mrs. Harmon said she saw you at the beach with a group of boys.

Thank god it was the Stantons' son, someone we know. God, if you had gotten a ride with some troublemaker—"

August shouted from the kitchen, "Are you kidding? He's bad news, just like our son. No different, just older."

Arthur was only half listening. He was too busy reveling in a giddiness only he could understand. He had escaped his father's wrath. Not forever, but at least for today, he was savoring a pleasant and most unexpected gift. Fate could be kind, after all. At least sometimes.

# Chapter 22

TWO DAYS WENT BY. All Arthur could think about was the cap gun he'd been promised. All he'd had to do to get it was open two doors. They happened to be two doors that were part of a building he had no business entering, but he didn't know that. Besides, even if criminal trespassing was nothing new to him, at least this time he didn't steal or wreck anything. Hadn't Pete told Arthur he was doing the owner a favor? The youngster's conscience was clear. He hadn't tasted the belt at home. That was the ultimate proof he's done nothing wrong. What troubled him was the fact he still didn't have his new gun.

What's fair is fair. After all, in Pete's own words, the young boy had "done his job."

Arthur set out for the Stanton residence. He took Rex along for moral support. On the way he remembered his father's warning to stay away from Pete, but the youngster was hell-bent on getting his pistol. The minute he had it, he'd forever treat the Stanton house as off-limits. As he walked on, he decided he wanted a holster thrown in as part of the deal.

Arriving at his destination, the young boy walked up to the front door and hit the doorbell. He kept the palm of his hand firmly pressed on it, producing a continuous loud clanging inside the house. Meanwhile Rex made himself comfortable lying down on the front lawn.

The door opened and a sleepy-looking older man grumbled, "Get your hand off that—"

The youngster did as told and announced, "I'm Arthur."

"I know all too well who you are. What do you want?"

"Are you Pete's dad?"

"Yes, I am. Now, what is it?"

"Well, I did something Pete told me to do and he said he'd give me a brand-new gun."

"Oh yeah, and exactly what did you do?"

"All I had to do was open some doors."

"What?"

"Yup."

"Look, I —"

The rumble of a powerful car engine—in a 1942 Buick Roadmaster, the only four-door car Mr. Stanton's son deigned worthy of driving—announced Pete's arrival. He spotted Arthur talking with his dad, an immediate cause for concern. Pete hurriedly parked the car, got out, and hustled up to the front door.

The elder Stanton questioned his son. "What are you doing hanging out with a kid his age? I don't know if he's fit to be around anyone, but, Christ, you're nineteen and he's what, six or seven? "

"We just used him as a gofer once. He's only been here a couple of friggin' times, getting tools for us."

"And what's this about opening doors so you're going to buy him some toy gun?"

"Yeah. I was doing some work on the inside of the Buick. He opened and closed the doors a few times. Got a kick out of seeing the interior lights go on and off..."

"Well, look. I don't want him on my property. What the hell would the neighbors think if they see me palling around with this kid, of all kids? " Turning to Arthur, "Son, you stay off this property, understand, and that means your dog, too." Rex took no offense and continued to snooze.

After muttering "Jesus Christ!" Mr. Stanton slammed the front door behind him. Pete yelled through the closed door, "All right. Whatever you fuckin' want. I'll take him home." Turning to Arthur, he continued shouting for his father's benefit. "Okay, kid. You can't be coming around here anymore."

"But you said—"

"I don't care what I said. I'm taking you home right now." Without waiting for a response, he pushed Arthur in the direction of his Buick.

As they distanced themselves from the house, Pete continued. "Is your dog okay in a car?"

"Yes."

"He won't shit in it or anything, will he?"

"Nope. He's a good dog. He's the best."

"Okay. Let's go for a ride."

All three hopped into Pete's car and headed out. "Remember, you can't take me to my house," Arthur reminded the older boy.

"Oh, you don't have to tell me. All I have to do is think of your old man's face. So, let me see if I remember. Roy Rogers, right?"

His face brightening, Arthur answered with a resounding, "Yup."

"Well, let's go down to Cooper's. No, let's go to Smitty's. He's got the best guns for kids. Hey, by the way, did you say anything else to my old man, besides the 'opening doors' stuff?"

"Nope."

"Smart kid. You know, we made such a great haul I should buy you two guns. But I won't."

"Is it really going to be Roy Rogers? You promised."

"Sure as shootin', pardner," Pete grinned. "Hey, I was talking like a cowboy. Laugh."

Arthur didn't.

"Can't interest you in Gene Autry or Hopalong Cassidy?"

"Nah."

"So what is it about Roy Rogers?"

"He's neat. I like his dog, Bullet. He's like my dog. He's a German shepherd, too."

"Well then, I guess Roy Rogers it is."

The unlikely trio arrived in downtown Port Jefferson. After parking the car, Pete escorted his young companion into Smitty's. Arthur's eyes lit up. There were all kinds of neat items: official-looking sports equipment, bicycles, tricycles, sleds, wagons, sling shots—the list went on. When they got to the toy gun and rifle section, Arthur immediately spotted and grabbed the latest Roy Rogers cast iron six-shooter.

"Can I get the holster too?"

"Hey, do I look like Fort Knox? " Pete gave it some thought. "Well, you know, you did help us make a small fortune so I guess I can spring for a holster, too."

"Neat!"

When they exited Smitty's, Arthur, wearing a holster around his waist, was clumsily trying to put the caps into his new gun while he walked. He gave up, put the caps back in his pocket, and contented himself with shooting blanks at passing cars.

Rex, his head stuck out a partially opened window, was anxiously waiting for the boys when they returned to the car. They took off and headed back to Suassa Park. Arriving at the intersection of Old Post Road and Lowell Place, Pete brought his car to a stop. He wasn't going to risk another confrontation with August Berndt.

"All out here. Now remember, you don't know me and I don't know you. At least for a while. Maybe we'll do business again in the future."

Arthur hesitated. "I'm not supposed to be walking around here."

"Why not?"

"Because of that man over there." Arthur pointed to a shack on the south side of Old Post Road.

Pete nodded understandingly. "Yeah, I know. There's a lunatic that lives there. He might be even crazier than your father. Don't worry, No one hardly ever sees him in the daytime. You go home. If he comes outside, I'll run him over with my car."

Pete extended his hand. Though they had shaken hands once before, Arthur still didn't fully understand the gesture. Pete grabbed the youngster's right hand with his and shook it. Then Arthur got out of the car, opened the rear passenger door, and let Rex jump out. Boy and dog started heading home. Arthur stopped in his tracks when he heard Pete's voice.

"Hey, didn't you forget something?"

Arthur turned around and asked, "What?"

"How about a thank you for the gun? You know, that honor among thieves thing. We gangsters got to stick together."

Not sure what thieves and gangsters Pete was referring to, Arthur simply replied with a childlike, "Thank you."

Pete's demeanor changed, and not for the better. "Get over here," he ordered.

Arthur walked up to the driver's window. Pete grabbed him by his shirt. "Remember, don't tell anybody nothing about why you got this gun. If you do, I'll take that gun and shove it up your ass. Nobody likes a squealer."

"What's a squealer?"

"Something you better not be. A stoolie, a rat. Just keep your mouth shut, got it? If your old man or old lady asks you how you got it, say I gave it to you for helping me work on cars. Understand? "

"Yup. Can I go now?"

"Sure, class dismissed."

Pete floored the accelerator and headed off. On the way home, Arthur kept admiring his new possession all the way up to his front door. He let Rex in and followed behind him. The young boy walked into the living room where he found Marguerite and

Ruth watching TV. Arthur proceeded to take aim and "shoot" his sister with his brand-new firearm.

Marguerite immediately asked, "Arthur, where did you get that gun?"

"David gave it to me."

"David Blake?"

"Yup."

"Really. Why?"

"He didn't like it. He likes the Lone Ranger better."

Pointing at her brother, Ruth chimed in. "I bet he stole it."

"Did not!" Arthur shot back defensively.

Marguerite wasn't satisfied. "Look, there's a price tag still on the holster. Why would Helen [Blake] buy a gun her son didn't want?"

"Well, he did want it. Then, he decided he liked the Lone Ranger's more."

"I'm going to..." Marguerite's voice trailed off. She went to the dining room and picked up the phone. Arthur didn't know exactly what she was doing, but guessed he should begin worrying. He followed her into the dining room, so he could gauge the temperature of the hot water he might soon be wading in.

"Helen? Oh, Diane. Would you put your mother on please?"

Arthur's heart sank. He was sure he was going to get caught for hanging out with Peter Stanton.

"Helen, this is Marguerite Berndt. I just wanted to check something with you. Did your son give Arthur a Roy Rogers gun?"

Listening to her neighbor's response, Marguerite's face became drawn.

"Oh, I see. Were the two boys playing today?"

Now Marguerite's expression was a thick mixture of concern and disappointment, one she wore all too often. "Well, thank you so much. No, nothing's the matter. Sorry to have bothered you."

After hanging up the phone, an exasperated Marguerite turned to her son and begged, "Arthur, when—*oh when*—will you stop this constant lying?!"

"But mom, I told you what happened."

"Well, it didn't happen. David's mom said her son has never owned a Roy Rogers gun and that the two of you weren't even together today. I want an explanation."

"But, my—"

"Just this once, tell me the truth."

"But I...I don't want to get in trouble."

From the living room Ruth shouted, "See Mom? I told you he stole it."

Marguerite looked her son squarely in the eye. "Well, did you?"

"No."

"So, how did you get it?"

"A friend got it for me."

"A friend? What friend?"

"That's the part I can't tell you."

"You know, your father is going to be home soon. He'll want to know the same thing. What will you tell him?"

"Like I said Ma, a friend got it for me."

Arthur wouldn't have to wait long to have a "chat" with his father. A car pulled up in front of the Berndt house. August was home from work.

As his father walked toward the house, a panic-stricken Arthur ran upstairs to his bedroom, took off the gun and holster, and hid them under his bed. He could only hope his mother would keep their secret; sometimes, she did. He came back downstairs just as his father entered through the front door.

Marguerite greeted her husband, he ignored the greeting and the children kept their distance from him—a common homecoming for August Berndt. Arthur sensed with cautious relief that his mother wasn't going to spill the beans, at least not for the time being. Cautious relief because Arthur spent much of his existence expecting the worst.

At dinner the family ate in the typical uneasy silence that characterized all the Berndts' mealtimes. However, this particular day, the silence was broken by Ruth. She was bursting with information she just couldn't keep to herself.

She directed a question at her brother. "Are you going to tell Dad about the gun?"

Angered by his sister's betrayal, the young boy responded with a defiant "No!" Ruth had a habit of ratting on her brother in a futile attempt to score brownie points with their father. Futile, because no one stayed in August Berndt's good graces for very long.

August's typically edgy look got a bit edgier.

"What gun?"

"It's nothing, Dad."

"I *said,* 'What gun?'"

Marguerite tried to keep her husband from getting too enthusiastic about his growing anger. "Why don't we finish dinner? Then we can talk about it."

August wouldn't let it go. "What's he done this time?"

Arthur, a boy of few words inside the house, was of even fewer when his father was about to lose it. Ruth also sensed the impending storm. "Mom, can I be excused?" Not waiting for a reply, she scooted up to her bedroom and closed the door.

August looked at Marguerite. "Don't try to baby him. What's he done now?"

"I'm not sure he's done anything, Gus," she answered optimistically.

"You know I work my ass off all day and have to come home to this?" Even though he didn't know exactly what this was yet, he was determined to find out.

Trying to act as if all was well, Arthur asked, "Dad, can I go outside with Rex?"

"*N-o-o,* you cannot go outside with Rex. Not until this gun thing is explained."

Marguerite lamely tried to defend her son. "Well, he came home with a new cap pistol. He said a friend bought it for him. Isn't that nice?"

August turned toward Arthur. "You must have some rich friends." Then he took a stab at humor. "Let me know who they are so they can buy me a new car. I don't know, a Mercedes-Benz or a Cadillac? Hmm...Tough choice."

He directed his next question towards Marguerite. "Who are we talking about?"

"Don't know yet. We were just getting to that when you came home."

"You weren't trying to cover up for him, were you? If our daughter hadn't said something, would I have heard about this? Maybe the two of you were going to pull a fast one on me, right?"

"No, Gus, that's not it."

"The hell it isn't."

Arthur didn't like it when his dad threatened his mom, especially when it was because of something he had done. Putting his mother in danger only added to the guilt that routinely streamed through Arthur's body. He shifted the focus back on himself by blurting out, "It was Peter Stanton."

Marguerite let out a poorly stifled gasp. She was sure this meant trouble.

"Peter Stanton? I told him to stay away from you and you were to stay away from him."

"I did Dad, I promise. But he said he'd get me a gun *before* you told me to stay away so..."

"So?"

"So I went to his house just one more time to get it."

"Why would he buy you a gun? What the hell is wrong with that punk, making friends with a kid your age? Must be something very wrong with him."

"Because I opened some doors for him."

"What's that supposed to mean?"

"I opened up some doors that he was too big to open. Him and his friends."

"What the hell is going on here? Why were they too big?"

"Because the buildings were too close."

August and Marguerite exchanged glances, his angry, hers confused.

The interrogation continued. "And just where was this building?"

"Far away."

"How far away?"

"You know West Meadow Beach?"

"Yeah."

"Well, way past that."

"I'm almost afraid to ask. What was inside the building?"

"Oh, it was just some car stuff, I think. And lots of boats outside."

"Jesus Christ, you son of a bitch. Do you realize what you did?"

Arthur didn't. He *did* sense his father's growing anger, which meant it was best to keep quiet.

August thought aloud. "I've got a good mind to beat the shit out of that Stanton kid. I don't give a crap if his old man owns Suassa Park."

Marguerite made a stab at calming her husband. "Gus, let's not jump to conclusions. There's probably a good explanation for all of this. You know, Art's only eight and he makes up stories."

"Yeah, and look at all the damage he's already done in his life. He can't be with anybody and nobody can be with him. That's it."

August stormed out of the dining room. Dinner was over, though nobody had finished their meal.

Uncharacteristically, August Berndt had not pursued the interrogation of his son any further. Perhaps, on this occasion at least, his thirst for alcohol trumped his thirst for dishing out punishment. The head of the family grabbed a beer from the fridge, cracked it open, and went outside into the backyard to stew. Ruth came downstairs, went to the living room, and practiced on the piano. Liz, who had remained silent during the conversation at the dinner table, took a bicycle ride. Arthur went to his room and stayed there until bedtime. Marguerite went about her chores, hoping the worst was over. It was, for the time being.

A few days later a letter arrived at the Berndt residence. Arthur was already riding a winning streak. He'd narrowly escaped two pummelings—one for disobeying orders and winding up in Pete Stanton's car, the other for possessing a cap gun he'd earned illegally. Not only that, someone way older than he (Peter Stanton) had owed him something—and he'd dared to collect it. Now this letter.

His mother read it to him:

*Dear Mr. and Mrs. Berndt,*

*Please be advised that your son Arthur has successfully completed the Red Cross Swimming Course # 1. As a result he is invited to participate in Course # 2 which begins on Monday, August 4th, at West Meadow Beach at 1 P.M. Please make sure your son wears a bathing suit and brings a towel. He should report to Miss Shirley Evan's group.*

*Sincerely,*

*Louis Edwards,*

*American Red Cross-Suffolk County Chapter*

Marguerite gave the letter to her son. "Arthur, this is certainly quite an accomplishment. You must be so proud of yourself. Good for you! I'm going to let you tell your father." Arthur took the letter and put it on the dining room table. He wanted it to be a surprise for his father when he came home from work.

The rest of the day the young boy spent outside roaming in nearby woods with Rex. He took along his new gun that he'd been hiding under his bed, just in case he and his dog ran into any bad guys on their travels. He made sure to get back to the house and put the pistol away before his father got home. His mom had no apparent issue with the gun, and his father, too, had surprisingly let the issue go. Keeping the gun out of his father's line of vision made sense. No reason to wake a sleeping tyrant.

Whenever August got home from work, he typically checked the mail first thing. Today was no different. Among the bills and advertisements, he spotted the letter from the Red Cross. He picked it up, read it, and put it back down. Turning towards Arthur, waiting nearby, he said, "Well, looks like you've found your calling. We've got a goddamn Johnny Weissmuller living with us."

August walked toward his son. Unsure what to expect, Arthur braced himself. His father extended his right hand. Having recently learned from Pete Stanton what to do in such a situation, Arthur gently clutched his father's rough hand. They shook. August sarcastically counseled his son. "Now let's see if you can start keeping dry when you're not swimming."

# Chapter 23

IT WAS NOW THE middle of August, which meant it was well past the middle of the professional baseball season. August Berndt't favorite team, the Brooklyn Dodgers, was in the thick of a pennant race. The Dodgers were the working man's team, affectionately called "Dem Bums." They'd had some good seasons but never good enough to win the grand prize—the World Series. The Dodgers shared the New York City metropolitan area with two archrivals, the Giants and the Yankees. Like the Dodgers, the Giants were in the National League, so the two teams played twenty-two fiercely contested regular-season games each year. The Dodgers' ballpark—Ebbets Field—was located in fast-decaying section of Brooklyn. The Giants played in the Polo Grounds, in a deteriorating section of Upper Manhattan. In the other league—the American—the Yankees reigned supreme. They resided in yet another neighborhood suffering a downturn, this one in the Bronx. The Yankees, however, were the epitome of success. For them, winning was an automatic as printing money was for the U.S. Department of Treasury. It seemed every year the experts penciled the Yankees in to win the American League pennant; the only question was who would represent the National League as the losing team when meeting the Yankees in the World Series. The running joke was that rooting for the Yankees was like rooting for General Motors.

These were the days before guaranteed contracts made players instant multimillionaires. Getting to the World Series meant several thousand dollars extra cash in each player's pocket, big money in the early fifties. Players saw other teams as obstacles to be eliminated on the way to a World Series paycheck. Hungry for that large payday, the players had as much antipathy for their opponents as their own fans did. That dislike expressed itself on the ball field in the form of extreme competitiveness: pitchers illegally doctored the baseball to make it less hittable and many of them had no problem throwing at opposing batters, often aiming for their heads (during an era that predated the mandatory use of safety helmets); runners sliding into bases utilized their spikes as weapons to intimidate and sometimes inflict injury on the other team's fielders; and throughout a game, opposing teams exchanged a steady barrage of verbal insults designed to rattle each other.

August's brother, Karl, had taken him to a Dodger game only weeks after he arrived in the United States. Karl, who had already been living in the U.S. for several years, explained the basics of the game and August was smitten with both baseball and the Dodgers. The other two Berndt brothers, John and Joe, were Yankee and Giants fans, respectively. When the four brothers got together, the arguments over players and teams went on well into the night, often fueled by beer.

Arthur was still too young to fully grasp the game, but he knew his father lived and died for the Dodgers, so he too became a fan of Dem Bums. In part, this was a child's natural tendency to follow his parent's lead, but, in Arthur's case, it was also a child's attempt to bond with the father he feared.

# # #

One Saturday afternoon, a neighbor invited Marguerite and her daughters to go shopping. The two men in the Berndt family stayed home and sat at opposite ends of the sofa, watching the ballgame—Arthur drinking soda, August drinking beer, with Rex stretched out comfortably on the living room carpet. When at home, Arthur usually did his best to stay out of whatever room his father was in. Today's chance to sit safely while in relatively close proximity to his father was a rare treat, giving the youngster a taste of father-son camaraderie. Arthur knew it was a fragile and fleeting timeout from their ongoing war, so he was determined to enjoy every moment of it.

The young boy could tell two things from watching his father's body language: the beer had taken effect, and because the Dodgers had the lead, all was well. In fact, August had entered that slaphappy stage that usually occurred during the early part of his drinking episodes. Typically short-lived, this afternoon it was prolonged because of the way the game was going. As a result, August was having one of the longest conversations he'd ever had with his son. "See, Erskine has already struck out eight. He's the best pitcher on the team, next to Branca, I guess."

Arthur asked, "What does 'struck out eight' mean?"

"It means he's gotten eight players to swing and miss or take a called strike. Has to happen three times. Could be a foul ball or two in there among the strikes. Anyway, three strikes mean the guy's out and has to sit down."

"Can a player stand back up after he sits down?"

August let out a rare chuckle. "Well, yeah. After the team makes three outs, players go out on the field and play defense."

Arthur wasn't really that interested in the game, but he was relishing this chat with his father so he did his best to extend it. "What happens if a team never makes three outs?"

"Can't happen. Sooner or later, they always make three outs."

Though he hadn't fully grasped his father's explanation, Arthur responded with a seemingly understanding, "Oh."

The game reached the bottom of the ninth inning. The Dodgers were three outs away from victory. The first batter on the opposing team—the Phillies—belted a two-run homer, much to August's disgust. "God dammit. Erskine got sloppy."

The score was now eight to three in favor of the Dodgers. August got into an expansive mood as he opened another beer bottle. “Hey, you wanna go to a ballgame someday?”

“Really, Dad?”

“Well, maybe in a year or two. You’re still too young to deal with at the ballpark.”

“I’d be good, I promise.”

“I say you’re too young. It’s a long drive from here. You’d piss in your pants. We’ll wait a few more years, till you finally grow up.”

“How long is it till I grow up, Dad?”

“Well, for one thing, stop pissing in bed. That’s what a goddamn baby does.”

The older Berndt turned his attention back to the TV. The Phillies had just scored three runs on a base-clearing double. The score was now Dodgers eight, Phillies six.

“Dammit. Get Erskine the hell out of there,” August shouted at the television. Then he hustled to the kitchen and came back with two beers. He popped both bottles open, tilted his head back and chugged one dry while standing, and then settled back onto the couch with the second bottle in his hand.

The room became silent except for the game’s announcer on the TV. Arthur knew what time it was—it was time for him to remain quiet. He sensed from the scowl on his father’s face that the game was taking a turn for the worse, and so was his dad. Arthur would have given anything to be outside and playing with Rex, but his father was still in a talkative mood, and would take offense and get nasty if his son walked out on him. Rather than leave the room, the youngster decided he’d stick around and try to prop up his dad’s sagging spirits.

“But our team’s still ahead, right? It’s eight to six. ”

“Yeah, but not for long. I can tell which way this game’s going. They don’t call them bums for nothing.”

The Dodgers brought in a new pitcher. August offered encouragement tinged with skepticism. "Let's go, Roebuck. For Christ's sake, don't blow it."

"Is he any good, Dad?"

"About the best they got for relief. The manager should have put him in sooner."

The first batter Roebuck faced greeted him with a run-scoring single. Dodgers eight, Phillies seven.

"Jesus Christ. Don't blow the game, you bastard."

With runners on first and third base, the relief pitcher struck out the next two hitters. August exclaimed, "Now you're pitching the way they pay you to!"

Two outs, two on. The pitcher and batter played a game of cat and mouse that brought the count to three balls and two strikes. Home team fans in the Phillies ballpark were cheering on the batter. Dodger fans, including August (and Arthur, in a show of solidarity with his father) yelled encouragement for the pitcher. Roebuck shook off two signs from his catcher. Then he nodded his head in agreement. He reared back and let fly a fastball. The batter slammed it, but right at the second baseman. Game over? Yes, but not the way the Dodger fans wanted it to end. The second baseman snagged the ball on one bounce and fired it to first base. The throw was out of the first baseman's reach and skidded on the ground into foul territory. The runner from third easily trotted across the plate to tie the score. Charging around third base, the runner from first was now making a mad dash for home. The Dodgers' first baseman corralled the wayward ball and let loose a desperate throw to his catcher. As the base runner neared home base, the catcher set himself up to snag the fast-approaching ball, at the same time bracing himself for the impending collision with the runner.

Catcher, runner, and ball simultaneously converged at home plate. The players' collision knocked the ball out of the catcher's glove and sent the two men to the ground. They both quickly scrambled to their feet. Unknown to the Phillies' player, he had failed to touch home plate. As he happily headed for the dugout, his third base coach and other teammates, who were now pouring out of the dugout, were yelling at him to hurry back to home plate. Meanwhile, the Dodger catcher had scurried to retrieve the ball and was running back towards home base to tag out his opponent.

This was a second race to home plate, a race the Phillies player won—at least according to the umpire. His "Safe!" echoed throughout the stadium. Final score: Phillies 9, Dodgers 8. Brooklyn players streamed out onto the field to argue with the umpire, but to no avail. Several fans threw bottles and other debris in the direction of the Dodger players and their dugout.

At the Berndt residence, August also reacted strongly. While screaming "God fuckin' dammit," he hurled the beer bottle he had been holding at the TV. Direct hit! With a loud explosion and puff of smoke the game had vanished—along with the television screen. The chaos scared Rex, who beat a hasty retreat upstairs to Arthur's bedroom. The youngster would have loved to follow his dog, or, even better, make a run for the front door, but instead sat expressionless on the couch. When his father was close by and this angry and unpredictable, Arthur's safest course of action was inaction—seeking shelter in the eye of the storm by locking himself in frozen silence. Fear-provoking thoughts raced through the youngster's head. Was he responsible for the Dodgers' loss? The damaged television? Would he pay a price and what would that price be?

"Fuckin' bastards. That asshole of a manager. It should never have even been a close game. Asshole!" August marched around the living room. "Jesus Christ. They had the damn game won. What a bunch of losers. No wonder the Yankees always beat 'em."

Arthur watched his father's angry face get angrier. The young boy wished more than anything that he had long ago dared venture outside to play with Rex. Now he feared making that move. His father was near the breaking point, and staying perfectly still and quiet remained the safest bet.

August realized that he'd thrown a half-full bottle of beer into the television set. He stormed out to the kitchen to get a refill. Arthur stayed fixed in place on the sofa, fearing what his father would do next.

From the kitchen, August mumbled—or was it growled?—half sentences. "God damn bastards...Fuckin' Dressen...Assholes... I could play better..." He came back into the living room, guzzled some beer and then resumed pacing and drinking while he fumed. Finally, he sat down on the couch, lit up a cigarette, and took a few soothing puffs.

Sensing a lull in the storm, Arthur dared to ask his father a question. "Are you going to call that repairman guy?"

August mulled over his son's question. "Yeah, I suppose so."

August walked over to the television, pulled the electric plug out of the socket, and reached inside the set to retrieve the beer bottle, cutting himself in the process. "Dammit!"

After he sucked some blood off his wrist, he turned to Arthur and said, "You keep your mouth shut about this, understand? If your mother asks you anything, as far as you know a tube went on the TV. Got it?" Arthur nodded knowingly. The young boy's life was all about cover-ups; keeping secrets came as naturally to Arthur as swimming to a fish.

The cut on August's wrist was still bleeding so he wrapped it up with a clean cloth. Then, he picked the TV up off its table. "Go out with me and open the door for the backseat," he ordered. The two exited the house, Arthur in the lead, August behind him, half walking/half stumbling with the television in his arms. As Arthur held the back door of the car open, his father slid the TV set onto the seat. Then father and son went back inside.

August got on the phone. "Hey, Mitchell. This is Berndt. Got a little problem with my television. My damn son was horsing around in the house and threw something...I don't know, a damn ball or something into it."

Arthur watched as his father impatiently listened to Mr. Mitchell's reply.

"C'mon Mitchell. I already got the damn thing in my car. It's of no use to me. At least let me drop it off." Following another response from the repairman, August replied, "Okay. I'll be there in fifteen minutes to drop it off. Hey, go easy on me. I'm just a poor working man."

August hung up the phone while muttering, "Damn guy wants you to beg to give him business." He turned to his son. "Okay, let's get going. You sit in the back and keep the TV from falling." The two went out to the car. August started the engine and was ready to back the car out of the driveway when he noticed something. Rex had come downstairs and was pawing at the front screen, hoping he'd be invited. He wasn't.

"Go close the big door. That dog has a habit of opening the screen door and getting loose."

"Dad, can we take him along?"

"No. This isn't some picnic we're going on. This is going to cost money."

Arthur knew better than to force the issue. After explaining to Rex that he was a flight risk, the youngster closed the storm and screen doors and rushed back to the car.

Off the two went, August driving extra slowly. Usually he was a speed demon, sober or not, but today he was carrying precious cargo—the television set. The duo reached Main Street and headed up the hill toward Port Jefferson Station. They didn't get far. A police car cruised up behind them, warning lights flashing.

"Shit. God dammit. What the hell now?" In the back seat, Arthur grabbed onto the TV as his father brought the car to an abrupt stop.

After exiting his car, the patrolman walked up to the driver's window and asked, "Hey, Gus. Something wrong with your car?"

"No, not that I'm aware of."

"I've been following you. Driving kind of slow, and a little herky-jerky, aren't you?"

"Yeah, I've got that TV in the back."

The patrolman glanced in the back seat. He recognized Arthur, whose reputation already preceded him with the local police department. "Hey, son, you staying out of trouble?"

"Yes, sir." In Arthur's world, policemen were a lot like teachers. Though they could be scary, they never hit the young boy. They were protective authority figures, unlike his father.

The officer turned his attention back to August. "Gus, I'm smelling something. You been drinking?"

"Yeah, just a little. Watching the ballgame. You know I don't drive drunk."

"Yeah...sure. Where you going?"

"Uptown to Mitchell's."

"Duane? He's a crackerjack with those sets. Worked on mine a couple of times. Cheap, too."

"I guess he's pretty good. Don't know that he's so cheap though."

Eyeing the TV a second time, the policeman offered his verdict. "Looks pretty bad. Total loss, I'd say. What the hell happened?"

"Long story."

"Looks like someone put their foot through it. So, Mitchell's is what, four or five blocks from here? You just dropping the set off?"

"Yeah. That's all we're doing."

"Okay. So drop it off and head back home. I don't get off until eight o'clock tonight. Don't wanna bump into you on the road again. It might make me look bad if I didn't do something."

"Nothing for you to worry about."

"Then, that's that. Say hello to the wife." The officer glanced at Arthur. "And you, young man, stay out of trouble. You do what your father says."

"He better," August mumbled.

As the policeman walked back to his car, Arthur felt he had lost a protector. When he was with his father, he always felt a bit safer if there were witnesses.

Father and son resumed their journey, which lasted exactly four more blocks.

Duane Mitchell was at work inside his garage-converted-to-repair shop. The garage door was open and he waved hello to August, who didn't reciprocate. Instead, he parked his car in the driveway and awkwardly carried the TV from the car into the workshop. The repairman pointed to the bench for August to unload the set on.

"Gus, this is real short notice."

"Well, look, I'm not happy about it either."

"What happened to your arm? Why the wrapping?"

"I cut myself getting the damn ball out of the set."

Chuckling, Mr. Mitchell admonished, "Gus, you got to teach your kid to play ball outside the house, not inside it."

"Nothing funny about it."

The repairman picked up on August's humorless mood and got more serious himself. "Kids. Sometimes I wonder if they're worth all the trouble."

"You can say that again."

"So, other than wrecking your TV, how's Arthur been doing? Shaping up?"

"I can't say that. He's got a long way to go. He still wets his bed, for one thing."

Arthur, wandering among the TVs in the shop, heard his father's comment. His face turned crimson with shame. Uncomfortably surprised by the unsolicited revelation, Mr. Mitchell changed the subject. "Don't think I can have it fixed sooner than Sunday after next, maybe Saturday. After scanning the set, he frowned and added, "That's if I can even fix it. Might not make financial sense. You need a new screen, picture tube..."

August suggested, half-jokingly, "Just take parts out of somebody else's set." Mr. Mitchell chose to ignore the comment.

August thought aloud. "Saturday or Sunday? Christ, that's a lot of ballgames I'm going to miss."

"You and your Dodgers."

"Your great Giants aren't doing so well, are they?"

"Yeah, but they got this new kid, Mays."

August shot back, "That nigger?"

"Well, you got Robinson. And Roy Campanella...what the hell is he? Heinz 57 varieties?"

"Yeah, I know. But he's a helluva a catcher. You gotta admit that."

"I guess so. You better watch out, Gus. I heard he's moving into Suassa Park."

"That'll be the day. Stanton would never let that happen."

"Oh yeah? He couldn't keep Cohen out. A Jew today, a nigger tomorrow."

Mr. Mitchell continued. "You know, I'd invite you to watch a game but don't take it personal, you sometimes get a bit out of hand, Gus. At least that's what I heard."

"Yeah? Who the hell says that?"

"I don't remember. Well, you know, maybe sometimes you fly off the handle a little bit."

"Everybody does."

"I know but...Well, forget it. Hey, the quicker you get out of here, the quicker I get to work."

"So I'll call you or you'll call me?"

"I'll take a look at it and call you later today. Got to decide if I can salvage it. It's a dinosaur, you know."

"Well, with all the crap on TV, why get a new set? Just to see crap on a bigger screen?"

"Gotcha. I'll phone you later."

August called to his son, who had been wandering throughout the garage, looking at the various television sets under different states of repair. The two headed back to the car. Because of the damaged TV set, Arthur had taken the trip to the repairman in the back seat. On the ride home, he had no excuse to sit there. He reluctantly slid onto the front passenger seat. The young boy always felt a bit more anxious when he was within his father's reach.

There was another reason for concern. August felt freer to drive with his foot to the floor since the TV was no longer a passenger. Arthur, however, was still young enough to be oblivious to the dangers of his father's erratic, high-speed driving. After all, didn't carnival rides always end safely? Arthur assumed they'd reach home that day in one piece, just like always—and they did.

When they got inside the house, Rex was there to greet them and immediately began his happy dance in front of Arthur, indicating he wanted to go outside.

"Dad, can I take Rex for a walk?"

"Yeah, go on. Just remember. What happened with the television set?"

"I was playing and broke it."

"Yup, that's it. And how'd you break it?"

"I don't know."

"Yes, you do. Remember this—no, you know what? "

"What, Dad?"

"I'll just tell your mother a couple of tubes went bad. I'll call Mitchell now and tell him to play dumb if she calls and say he can't fix it. He can tell her they don't make those parts anymore. I'm not going to miss all those ballgames. Damn Dodgers are going to cost me the price of a new set."

Arthur thought this over and asked, "So, Dad, what am I supposed to say?"

"The TV just went kaput. We were watching the game and the set punted. You got it?"

"Yup!"

With that, August went into the kitchen and turned on the radio. The hated Yankees were on and he spent the rest of the afternoon drinking beer and rooting against them. Arthur burst out the front door with Rex and the two headed off for the nearby woods.

A strange day, even by Arthur's standards. He went from potentially taking the blame to being let off the hook for something he hadn't done in the first place.

# Chapter 24

IN SEPTEMBER OF 1952, just weeks after his father had blown up the televisions set, Arthur headed back to the Port Jefferson Elementary School to begin the third grade. A few days into the new school year, Arthur's past caught up with him.

Over the intercom, the voice of the school principal's secretary interrupted Mr. Junior's third-grade classroom. "Could you please send Arthur Berndt to Mr. Tolleson's office? It's important."

"Why sure." The teacher turned and addressed the young boy. "Okay, Arthur. You're wanted in the principal's office."

"But I didn't do anything."

"Oh, I'm sure you didn't. Hopefully, everything is okay at home. Don't worry. You'll be back here in class in no time. By the way, do you know where Mr. Tolleson's office is?"

"Not really. Somewhere upstairs?" For all the trouble Arthur had gotten into outside of school, in school he had never been anywhere near the principal's office. In fact, not one teacher had ever even threatened to send him there, not even Mrs. Goward when his stealing spree had come to light.

"Yes. We don't have a hall monitor today to help you, so listen carefully. Take the stairs outside our room up to the second floor. When you get to the second floor, walk past the two classrooms on your right side. Which is your right side?"

The young boy gestured correctly.

"Okay, good. So, go past the two classrooms on your right side. Mr. Tolleson's office is the next room on the right. His door is usually open but, if it isn't, knock first, and someone will open it. Now, don't just go barging into the principal's private office. Wait in his secretary's room until you're asked to be seen by the principal."

Arthur got up from his seat and headed for the door. As he passed by other students' desks, he heard Richard whisper, "You're in trouble. You're gonna get it."

Arthur stopped in front of his perennial antagonist and shot back defiantly, "Am not."

"Are so."

"Prove it!"

Mr. Junior interceded. "Okay, that's enough. Arthur, get moving."

Arthur responded obediently to his teacher's order. He left the classroom, walked to the staircase, and began his ascent to the second floor. On the way, he feverishly struggled to make the unknown known—why would the principal want to see him? There seemed little reason for concern, but in cloudy situations like this one, it had become second nature to fear the worst, while holding out scant hope for the best.

Reaching the second floor, he headed for Mr. Tolleson's office, still desperately trying to convince himself that whatever he was headed for, it wasn't trouble. As he neared the open doorway, he heard crying. He walked into the office waiting room, marched up to the principal's secretary, seated at her desk, and announced, "My name is Arthur."

"Oh. Yes, Arthur. Just—." She was stopped in midsentence by Marguerite Berndt, who had appeared in the doorway of the principal's inner office. She was dabbing her eyes with a tissue. "Arthur...Arthur...why?"

Now the young boy was not only bewildered, but fearful. Marguerite ushered her son into the principal's office. The young boy instantly recognized Mr. Tolleson seated behind an enormous desk. There was another man, tall, mustached, wearing a suit and tie. He had placed his dress hat on the window sill he was seated on. He was wearing the look of someone who had just reluctantly reported bad news.

The school principal got up from his desk. "I'll leave you folks to discuss this matter in privacy." He exited his office, closing the door behind him.

The well-dressed man took control. "Mrs. Berndt, why don't you sit down on the couch with your son?"

She did, telling Arthur to sit beside her. After pulling up a chair in front of them, the man sat down and, directing his attention at the young boy, began talking.

"Arthur, my name is Ted McIntyre. Detective McIntyre. Do you know what a detective is?"

"I'm not sure..."

"Do you ever watch that new show on TV, *Dragnet?*"

Marguerite interrupted. "Mr. McIntyre, that comes on too late for my son to watch. Besides, it might not be the right kind of show for him to watch."

"You're probably right. Hadn't thought about that. I don't have any kids."

He turned back to Arthur.

"Well, do you remember—what was it, last year? No, more like two or three years ago—when you had a little trouble? You know, you and that other boy broke into that house in your neighborhood?"

"No."

"Well, I'd probably say the same thing. Not something you'd want to remember or talk about. But you boys did a lot of damage and cost your parents money, I'm sure." Marguerite, again sobbing, nodded her head in agreement. Her attempts to dry her eyes were futile. "Those men from the police department you talked to about it—one of them was me. Maybe you don't recognize me because back then I didn't have this mustache and I've put on a bit of weight."

"Yeah?"

"Well, I'm still a detective. I have to investigate, you know, collect information when something bad happens. I have to figure out who did what. The people who do bad things have to be brought to justice, punished, so they don't keep doing wrong things. Does that make sense?"

"I guess so."

"Have you ever been to Juska's Marine?"

A jolt of panic-produced adrenaline shot through the young boy's body. The young boy didn't exactly know why, but his well-developed instincts shouted silently Watch out! Be careful! He went into denial.

"Nope. Not me."

"Are you sure?"

"Yup. I don't even know what a juice cup marine is."

"It's pronounced Juska's. It's a store. It's all the way over in St. James. Now, I know you couldn't get there by yourself. Do you ever remember anyone, any young men taking you there?"

"Nope. I—"

Marguerite interrupted. "Don't lie to the detective. Tell the truth. This is all going to come out anyway. It always does."

Arthur pleaded his case. "But I already told you, Mom. I didn't do anything."

The detective continued the interrogation. "Okay, son. You didn't do anything. But maybe you can help us. Were you there when maybe somebody else did something?"

"Where?"

Fighting to hide his frustration, Detective McIntyre repeated, "Juska's."

"But I couldn't be there. You said it was too far away."

Exasperated, the detective tried a different approach. He pulled his chair directly in front of Arthur, just inches away, leaned forward, and stared into the young boy's eyes, unnerving the eight-year old. Arthur immediately feared he was about to be hit. What would he do if it became an all-out assault? What would his mom do? Anything? He remembered that when the police caught him for breaking into the Cohens' house, they didn't hit him; his father had done that after the policemen left. In fact, so far in his life, no other man besides his father had ever hit him. He guessed that a dad was the only person designated to dish out the really serious punishment to his son. For this moment at least, he hoped so.

The detective, noting the young boy's panic, switched tactics and slid his chair away from his precocious suspect, adopting a more laid-back strategy. He asked for the young boy's assistance. "Look Arthur. You want to help me, right? That's all I'm asking. Can I get your help?"

That question brought about a look of bewilderment to Arthur's face and a feeling of suspicion to his mind. The only other time Arthur had talked to this man, the young boy earned a severe beating for his honesty. Besides, adults rarely asked for his help. Why would this one?

"Help?"

"Yes, help."

Sensing an avenue of escape without knowing exactly what he was escaping from, Arthur asked, "What do I have to do?"

"Just help me out. Your mother told me that last summer you took a ride in a car with some young men and wound up in Setauket. St. James is the next town over."

"You mean Pete. We went on a couple of rides. I don't know the names of the towns."

"Pete? Is that Peter Stanton?"

"I call him Pete. So does everyone else. He lives far from me. He's all the way on Emerson Street. I can walk all the way to his house by myself."

The detective glanced at Marguerite and nodded his head. "It's him, all right."

"Did anybody else go with you two?"

Arthur was warming up to the interrogation, taking comfort in Detective McIntyre's now friendlier demeanor, so unlike his father's.

"Yup. There was a kid named Scott, and Four Eyes and Richie, but Richie didn't go that time. Richie—he's my favoritist."

"Four Eyes? Does he have another name?"

"Nope."

"So, it must've been exciting to go that far in an automobile, right?"

"Yeah, it's real far away from my house."

"Did you stop anywhere?"

"We went behind some building."

"What kind of building was it?"

"I don't know. There were a lot of boats there."

The detective was jotting things down on a pad. "Remember the name of the place?"

"Not exactly. Some funny name. I think it was that name you said or something."

"So, did you go inside?"

"Well, they had to get the door open for the owner, but I was the only one that fit."

"Fit? What do you mean?"

"I was the only one that could open the door. The other guys were too fat."

"Really? How'd you do it?"

"I had to walk like this..." Arthur got up and walked sideways a few steps. Then he sat back down. "The buildings were real close. It was kind of dark and scary."

"Then what?"

"I opened the secret door and went inside. There was a lot of grownup stuff inside. No toys or anything neat."

"And then?"

"I opened another door so Pete and Four Eyes could come in."

"What did you boys do next?"

"Well, then we went back to the car and they took me home."

"That's it? They didn't take any of the grownup stuff with them?"

"Nope."

"You sure?"

"Yup..." Arthur got lost in thought. Then he looked at the detective and, in a tone laced with equal parts naiveté and fear, asked, "Am I getting in trouble now?"

After briefly glancing at Arthur's mom, the detective turned back to Arthur. "Hopefully not, at least with the police. But your mom and dad are going to have to have a long talk with you. You always have to tell them who you're with and where you're going, so something like this doesn't happen again."

"Something like what, sir?"

Ignoring the youngster's question, the detective asked, "Did you ever go back there with them?"

"Uh, uh. My dad told me not to."

"He's a smart man. You're way too young to be hanging around with people that old, especially those guys. You don't want to be a bad guy, do you? You've already had some problems with the law. You're off to a bad start. Your parents want to be proud of you, you know that, right?"

Though he didn't, Arthur dutifully answered, "Yes."

The detective turned to Marguerite. "I think I have what I need here. Like I told you, loose lips sink ships. This Scott kid and one of his buddies were in a local bar bragging about stealing a whole bunch of stuff and said they used some brat—er, kid to do it. One of them called the kid Artie. The bartender happens to know Mike Juska and already knew about the break-in. He also knows Pete's cousin works for Mr. Juska. We've had our eyes on Mr. Stanton for quite a while. And that Scott kid has already had some run-ins with us. I did a little canvass near the store and found a neighbor who said he saw two people—an older teen and a very young boy—going over the fence at Juska's place. He kind of ignored it, but when he was on his porch later, saw the same two boys and another one, wearing glasses, come out from inside the store. This guy didn't think much about it until he found out Juska had been robbed. But, you know what? He didn't call anyone. We had to weed him out going door-to-door. Sometimes the public makes our job tougher than it should be."

The detective shot a quick look at Arthur. Then he continued describing the crime to Marguerite. "The locks weren't tampered with on the doors. That's where your son came in. They had him squeeze between Juska's and the meat market next to it and open a side door that's never used. Your son gets inside and goes to the rear door to let the others in. My guess? They took Arthur home and returned that night to clean things out. Got a lot of stuff—oil, tranny fluid, spark plugs, lots of tires, and mufflers. Quite a haul. Probably had to make a couple of trips."

Marguerite's eyes began to well up again. "What does all this mean for my son?"

"Well, I'm not sure. He's awfully young. That whole matter with the Cohens—as I recall he suffered no legal consequences. You settled matters with the Dr. Cohen, right? I know he didn't press charges."

"Yes. It was quite costly. We're not wealthy people."

"I bet. I bet you had a long talk with your son, too."

"I did. My husband was very angry. He... Well, he handled it as he saw fit."

"I completely understand. I'm not making excuses for your son, but this time I'd like to believe he didn't actually know what was going on. After all, apparently they didn't take anything in his presence. You said your husband said the car was 'full of punks' when they brought your son home. My guess is they went back that night with Scott Olsen's truck. Dead of night. No streetlights in the area. Easy pickins."

Suddenly feeling the need to defend himself, Arthur blurted out, "They told me we were opening the door for the owner."

"I'm sure they did," the detective replied, fairly certain the youngster had been used as a pawn.

"They said he lost his keys or something."

All three sat in an uncomfortable silence, until Arthur chimed in. "Can I keep my cap gun?"

"Your cap gun?" asked the detective.

"Yup. I got one for opening the door. Pete gave it to me."

"Well...I'll let your parents decide that one."

Slightly more resigned to her son's situation, Marguerite composed herself and asked, "What happens now?"

"Well, for one thing, your son's technically not too young to testify in court. At least I think that's the case. I can't see him being charged with anything, though. If Mr. Juska sues for his loss I don't know exactly how that would work. I don't want to get you upset Mrs. Berndt, but you folks might be held responsible for your son's actions. I can't say for sure. The question might come up if you as the parents should have known your son had the potential to do...but, I mean he only opened a door. By all accounts, they didn't even take anything while he was there. The problem is he has a track record with that Cohen matter." The detective thought a bit, turned towards Marguerite, and said, "Again, I don't want to upset you needlessly, Mrs.Berndt, but there is also the possibility your son could be subpoenaed as a material witness. Remote, but possible. In that case, Arthur here is going to be counting on you and your husband for support. In a courtroom, all those serious-looking adults—no doubt the scariest situation he'd be dealing with since we visited your house that time a few years ago."

The detective continued. "I'm hoping for pleas from Stanton and Olsen. Stanton's father wants to get this over with. As far as damages go, all the other boys are eighteen or better. Figures they'd be the ones to make restitution. But, you know, in a civil suit, the lawyer would probably go after everybody. Maybe you could talk to Mr. Juska and reach some kind of agreement."

"Oh, I don't think so. Did you know he lives on the same street as we do?"

"Yeah, I saw that. Small world."

"Too small, sometimes. Gus—my husband—and Mike have had some...well, there's friction between them. My husband accused him of selling tires on the black market during the war. Mr. Juska calls us a bunch of Nazis. I think he lost some relatives over in Lithuania during the war. We had nothing to do with that, but he doesn't see it that way. They got into a fight at a gas station once. It was awful. Now my husband and Mr. Juska don't talk to each other. He won't even drive by our house; he takes the long way around."

"Geez, I'm sorry to hear that. Might complicate things."

Marguerite continued. "Because of that fight, Arthur can't play with the Juskas' two boys. That bothers me a lot because they're my son's age. My son has this habit of seeking older boys to associate with. I've tried to talk to Roslyn Juska. You know, why should the kids suffer? But, her husband just won't budge, so that's that."

Detective McIntyre got back to the legal issues. "I've never really seen a case like this, you know, with a kid so young. My understanding is that if a child Arthur's age appears in court he has to prove he is competent, he has to be able to recall events accurately, he's got to be able to communicate...what else ? Know the difference between truth and lies and... There's something else... Yeah, understand it's important to answer questions truthfully. He seems to remember what happened. That's if he's telling me the truth." He turned to Arthur. "Are you, son?"

"Yes, sir."

"You haven't been lying or holding out on me, not telling me things you know, have you?"

"No, sir."

"Well, Mrs. Berndt, I can't guarantee how this will go. I'm not a judge or prosecutor. The Olsen kid is on probation. He's probably the weakest link in that gang. He might be willing to fess up the details to save his hide. If they all cop a plea, that'd make things a lot easier for all of us, including your son."

Arthur burst out in tears. "I don't wanna go to jail."

"Son, you're not going to jail. Not this time. But if you keep this up, if you don't change, some day you will be old enough to go to jail. When you get older, you can't just say 'I didn't know what was going on.' You'd be an accessory, you know, somebody that helped someone else do something bad. Or, maybe even worse, a perpetrator."

"I don't wanna be a accessory. Mr. Detective, that other thing you said, a witness something, is that better to be?"

"You mean material witness? Well, legally speaking, I would think so."

"So, I'll be that then."

Stifling a slight chuckle, the detective responded. "Son, other people have to decide that matter. Hopefully, you won't have to be either."

Marguerite expressed her dismay. "My god, I still can't believe this is happening."

"It's tough, I know."

"So what do I do? What does my son do?"

"For one thing, he has to stay away from the Stanton gang. Completely. Totally. No contact. I have to admit I have a hard time understanding how a kid his age winds up with a crew like that."

"I don't understand either. We try to do our best with him."

"Don't take this the wrong way, but I think your son's just one of those kids that has to be watched closely."

Marguerite answered with a mixture of confusion and self-defensiveness, "I always thought we did."

The detective directed his next remarks at Arthur. "Shouldn't you be playing with kids your own age?" Without waiting for an answer, he continued. "Seems to me you should be looking to your parents for guidance, not a gang of lawbreakers."

This well-intentioned advice made no sense at all to Arthur. Yet he felt obligated to pacify the adults in the room, especially his mother, who would be reporting to his father. He responded with a lukewarm, "Yes, sir."

The detective turned back to Marguerite. "Talk things over with your husband. Maybe he has some ideas. Maybe he could spend more time with his son. You know, a good role model. Of course, he can't be getting into fights with the neighbors. I'm guessing that was some isolated incident."

Marguerite offered an ambiguous answer. "Well, yes. I guess so, for the most part." Uncomfortable with the conversation, she tried to head it in another direction. "But, as far as his father spending more time with him, that's hard. August works an awful lot. Always asks for overtime."

"Well, I'm just saying...Arthur seems to be headed down the wrong path."

Marguerite again burst out in tears. "I know, I know."

"I'm sorry. It's got to hurt....Well, I'm done here. You have my card. Anything comes up, give me a call."

Collecting herself, Marguerite asked, "Can I call you to find out what's happening, how things are progressing?"

"Certainly."

"Well, thank you very much, Detective McIntyre. I'm so glad we met today here in school. I took a cab just so I wouldn't have to bother my husband at work. He wouldn't handle this sort of thing well. I'm so glad you didn't drop by our house."

"I would have, if you hadn't answered the phone."

Grateful for such good fortune, Marguerite wanted to dodge any further bullets. "Sir, could I ask a favor of you?"

"Yes?"

"Would you please not call my residence? I'd rather call you or stop by the station. You're on East Main Street, right?"

"Yes..."

"I'd prefer to be responsible for touching base with you. I'd rather not get my husband upset if it's not necessary. "

"I understand, I guess. One upset parent is enough. I'd say give me a call once a week, or stop by the station."

Marguerite mumbled to herself, "I've got half a mind to say nothing to my husband and just pray this goes away." The detective heard her. "I can't give you advice on that, ma'am."

"Oh, I know."

Detective McIntyre rose to his feet. Mother and son did likewise. The detective shook hands with Marguerite and then with Arthur. "Young man, you mind your parents. They know what's best for you. Remember, you're at an age now where if you keep getting in trouble with the law, you could be classified as a juvenile delinquent, something called a lower age delinquent—at least that's my understanding."

Arthur was familiar with the term. "My father told me I'm already one of those kind of people."

Eager to avoid any further scrutiny, the youngster asked the detective a question of his own. "Can I go back to my class now?"

"As far as I'm concerned, you can."

The three left the principal's office, and after briefly exchanging pleasantries with Mr. Tolleson, they exited the secretary's room. As they walked through the hall, Marguerite commented to the detective in a puzzled frustrated voice, "He does so well in school."

"Well, school has structure. Maybe he needs a little more of that outside of school. I get the impression he's a bit of a live wire."

Marguerite admitted as much. "Oh, he can be a handful. It's just so difficult. Every time I get my hopes up, something like this happens."

"You've got your hands full. I don't envy you. But I can see you're doing your best. That's all you can do. Odds are good he'll grow out of this."

"That's what I keep hoping for. I keep telling myself this is just a stage he's going through. We don't have any problems with his sisters, but—he's a boy. I guess that means more work."

"Probably true."

After descending the stairs and reaching the first floor, Detective McIntyre shook Marguerite's hand. He then shook Arthur's, admonishing the youngster. "Now listen, son. I don't want to hear you're up to no good. You listen to your parents, you got it?"

"Yes, sir."

The detective headed down another flight of steps to leave the building. Marguerite escorted Arthur over to his classroom door. Along the way, she offered unexpected and comforting words to her son.

"Okay. I'm not going to tell your father about this for the time being. There's no reason to get him upset. Hopefully, things will get straightened out...somehow."

A wave of relief fell over the young boy. All the while he was being grilled by the imposing detective, his mind had worked overtime, visualizing what lay in store for him if his father found out about any of this. Now his mother had granted him a temporary reprieve.

After giving her son a tentative—and unexpected—hug, Marguerite headed down the hall. The young boy watched her walk for a bit and then he called out, "Mom!" She turned to see her son waving goodbye. This was more than a typical young boy's sign of affection for his mother; it was a silent show of gratitude from a child who had been spared the wrath of the most fearsome person in his life—his father.

Arthur returned to his classroom. The minute he entered the room, fifteen sets of young eyes began scrutinizing him. His classmates already assumed he was in trouble; they wanted to know all the juicy details.

Mr. Junior reined in the young inquiring minds. "Larry, no need to stop reading. Arthur, go to your desk and get out your reader. We're on page seventeen. The Smith family has gone for a ride and now they're in the park. Larry, please start from the top of page seventeen again."

That got an "Okay, Mr. Junior" from Larry, and the students settled back into their routine.

Arthur was a child who relished the safety that school provided him and, today, when the dismissal bell rang, he was even more reluctant than usual to leave the sanctuary of his classroom and head home. He wanted to believe he was in the clear, but was never completely certain his mom could be counted on to spare him from his father's rage. Though his mother had a soft side that her husband didn't, she rarely kept him in the dark regarding issues with their son. Whether his mom would eventually feel duty bound to tell her spouse about the store robbery or his father found out some other way, either scenario would lead to a beating. Arthur engaged himself in the conflicted thinking that by now came so naturally to him, holding out hope his father would never learn about this latest brush with the law, while at the same time fearing he would. If the latter proved true, the young boy could only pray it would be in the late evening when he'd already be fast asleep. That way he wouldn't have had to spend any waking hours dreading what was to come. August would jolt his son out of his sleep and get down to the business at hand immediately—just like he so often did when rousing Arthur and finding he'd wet the bed. The punishment would be over almost before the half-asleep youngster knew what hit him.

When he got home from school, Arthur immediately went outside with Rex, trying to enjoy as much of the calm before the storm as he could. He wandered aimlessly with his dog through the neighborhood. Reaching Emerson Street, he put on the brakes. That was Pete Stanton's street. Arthur had steered clear of the older boy for weeks, though he'd never understood why he was supposed to. After today's conversation with Detective McIntyre, he sensed it was more imperative than ever to avoid the older boy, even if he still wasn't sure why. What he was sure of—when the police are involved, things can't be good.

Arthur turned around and headed back to his house. He wanted to be there when his dad got home. He hoped his mother would feel sorrier for him if he was standing in front of her, making it harder for her to give his father a heads up on what had happened at school that day.

Arriving at Twenty-one Lowell Place, the youngster saw the family car was sitting in the driveway. That meant his father was home. This called for a change of plans; he had to determine if entering his house was safe. It was a warm late summer afternoon and the windows were open at the Berndts' residence. There was a small wooded lot between their house and the next-door neighbor's. Arthur left the street and, crouching down, carefully wended his way through the brush between the two homes until he got as close to his house as he dared. He planted himself on the ground behind a laurel bush, and with Rex at his side, listened intently. He could make out his father's voice.

"...and Chuck was trying to unload tickets for the ball game for ten bucks each. What a chiseler. He's not a kike, but he might as well be."

"Gus, it would be great if you and Art went to a game together. He'd be so excited."

"Yeah, well ten dollars is way too steep. Of course, since Chuck can't go, maybe I can jew him down. Besides, Arthur's a kid, so I should get a discount."

"I could pack a lunch so you wouldn't have to spend any money at the ballpark."

"Christ, I'll have to drive all the way to Brooklyn and then make a run for it to the ballpark. Karl took me there years ago and it was already getting 'dark' back then, if you know what I mean."

"Oh, Gus, you shouldn't talk like that. You know you like Robinson and Campanella."

"Yeah, on the ball field. That's it!"

"Well, anyway. We do have the money. When is the game, next Saturday?"

"Yeah. Next to last game. By the way, where is Arthur? Shouldn't he be home by now?"

"Oh, he went out with Rex."

Arthur, who had been listening intently, took his father's question as the cue to show up. He got up from his lookout post and headed for the front door, his confidence bolstered by the absence of the names Juska, Stanton, or McIntyre in his parents' conversation. In fact, his attention shifted to the exciting possibility of seeing his Dodgers in person.

Once inside the house, Arthur headed for the living room and the TV. Then he remembered he couldn't turn on the set without his parents' permission. He went to the dining room, where his parents had been talking.

"Mom, can I watch *Howdy Doody?*"

Before his mother could answer, August carped, "*Howdy Doody?* That nonsense?"

"Gus, he's just a kid. All the kids his age watch it."

"Christ almighty, I guess so."

Then, turning towards his son, August asked a question that brought a smile to his wife's face. "Hey, how'd you like to go to a ballgame?"

"What game?"

"A Dodgers game."

Arthur's eyes lit up, partly an act since he'd been eavesdropping and had expected the offer, partly the real deal, because going to a Dodger game was a dream come true. "Wow, can we really go? Dad, you told me I had to wait."

"Well, I lied. Something came up. I'm not promising anything yet. I have to work on the price of tickets. It's the next-to-last game of the season. Everything might be on the line. The damn Giants just won't quit."

Normally, a long drive with his father anywhere was to be avoided. Though the youngster was used to being on guard around his dad under any circumstances, there was something extra tension-provoking when in a car. In dicey situations outside an automobile, the young boy fed himself the comforting thought that if things got bad enough, he could make a run for it. Trapped in a speeding car with his father, even his fertile imagination could not cook up a plan of escape if his father started smacking him around. On a long drive to Brooklyn, his father would have plenty of time to get angry about something. But if they were going to a ballgame, the young boy figured his dad would be upbeat and safe to be around, even inside a car. To increase the odds of a pleasant ride, Arthur vowed he'd force himself to stay up all night before the game, just to make sure he didn't wet the bed. That way, the day of the ball game wouldn't get off on the wrong foot. There was another concern. A Dodger loss might doom the youngster to an uncomfortable ride back home. Arthur handled that fear with a youngster's blind optimism—the Dodgers would win, for sure!

August turned to his wife. "Right now, got to get to work on that damn drainage ditch in the backyard." With that, August headed out to the backyard. Marguerite got back to preparing dinner and Arthur, reveling in his father's offer, made a beeline for the living room and Howdy Doody.

For the moment the Berndt house was enjoying a rare cease fire. Rare and short-lived.

# Chapter 25

TWO WEEKS LATER, A furious neighbor stormed up to the front door of the Berndt residence and, refusing to passively ring the doorbell, instead banged on the front door screen. Marquerite rushed to it and found herself face to face with a red-faced Mike Juska, steaming mad. Her son eavesdropped from inside the house, crouched behind an open window in the living room. He hoped this unhappy neighbor would go away soon. Arthur's father was not yet home from work, but he soon would be.

"Where the hell is that bastard kid of yours?"

"That's a nasty thing to say." Marguerite never mentioned her meeting with Detective McIntyre to her husband and had not called the police since. She let herself believe the whole thing had evaporated into nothingness. It hadn't. The last thing she wanted was for her husband to come home to find a neighbor, one he already disliked, standing on the front stoop. Especially since he was there complaining about their son's most recent criminal activity, activity Marguerite had kept August in the dark about. Disclosure of such a cover-up would likely lead to a beating for the young boy, and possibly for her, too. Hoping to do whatever it would take to get him to leave her property before August arrived, she continued her conversation with Mr. Juska, speaking softly, hoping to calm him. "What seems to be the problem?"

"What's the problem? I'll tell you what's the problem. That s.o.b. kid of yours is a criminal, that's what."

"Why, what do you mean?"

"Don't play dumb. And don't cover up for that brat. That's the trouble. You go too easy on him. I suppose you didn't hear about my store?"

"Well yes, I did, some weeks ago. I thought it all got straightened out."

"Well, it didn't. I'm suing the whole goddamn bunch of youse—Stanton, those other punks, and your damn son. What is he? Seven? Eight? I don't give a shit. If you can't control him, you have to pay the price. I can't wait for the law on this. I lost over a thousand dollars. This is bullshit."

"Well, I spoke with Detective McIntyre. He feels my son didn't know what he was doing."

"Oh, yeah? Good for him. How about when he broke into the Cohens' place? Or (pointing across the street) the Harrisons'? 'Didn't know what he was doing' my ass."

"Well, I don't know what to say. We don't have a lot of money—"

"So, then keep that kid on a shorter leash. He's only going to get worse."

"Look, Mike. Why don't I stop by your house sometime soon so we can discuss this? I don't want any problems between you and Gus."

Too late. The Berndt family car pulled into the driveway. August bolted out of the vehicle and, lunchbox in hand, walked up the steps towards the front door. He was already in a foul mood. He'd gotten into an argument with Chuck, his coworker, over the asking price of the tickets for the Dodgers game. Words were exchanged, the two almost came to blows, and Chuck canceled his offer. Due to that fracas, the frown August typically wore was a bit more pronounced than usual. It transformed into a deep scowl as he neared the stoop where his wife and their angry neighbor stood.

August warmly greeted his neighbor. "What the hell do you want?"

"Money. That's what I want. I'm here looking for $220 bucks. I figure that's your son's share of the take."

"What 'take'? What the hell ya talking about?"

"Don't play dumb. Your brat and those punk teenagers broke into my store. You know all about it, I'm sure."

August looked at his wife suspiciously. It was easier for him to suspect Marguerite had purposely withheld damaging information about their son than it was to believe his son might be innocent. To make matters worse, he'd had a tough day at work, didn't like Mike Juska, and was itching for a rematch.

"Look, you leave my wife alone and stay off my property. You got that?"

"I'll leave when I'm ready."

August's eyes glazed over with hatred. His face was wearing an all-too-familiar look. He dropped his lunch box and picked up a shovel lying on the grass. He grasped it like a baseball bat and began taking swings at imaginary pitches.

Mike Juska edged his way off the stoop, all the while keeping a wary eye on his neighbor, a wild man brandishing a weapon.

All this time, Arthur had been watching the activities from the dining room window, relieved that the object of his father's rage was someone other than himself, at least for the time being.

"Get the hell off my property. Last time I'm telling you." August swung the shovel, narrowly missing his neighbor, who agilely jumped out of harm's way.

"Berndt, you're nuts! Just fuckin' nuts! I can see there's no talking to you. See you in court, asshole."

Taking his leave, Mr. Juska briskly and purposely walked across the Berndts' front yard, knowing what everybody else in Suassa Park knew: August Berndt hated anyone trespassing on his manicured property. August, now leaning on the shovel, watched in fuming silence as his neighbor, after daring to tread on the lawn, walked off towards his own house. As soon as Mike Juska was out of sight, August switched his attention towards a more customary target, his son. Arthur was standing inside at the screen door, the only line of defense between him and his father.

Eyes aglow with anger and suspicion, August demanded of his son, "What the hell was that jackass talking about?"

Arthur was too fear-stricken to answer. Marguerite rushed to his defense. "Oh, his shop was robbed some time ago. He's very mad because he lost a lot of money. He thinks somehow Arthur was involved. You know, Peter Stanton was apparently involved and maybe Mike saw Art with him—but that was months ago. A detective—"

"Jesus Christ," August muttered under his breath.

"Oh, it's okay. This detective—Mr. McIntyre—talked to Arthur and told him there was no problem."

"Well, why did the cop wanna talk to Arthur in the first place?"

Marguerite thought aloud, struggling to keep her son out of his father's crosshairs. "I guess Peter wanted...No, that wouldn't make sense, a boy his age blaming an eight-year-old. Probably Mike Juska did. You know how he feels about us. Oh, I just don't know."

"Why would Juska blame him? Juska's way over in Saint James. What an idiot. How the hell—" August stopped himself in midsentence. "That time that punk drove him to the beach. Saint James isn't that far from there. So, when did this so-called robbery take place?"

Marguerite was determined to defuse the issue. "I'm not really sure."

The Grand Inquisitor turned towards his young son. The scrutiny continued. "Well, what do you have to say about all this?"

"I didn't do anything."

"So, that day at West Meadow, where did you go with Stanton?"

"He took me right home."

"He better have."

August picked up his lunchbox and, muttering " fuckin' Juska asshole," entered the house.

Marguerite silently recited the Serenity Prayer, then let out a sigh. Arthur, not familiar with the Serenity Prayer and not given to sighing, instead gave silent thanks his father had not hit him. No matter how sure he was he'd done no wrong, his father was always the final arbiter of that.

As far as Marguerite was concerned, the worst was over. Arthur still wasn't sure what the fuss had been all about. In his mind, whatever he had done to earn his Roy Rogers cap gun, the end justified the means.

For the time being, August focused his anger on Mike Juska. That was comforting to Arthur. Whenever his father was distracted by someone or something else, that provided the youngster a temporary reprieve from his father's fear-provoking attention. That evening, August became even more distracted.

Meals were always uncomfortable in the Berndt residence. Except for August, the family rapidly ate dinner in silence. The goal was to get away from the table as quickly as possible before anyone said or did something to set off the head of the household. If any questions were asked during a meal, they were asked by August. At dinner that night, Liz didn't wait for questions from her father and instead spoke up with unaccustomed fearlessness. "You had a chance to go into business with Mr. Cawley. That's a way better job than the one you have now. You should've taken it."

The tension meter immediately shot up to a dangerous level. While August glowered at his oldest daughter's impertinence, the rest of the Berndts experienced an all-too-familiar increase in uneasiness. Though his guard was up like everyone else's, Arthur privately savored his older sister's surprising show of courage. At times Arthur challenged his father with deeds; now Liz was challenging him with words.

"For your information, I've been the head caretaker at RCA for three years now. Cawley's business is too risky. I'd be giving up a pension and a steady paycheck for nothing guaranteed."

Marguerite tried to defuse the growing tension between her husband and daughter. "You know, Mr. Cawley has a lot of respect for your gardening talents. That's why he offered you a partnership in his flower shop. Even if you didn't take it, that's a feather in your cap."

"Yeah. I'd be doing all the work; he'd be making all the money. Don't know if I could trust him."

Liz wouldn't stop. "It'd be a lot better than cutting a lawn for a living. That's pretty much what you do, right?"

August picked up his dinner plate, half full of food, and threw it at his daughter. Liz ducked and the plate and its contents slammed against a wall. As strands of spaghetti slid down to the floor, the rest of the family froze in place as August Berndt glowered at his daughter. "Go to your room!"

"I'll go when I want to. You can't make me."

Flustered by his daughter's show of defiance, August turned to his wife at the other end of the dinner table. "Tell her to go to her room."

"Liz, do as your father says. He's your dad."

"So? Who cares if he is? You never stick up for us."

August started to get up from his chair. That was enough of a threat for Liz. She leapt to her feet and ran around the dinner table, heading for the stairs that lead up to the second floor. On the way, she lost her balance and hit the floor. She collected herself and clumsily scrambled up the stairs mumbling "shithead" under her breath, just low enough so that her father couldn't hear it—a bit of camouflaged rebellion. When she got upstairs, she entered her bedroom, slamming the door closed with her foot as loudly as possible.

"Dammit. I work my ass off and those kids have no idea. Yeah, the grass always looks greener until you have to pay the bills. Jesus Christ."

August got up and headed for the kitchen and his beer reserve in the refrigerator. He took out the last can and popped it open. He went out onto the back steps where he sat down, lit a cigarette and silently fumed.

The rest of the Berndt family that remained at the table heaved a collective, silent sigh of relief and then went their separate ways. Marguerite cleared the table, cleaned up the spilled food, wiped down a sauce-spattered wall, and began washing the dishes. Ruth went over to the Regalmutos', her home away from the house she was forced to live in. Arthur went to his room to read, biding time until his father to cooled off.

A half hour later, Liz decided to venture back downstairs. She chose not to directly confront her father, now sitting in the kitchen drinking Scotch whisky, his backup drink of choice when the suds ran dry. Instead she went into the living room and vented in the company of her mother, making sure she spoke loud enough for her father to hear.

"He is too much to deal with. I can't stand him. Why don't you ever do anything about it?"

"Now, Liz, he had a very tough day at work. He told me. Please calm down. This isn't like you."

"He always has a 'tough day at work.' That's just an excuse. I hate this house. I can't wait to get on that train for college tomorrow."

Marguerite's face winced in a combination of disappointment and hurt. "Oh, don't say that. Please. That's very upsetting to hear. You've never talked like that."

"Well, there's a first time for everything. And, by the way, I have talked that way. You just never listen."

Marguerite wanted this conversation to go away. She got up, went over to turn on the TV, and stood waiting for the picture to come on. She put on the news and went back to the couch.

"Just like always. You stick up for him and ignore me."

"I just don't want any trouble—"

From the kitchen, August threatened, "Tell her to shut the hell up."

"Oh, the hell with it!" Liz stormed back upstairs, again somewhat awkwardly.

Arthur had listened to all this from his bedroom. He felt relief—and a twisted satisfaction—when the other members of the family were arguing and he wasn't the subject of the conversation. From his doorway, he watched his sister reach the top of the stairs, stumble past him, go into her room, and slam the door shut, louder than she had the first time. Arthur went back to lying on his bed, reading a comic book.

A stillness washed over the Berndt household, except for the newscaster babbling from the television set.

A half hour later, Arthur heard an odd sound coming from his sister's bedroom. Liz was choking! Arthur flew out of his room and ran to open her door. The warped door always stuck, so he had to throw his small frame against it several times to open it up. When he did, he looked inside and found his sister, sitting at her desk, doubled over. She had vomited into a wastebasket. Most of the vomit had found its target but there were splatters on the floor. Arthur wasn't sure what was happening, but instinctively sensed this was something their parents must not find out about. He closed the door behind him while Liz pulled herself together. The two then cleaned up the floor with Kleenex and two of Liz's sweaters. When they were done, the tissues and soiled clothing were thrown into the wastebasket that Liz then hid in her closet.

On her desk sat at half empty bottle of gin. She'd been drinking from it, not bothering to use a glass. She capped the gin bottle and shoved it under her bed mattress. Then she plopped onto the bed.

"I'm tired. Turn off the light and go back to your room. Don't you dare say anything to anybody. Got it?"

"I won't, I promise."

Arthur, used to a life of stealth, knew what to do and what not to do. He turned out the light switch, leaving his sister, still fully dressed, lying on her bed in the dark. He left her room and, as cautiously and quietly as possible, closed the stubborn door behind him. He carefully listened for any activity downstairs. All he heard was his father yelling back at a television news report that was not to his liking. The young boy carefully inched down the hall and back into his bedroom, closing the door behind him.

Arthur went to sleep with the muffled rantings of his father serving as a lullaby.

# Chapter 26

ARTHUR STARED STRAIGHT AHEAD. Not at his third-grade teacher. The youngster had no interest in the math lesson Mr. Junior was presenting on the blackboard. He was in his own world, busy hatching a plan that had his undivided attention.

When he was finished, Arthur had come up with a novel way to feed his insatiable sugar craving. Every school day, he left home with the thirty cents his mother gave him to purchase lunch in the school cafeteria. Why not skip lunch and use that money to buy candy? Thirty cents could buy a lot of sweets. Plus, he already had practice missing meals. It was one of the punishments used at home. This was such a great idea, he put it into action immediately.

Lunchtime. The procedure was for all the school children to eat in the cafeteria and then go out onto the playground until it was time to go back to class. Today, Arthur skipped the lunch line and immediately sat at one of the tables in the dining area. Soon, other students, holding full lunch trays, began to file in and find seats. One sat down at Arthur's table and immediately asked him, "Aren't you gonna eat?"

"Nah. Don't like Welsh rarebit. Yuck."

Having nothing to do inside the school, Arthur was the first to go outside. Mr. Dennis was the teacher assigned to monitor playground activity.

"Wow! Art, you must have wolfed your lunch down."

"Yup. I was really hungry."

"Well, why don't you use the swings until the other kids come out? Then you can play Elimination."

"Okay, Mr. Dennis."

Arthur killed some time on a swing until other students, freshly nourished, began streaming out from the cafeteria exit. Some ran to the seesaws, others entertained themselves on the swings, still others chose Elimination. The latter was Arthur's favorite and he joined in with a group of his peers just as the game began. A soccer-sized red ball was thrown up in the air by Mr. Dennis. Some twenty children scrambled to catch it. Per the rules, the one that did could give chase and throw the ball at any of the other participants. If the intended target was hit by it, he or she was out of the game and had to wait on the sidelines until the next round started. If the ball was caught, the one throwing it was out. Should the ball miss all the participants, whoever retrieved it got to throw next. The game continued until only the winner was left. This day, Arthur survived until there were just six kids remaining, but then he got clipped on the ankle by Skinny's throw.

There was time for three more rounds of Elimination before the kids had to go back to their classrooms.

During the afternoon, hunger pangs came on with a rush while Mr. Junior showed the class a film. Although it dealt with how children lived in different parts of the world and was the kind of movie that normally would keep Arthur's attention, his painfully empty stomach nagged at him mercilessly. By the time the film ended, Arthur's gut was desperately crying for food. He dragged himself through fifteen minutes of penmanship. Arthur's writing was deemed excellent by his teacher, but the youngster couldn't have cared less. Next, a half hour of reading, with students taking turns. Normally Arthur, a superior reader, eagerly volunteered, but not today. With such a dire need for food, it was difficult to focus on anything happening in the classroom.

By 2:15 p.m. students in the class began to fidget, since three o'clock was release time. Mr. Junior had a rule. While school was in session, no one could turn around to look at the clock on the wall in the back of the classroom. As the end of the school day got closer, many students did anyway, ignoring Mr. Junior's admonitions since they all knew that he was pretty much of a pushover.

To keep the students too busy for clockwatching and for his own sanity's sake, Mr. Junior decided to end this school day with a spelling bee. After asking all the students to stand by their desks, he challenged individual students to spell whatever word he pronounced. Every time a word was misspelled by a student, he or she had to sit down. In a sense, good spellers were punished because success meant they had to stand longer. Nevertheless, hoping to stay alive in the contest, each student privately prayed the word he or she got was an easy one. Always, camping, smell, summer, vase, yesterday—thanks to words like these the number of students sitting quickly surpassed the number left standing. Throughout, Arthur, still alive in the contest but shaky from hunger, struggled to keep from collapsing to the floor.

The contest went on until only three contestants were left—Richard Blaskowitz, Kathryn Thomas (the smartest student in the class), and Arthur. The new word was "evaporate." Richard spelled it e-v-a-p-p-a-r-a-t-e. Dejectedly, he took his seat. Kathryn and Arthur both nailed it. Mr. Junior asked the two remaining contestants to come up to him and face-off in front of their classmates. Because of his chronic fear of failure, Arthur's anxiety level skyrocketed. The hunger pangs were temporarily forgotten as panic-induced waves of adrenalin shot through every inch of his body. Both students walked up their respective aisles and stood alongside each other next to Mr. Junior's desk. He announced the new word—ocean.

Arthur regained his confidence as he was certain he knew how to spell it. His self-assurance quickly dissipated. He was just as certain Kathryn could spell it, too, so they'd have to go on to another word. He wondered if that next one would be too tough for him. Disaster lay just around the corner. Humiliation at home was easier for Arthur to endure than humiliation in public.

Kathryn confidently spelled out the letters o-s-h-u-n. Arthur knew that was wrong; he sensed victory. Mr. Junior advised Kathryn her response was incorrect. Glumly, she went back to her seat. Only Arthur was left standing. If he got the word wrong, the contest would be considered a tie as time was running out on the school day; if he spelled it correctly, he would be the winner. A fresh rush of adrenaline shot through Arthur, generated not by anxiety, but by confidence. He knew it! He knew how to spell a word Kathryn couldn't! With his hunger pangs still on hold, Arthur decided to milk the situation.

"Arthur, can you spell ocean?"

"Could you repeat that sentence you used it in?"

"Sure thing. The ship sailed over the ocean."

Arthur hesitated, pretending he was searching for the right letters.

"I'm not... o ... Is it uh, o – s... No. Maybe o – c – e –....a... Wait...-n?"

"Spell it again, clearly."

"O-c-e-a-n?"

"Yes. Excellent. Arthur wins the spelling bee!"

The classroom broke out in spontaneous celebration. As Arthur walked proudly down the aisle towards his desk, he was saluted on the way by cheers from the smiling classmates he passed. It felt like the whole world was giving him one big thumbs up.

As soon as the euphoria of victory wore off, his stomach felt emptier than ever.

The bell rang; school was over. Arthur shoved his books into his desk and scurried to be the first out of the classroom. He scooted down a flight of steps and burst out into a clear, brisk fall day. Usually, when the school day ended, he walked straight home. Today, a boy on a mission, he had a stop to make along the way.

Arthur passed the Crystal Fountain in downtown Port Jefferson every day on the way home from school, but he'd never gone inside. Now, here he was, standing in front of it, both eager and afraid to enter. The Crystal Fountain had the reputation of being primarily for big kids. That's why Arthur hesitated before getting up the courage to pull open the door and enter.

Once inside, the youngster quickly saw for himself that the Crystal Fountain was an older crowd's hangout. Except for Arthur, all its patrons were teenagers. A few of the male teens looked especially menacing with their long slicked-back hair, heavy-duty Garrison belts and engineer boots. Several of the female patrons looked older—and more socially advanced— than their age, thanks to a liberal dose of makeup and tight-fitting sweaters and jeans. Some of the teenagers were sitting at the soda fountain, others were dancing to popular music blasting from a jukebox, while still others were standing in small groups smoking cigarettes. Intimidated, the typical child Arthur's age would have headed for the exit. But Arthur would not be deterred. He wasn't there for the jukebox, the dancing, or the soda. Rumor had it the Crystal Fountain featured a huge selection of candy—the largest in town—spread out in a mammoth glass case. Arthur immediately spotted it and, within seconds, stood gazing into a mesmerizing magical paradise, a candy lover's dream-come-true. The intimidating older kids, the thick cigarette smoke, the shouting, and the blaring jukebox all receded into a hazy backdrop. Arthur was a candy specialist and his eyes and thoughts were fixated on the collection in front of him. Pom Poms, BB Bats, Mary Janes, Good & Plenty, Bonomo Turkish Taffy—the candy went on for miles.

"Whadda ya want, young feller?"

Arthur looked up. A man was standing behind the case. His skin was mostly milky white but with a few large blotches of pink. He had no hair. At first, Arthur thought the man had some kind of creepy disease, but then decided he had been burned in a fire. Believing the latter, it wouldn't be so scary eating candy the man had touched.

"What can I do for you?"

Arthur made his selections, though he found it almost impossible to narrow down his picks among so many attractive choices. The owner added up the mountain of selected goodies.

"That comes the forty-five cents."

"Aw, heck." Arthur had to make tough decisions to get the cost down to thirty cents. Back into the case went the Necco Wafers, Root Beer Barrels, and Chocolate Babies.

Arthur exited the Crystal Fountain with pockets bulging. He walked home, sampling goodies along the way. What a great day! He had beaten Kathryn Thomas, the class genius, and Richard Blaskowitz, his arch enemy, in a spelling bee, and he had more candy than he knew what to do with. Life was good.

Arthur first put this "skip lunch, buy candy" scheme into action in early November. Initially, he was content to indulge his sugar cravings a couple of school days each week. The hunger pangs took getting used to so, on days when they were particularly strong by lunchtime, he'd give in and eat in the cafeteria. When he did, he cherished every minute of filling his empty stomach. Later, he'd glumly mope past the Crystal Fountain, its delicacies out of sight and out of reach, but not out of Arthur's mind.

Eventually, the youngster's addiction to sugar became uncontrollable. By midwinter he was skipping lunch every school day. Before long, the Crystal Fountain's best customer was an eight-year-old boy. The older kids greeted Arthur when he entered.

"Here comes Sweet Tooth."

"I bet the dentist loves you."

"Hey kid, how come you're not fat?"

In fact, Arthur was losing weight. During the school year, five report cards were issued: one at the end of October,

December, February, April, and the final one in mid-June. Among other statistics, it provided the student's most current body weight. Arthur weighed fifty-five pounds in October, fifty-four in December, fifty-one in February and, in April, forty-nine. At an age when a healthy child adds weight, Arthur had not only stopped getting heavier, he was shrinking.

The April report card elicited a phone call from the school nurse to Arthur's parents. She reached Marguerite.

"Thank you for calling, Mrs. Cagney. His weight has been troubling me. I thought he was losing..." Marguerite's voice trailed off as she lost her train of thought.

The nurse expressed concern. "His overall health seems okay but something isn't right here. He hasn't gotten any taller for a while. That can happen. But, his weight...Does he eat enough at home?"

"Oh, yes. At least he used to. I noticed at supper the last few months or so, he tends to pick at his food." Marguerite had no idea her son was skipping lunch and spoiling his appetite for dinner, all for the sake of his late afternoon candy binges.

"I strongly recommend you have him seen by a physician."

"I will."

A week later Arthur was sitting with his mother in the office of the family doctor. Dr. Mills did a cursory examination. Throughout, the young boy grew more and more fearful that, at any moment, the lid would be blown off his secret. He began searching for a defense before even being charged with a crime.

Exam over, the physician sat down behind his desk, asking that Marguerite and her son do likewise in the chairs at the other side of his desk. Stressed over what he was sure the doctor was about to say, Arthur fidgeted in his chair.

*Mrs. Berndt, the reason your son has been losing weight is that he's been skipping lunch and using your hard-earned money to buy candy instead.* That's the report the trembling youngster braced himself for. How would he talk his way out of this one?

"Arthur, no need to be so nervous. I'm here to help you. How do you feel?"

"Good."

"Maybe a bit tired, weak?"

"Nope."

"Well, I'm glad to hear that. So son, how's your appetite?"

"Okay."

Marguerite chimed in. "Doctor, he hasn't been eating well at dinner. Breakfast is okay, but not dinner."

Dr. Mills turned back towards the patient. "Arthur, don't you like food?"

"It's okay, I guess. Yes, I do."

"Mrs. Berndt, we're not going to do anything further right now. I'd like you to closely monitor Arthur's eating habits. Do you give him lunch for school?"

"Not very often. Usually, he takes money for the school cafeteria."

"Arthur, do you like the food in school?"

"Yes."

"If you don't, maybe your mom could make you something to take to school."

*Oh no! There goes the automatic thirty cents. A bagged lunch every day just wouldn't cut it.* "No, I really like school food a lot."

"Good. Son, don't skip any meals, and clean your plate. I'll see you both in a month—no, make that two weeks. We can't fool around with this."

Marguerite thanked Dr. Mills, made a follow-up appointment, and left the doctor's office with her son.

Arthur knew what he had been doing to himself yet, while a bit bothered about the weight loss, had refused to give up his sugar binges. It had been a matter of priorities. Now adults were complicating things. He'd be reporting back to the doctor in a couple of weeks and the scale wouldn't lie. The jig was up. Or, was it?

Brainstorm! Arthur decided he'd start stealing money from his mother so he could eat the school lunch and still buy lots of candy, too.

Every school day morning, there was a period of about fifteen minutes, after his father had left for work and his sisters for school, when Arthur and his mother were the only ones in the Berndt house. Marguerite spent most of that time upstairs getting ready for work. This gave Arthur the opportunity to rifle through her pocketbook, which she always kept on her dining room chair. The first time he pulled off this caper he fumbled a bit with the handbag, unsure exactly where the treasure lay. It turned out her pocketbook contained a change purse in which she kept both bills and coins. For starters, Arthur took two dollars and fifty-five cents in coins. Was he nervous about being caught? Very much so, but it was a thrilling nervousness. Did he feel guilty? Not really. He was simply rewarding himself.

Before he left for school, Arthur got one more reward: the thirty cents his mother fished out of her purse for his lunch.

That day, for the first time after a long absence from the lunchroom, Arthur happily rejoined his classmates on the cafeteria line. Today's menu? Baked macaroni, one of his favorites. Following lunch and recess, he spent the afternoon in class without hunger pangs and, after school, headed for the Crystal Fountain to get his sugar fix.

# # #

Arthur had tapped into a rich vein of money. Unlike most other school kids, he had a yearning for Mondays to roll around so he could resume his criminal activity. Every once in a while, the fifteen-minute window of opportunity to steal didn't present itself and the youngster had to make a decision that day—buy lunch or candy. Candy always won. After all, unlike people, candy never let Arthur down.

As proof of his addiction, Arthur's tolerance for sweets increased. Therefore, his need for more money also increased.

This presented a new challenge: stealing a greater quantity of money from his mom without her noticing. Arthur pushed the envelope. He continued to take coins, but now began regularly adding paper money into the mix. He figured if his mom had a lot of singles, a couple of dollar bills missing would go unnoticed. They did.

Weeks went by. Arthur was living the sweet life, literally. Candy galore. He bought so much he was able to keep some hidden in his bedroom to tide him over on the weekends.

# # #

It was bound to happen. One weekday morning Arthur dug into his cash cow (aka mom's pocketbook) and found about seventy-five cents in coins, two singles, and a twenty-dollar bill. What to do? Until this day, four dollars was the most he'd taken in one pop. Seventy-five cents and/or two dollars would no longer cut it. Twenty dollars would. He sensed he was pushing his luck, but he couldn't help himself. He took the twenty.

After his mother came downstairs, Arthur held his breath as she opened her pocketbook to get him his lunch money. She let out an "Oh!" and began rummaging through her pocketbook. "I know I had a twenty...where did it go?" She dumped the contents of the pocketbook onto the dining room table. Still no twenty-dollar bill. She looked quizzically (or was it suspiciously?) at Arthur. He was prepared to be frisked, having put the twenty inside his sock. A concerned expression on her face, Marguerite thought out loud, "I've got to get to work."

This was the richest Arthur had ever been in his life. Besides the thirty-five cents in his pocket for lunch, Arthur left the house with twenty dollars burning a hole in his sock. He'd put the fire out later at the Crystal Fountain.

On the walk to school, Arthur envisioned all the candy he'd buy that day. He toyed with the idea of making a great day even greater. Why not include Cooper's Stationery on his itinerary and purchase a few comic books? He did his best to suppress the nagging fear that, sooner or later, his mother would catch on to his larcenous ways.

During the school day, Arthur could barely pay attention in class. He was mentally lining up the goodies he'd be getting later. He still couldn't believe his luck. His mom's pocketbook was a gold mine, and today he had struck the "mother lode." According to some experts in such matters, when a child steals money from his parents, it's done due to a lack of love. They are wrong. Arthur just loved candy.

Three o'clock bell. Arthur flew out of his seat, through the hall, down the stairs, out into the street and down to the Crystal Fountain. Gilbert (the owner—by now the two were on a first-name basis) headed over to the candy case when he saw Arthur burst through the door.

"Okay, Art, what's on tap today?"

Arthur rattled off one treat after another. Shopping done, he had to cough up nearly fifteen dollars. He paid it with a smile. After all, money was no object. Arthur left loaded down with two sizable bags of candy. Gilbert stayed behind, richer by fourteen dollars and twenty-five cents.

Having made up his mind earlier and with a purpose in his step, Arthur headed to Cooper's Stationery store. Seeing the two bags of candy Arthur was carrying, Mr. Cooper asked, "Hey son. Did you win the Irish Sweepstakes?" Taking that as a serious question, Arthur replied with a straight face, "No. I didn't." Then, he purchased numerous comic books and three packs of baseball cards.

Arthur left Cooper's and took the nearby alley that came out behind the Bohack supermarket. This was the quickest way to his house. He tried to run, but was constantly slowed down by all the goodies he was carrying. Nonetheless, he got home before anyone else did. He hid some of the candy in the woods bordering his house. The rest of it, along with the comic books and baseball cards, he stuffed under his mattress. Mission accomplished before anyone else got home.

That evening he heard his mother and father downstairs.

"I know I had a twenty. It didn't just disappear."

"Well, did you ask the boy?"

"I did. He swore he didn't take it."

"Well, let me find out. I'll get to the bottom of this real quick. He's—"

"Gus, you don't have to bother. I remember now. I got gas and some groceries yesterday. Oh, my memory! It'll be the death of me." The subject was dropped.

Arthur was sure his mom was on to him and had given him a pass. Next time he wouldn't be so lucky. He forced himself to stay away from her pocketbook for the next few days. Then, the sugar monkey on his back started running the show again. He lapsed into his old routine. Thankfully, now every time he looted his mom's purse he found a supply of coins and singles, sufficient enough to help Arthur resist the temptation of taking a larger bill and risk capture.

Arthur was all set. He had some of his purchased candy under his mattress, saved as a backup, emergency stash to be utilized on days he couldn't steal money. As for the comic books, he read them on the sly, shoving them back under the mattress in between reads. The baseball cards also found a home under the mattress, left unopened and saved as a special treat to be enjoyed in the future. He also had that supply of sweets buried outside. Sugar, sugar everywhere!

One school day, Arthur decided to share his good fortune and impress his peers. He invited his classmates Ronnie and Peter to go with him to the Crystal Fountain. They did, both highly skeptical about his alleged unlimited purchasing power.

By the time they came out of the store, they were convinced. Arthur had let each boy buy a dollar and fifty cents worth of goodies. Arthur bought himself nothing. No need to. By now he had so many goodies stuffed under his mattress, he could have opened his own candy store. Since he was the one stripping and making the bed when he wet it, the stash remained his personal secret.

###

Following that first visit to Dr. Mills' office, Arthur had dedicated himself to eating lunch at school as often as possible and forcing himself to eat as much as possible at dinner, despite his candy-damaged appetite. As a result, his final report card for the year indicated he weighed fifty-three pounds. He was back on track to reaching a normal weight and without having to sacrifice his sweet tooth. He had a ton of candy at home and more stored outside, although most of the stash outside would prove to be no longer edible; sugary products don't hold up too well when exposed to the elements. The problem was he knew there wasn't nearly enough to get him through the entire summer. With school about to end, how would he keep stealing money? Ruth, also off from school, would be home during his peak stealing time; she'd snitch on him for sure. What to do? As fate would have it, he never had to figure that out.

A few weeks after the school year ended, Arthur came home after going to the beach for his first Red Cross swimming lesson that summer. During that initial session, he'd perfected floating on his back, something he'd been unable to accomplish throughout his entire set of lessons the prior year. The young boy was excited and eager to share his accomplishment with his mom.

A neighbor, who had taken Arthur along with her son to the swimming class, dropped him off in front of his house. As Arthur walked towards the front door, he could see his mom through the screen, holding something in both hands. As he got closer, the bottom fell out of his stomach. She was holding his stash, at least a small part of it. Suddenly the joy of having learned how to float lost all its luster. The young boy was in big trouble and he knew it.

"Arthur, what is this all about?"

"It's candy."

"I know that. Do you know where I found it?"

"No."

"It was under your mattress. Where did it come from?"

"The store."

Then, Marguerite asked the question Arthur couldn't answer.

"Yes, but who paid for it?"

"I got it from friends."

"If you don't stop your constant lying..."

"I did, really."

"And who are these friends?"

"I don't remember."

"Wait till your father hears about this. I'm afraid I've got to tell him. And don't worry. I threw out all the rest, the comics, the baseball cards, all of it, just like I'm going to do with this junk." She waved her two candy-filled hands in Arthur's face. Even in such dire circumstances, Arthur couldn't help but be tantalized by the sweet contraband fluttering inches from his mouth.

Arthur used his last line of defense, one that rarely, if ever, worked. He began crying. No luck. His father was still going to find out.

In the midst of his panic, Arthur still had room in his brain to fret over the fact that he'd never find out what players were in all those unopened packs of baseball cards he had bought. Maybe later, when no one else was around, he'd rifle through the garbage can to retrieve them.

Earlier that day, Arthur's mom had purchased a new larger rubber mat to replace the one she'd been using to protect his bed from urine. While tucking it under the mattress, a Tootsie Roll popped out and fell onto the floor, provoking further investigation by his mother. She discovered her son's cornucopia of sweets. Arthur's penchant for bedwetting had exposed him as a thief. Bed-wetting—it was a curse all the way around.

As promised, his father heard about it later that day. He kicked his son all the way to his bedroom and ordered him to stay there until told otherwise. That was one part of the punishment. The next day, he found out the other part. His parents had calculated the approximate value of the hot property found, coming up with a figure of twenty-two dollars. Thank God, he had either already eaten or hidden outside all the rest of his ill-gotten goods!

Arthur was given a weekly allowance of twenty five cents if he did chores: cleaning his room, drying the dishes, raking the lawn, etc. To pay back those twenty-two dollars, he was looking at no allowance for almost two whole years while still having to do all his chores. His sentence would be shortened to six months if he promised to never steal money again. It was an offer Arthur couldn't refuse. He promised.

It was a promise he couldn't keep. Three days later, with his father outside mowing the lawn and his mother upstairs making the bed, Arthur clipped eighty cents from his mom's pocketbook. He spent the rest of the summer taking advantage of the rare opportunities he got to enrich himself. The youngster longed for September and those early mornings on school days when the pickings were easier.

In order to make it to September, the young boy would have to survive two challenges, one legal, the other unworldly.

# Chapter 27

ONE SATURDAY, A FEW weeks after Arthur suffered his candy crash, a noteworthy phone call was made to the Berndt residence.

"Hello!"

"Mr. Berndt?"

"Yes."

"This is Detective McIntyre. I was calling to speak with your wife, but I'll tell you the good news."

"And that would be...?"

"The whole matter with Mr. Juska has been settled. Those boys your son got caught up with came clean."

"Why does your name sound familiar?"

"I'm the same guy that stopped by your house a few years ago. That Cohen situation."

"Yeah. Okay. So you say settled. What do you mean by 'settled'?"

"Those four teenagers admitted to breaking in and stealing merchandise. Mr. Juska claimed losses of about $1,400 total, but I think the matter was settled for around $1000 or so. Peter Stanton's father is kicking in a significant amount because Mr. Juska refused to deal with any payment plan. Juska refused to get his insurance company involved. There was a lot of haggling about the dollar value of merchandise. Some of the goods were returned. It all took a lot of time. I was a bit concerned about your son for a while. He could've been in a real jam."

"So, exactly what did he do?"

"Well, the others used him to gain access. He opened the side door only a kid his age could get to."

"Jesus Christ! That little—!"

"Mr. Berndt, I don't think he had any idea he was doing anything wrong. Peter Stanton told him a tale about the owner locking himself out, and that your son was doing him a big favor. They even bribed him, bought him a cap gun."

"I don't care how young he is. What the hell would he think when they were taking all the crap out of the store?"

"Oh, they did that later at night. Your son wasn't there for that."

"And he got a cap gun?"

"Yes, sir."

"I'm going to have to teach him that crime doesn't pay."

"I'm not sure your son had any idea what these boys were cooking up. In fact, I'm pretty sure he didn't. I'd give him the benefit of the doubt. "

"Yeah, well I wouldn't. You don't know my son like I do. He's a little thief. He's got to smarten up."

Detective McIntyre sensed it was time to bring the conversation to a close. "That's about it, Mr. Berndt. Can I answer any questions for you?"

"Well, you can tell Juska to stay off my property. He came over here raising all kinds of hell weeks ago. He's getting his money, so he can leave me alone. I don't want him trespassing on my property."

"Do you want to lodge a formal complaint?"

"Nah. Not worth the bother."

"Okay, sir. Hopefully, things should calm down now. Please say hello to your wife. I know she was very concerned."

"So did she know what happened, all the details?"

"I was keeping her updated."

"I see..."

"Well, nice talking to you, Mr. Berndt."

"Yeah. Thanks for calling."

August Berndt hung up the phone and immediately yelled, "Get down here!" as if knowing his son had been eavesdropping from upstairs. Arthur did as told. He slowly descended the stairs and entered the dining room where his father awaited him.

"Well, looks like you're not in trouble with the law again—no thanks to you. You have any idea what you did?"

"No, Dad."

"Listen closely. I'm going to explain it to you. You opened the door so some goddamn thieves could break into a store. That's what you did."

"Am I in trouble?"

"I just told you. No. They all think you didn't know what you were doing. I'm not so sure. Either you're a smart crook or you're a stupid accomplice. Either way, you shouldn't have been there. Where's the cap gun?"

"You mean the one Peter gave me?"

"That's exactly the one I mean."

Arthur didn't want to give up his prized Roy Rogers pistol no matter what, so he lied. "Mom made me throw it out."

"Did she? Well, finally she's smartening up. So listen. I'm telling you this for the last time. You stop hanging around kids twice your age. From now on, stick with children your own age. I can't follow you around all day, so I'm warning you. If I ever find out you're with the wrong people, you'll pay a price. Got it?"

"Yes, Dad."

Arthur sensed the conversation had ended—and peacefully! He turned around and headed back upstairs to distance himself, just in case he had misread his father. Arthur briefly reveled in that special sense of relief he experienced whenever he avoided physical contact with his father.

Later that day, when Marguerite returned with Ruth from shopping, August recounted his conversation with Detective McIntyre. "I'm glad you took the gun from him. Can't be rewarding him for his misbehavior."

"I never actually—" Marguerite caught herself in midsentence. After collecting her thoughts she continued. "I found out about that cap gun from the detective. I explained to Art how those kids took advantage of him."

"Yeah, I doubt they had to twist his arm very much. You should know better than anyone. Look how much he's stolen from you."

"Well, he hasn't been doing that lately. He'd probably do whatever they told him to do. Look at the age difference."

"Yeah. I made it clear to him that he better hang out with kids his own age. We're just going to have to keep a closer eye on him."

"I agree. I did promise Arthur I'd get him another cap gun."

"Well, isn't that still rewarding him?"

"I don't think so. I told him it would be a less expensive gun. Gus, these days all the boys his age have a cap gun. If we want him to play with kids his own age—"

"I guess so. Maybe Smitty's has something on sale."

"I'll do some window shopping at Woolworths. They might be the cheapest."

Marguerite had never gotten rid of Arthur's gun. She lied to her husband to cover up her son's lie—all in the name of keeping the peace at home. In order to make sure war didn't break out, Marguerite had more work to do. She now had to get rid of Arthur's pistol and do it under her husband's radar.

The following morning, after August had gone to work and Ruth to school, Marguerite had a conversation with her son. "Art, will you please go upstairs and bring me your cap gun?"

"What for, mom?"

"Bring it to me. I have to talk to you about something."

Arthur reluctantly went upstairs to his bedroom. He waited a few minutes and then came back down empty-handed. "I can't find it, Ma."

"Art, I know you like your cap gun very much. But your dad and I had a discussion about it yesterday. Those boys that gave you that gun didn't do it because they were nice. They did it to get you to help them do something wrong. They fooled you."

Marguerite searched for the right words, clinging to the belief that her son had naively and unintentionally aided and abetted a crime. "They got you to do something that you thought was okay and they knew was wrong. They're older and had no business involving someone your age."

"Is that why that police guy talked to us in school?"

"Yes. Fortunately, the whole matter has been settled. But your father just isn't comfortable with you having that gun."

"Why, Mom?"

"Well, there's an expression about ill-gotten gains."

"Yeah? What are they, Ma?"

"They are...well, it means getting something dishonestly. The wrong way."

"All I did was open a door."

"I know, Art. But, those boys took advantage of you. They came back and stole a lot of things from Mr. Juska's store. They're in trouble for it. That cap gun is tainted. I agree with your dad. Now, let's quit stalling."

Arthur cried out, "Mom, I want to keep my gun. Why can't I have it?"

Instinctively, Marguerite put her forefinger to her lips. "Shh!" After realizing her husband was not in the house, she continued. "Your father doesn't know you still have it. He'd be very mad at me if he found out you did. Look, I'm done talking with you about this. Do you want me to go upstairs and help you look for it? You know, I haven't seen you with that gun for weeks."

"You won't find it."

"Why, where is it?"

"Outside." Sensing the gun might be "hot," just to be on the safe side, Arthur had kept it out of his father's sight.

"Outside? Didn't it get dirty and rusty?"

"I wrapped it in tinfoil."

"Oh. And where is it outside?"

"In the woods."

"The woods?"

"Yup."

"What woods?"

I can't tell you. It's a secret."

*"Arthur!"*

"Well, it's on the other side of Old Post Road."

"Arthur you shouldn't go up that way. Cars fly on that road. It's not safe for Rex, either. Besides, I don't want you going anywhere near the shack where that crazy man lives. I've told you that more than once."

"I'm careful."

"Well, you know that man that lives in that old shack? I don't want you going up that way at all. He's not to be trusted. Tomorrow afternoon, when you get home from school, I want you to get that gun. Bring it home. I'm going to leave work early and buy you a brand-new gun—and you can keep it at home. Okay?"

"Will it be a Roy Rogers?"

"Well, we'll see what's available. Do you have any other choices? Wild Bill Hickock? Gene Autry? Aren't those some of your favorites, too?"

"Nope."

"Don't forget! Bring that gun right home tomorrow. And don't you ever go near that shack again!"

Arthur replied with a defeated, "Okay."

After school the following day, Arthur reluctantly retrieved his prized possession and then went home. His mother was already there.

"Okay, Art. We'll make a trade. I'll take that gun and you get this brand-new one." She handed Arthur a toy six-shooter. "Here. Try it on for size."

Arthur took the gun from his mother. Since it was larger than his Roy Rogers cap pistol, he handled the new firearm somewhat clumsily.

He examined it and said, "Who is the cowboy for this gun?"

"You are!"

"No, I mean somebody on TV?"

"Oh, I don't know. I threw away the packaging." Marguerite *did* know. She had purposely left the packaging at the store. She had purchased a less expensive cap gun that featured the endorsement of a generic cowboy. She had done that to placate her husband. Now, she had to placate her son.

"This gun stinks. Mom, do I have to lose my real gun?"

"I told you. It just bothers your dad and me. It was purchased with money that didn't get earned the right way. Remember when you used to take money from my pocketbook??"

Alarm bells briefly went off in Arthur's head. He'd never completely stopped pilfering from his mother. Was she on to him? The youngster felt a wave of relief wash over him when he realized his mother was talking about his thievery in the past tense. "Well, we were upset because that's just wrong. Remember when I threw out so much of your candy and comics. Those were the kind of ill-gotten gains I was referring to yesterday."

"But I didn't steal anything this time."

"No, but those other boys did, and that's why they bought you that cap gun. Now do you understand?"

Though he didn't, he replied with a halfhearted "I guess so."

"And the good thing is you don't have to hide this gun. You can keep it in your room."

"Mom, I have the holster up in my closet. Can I keep that?"

"I don't see why not. The new one didn't come with one. I'm sure your father won't have a problem with that. At least, I hope not."

Arthur went upstairs. The new slightly bigger gun was a tight fit in his holster. But the holster had Roy Rogers' name on it—a consolation prize.

Downstairs, Marguerite put "Roy Rogers" into her pocketbook, the gun destined for the garbage can at her place of work. She'd been less than honest with her husband—a small price to pay to keep the always stormy seas in the Berndt household from getting even more turbulent.

# Chapter 28

NOT FAR FROM ARTHUR'S home sat a long nameless dirt road bordered on both sides by thick, sprawling woodlands. Long ago, there had been plans to pave this trail and build houses along it, but that never happened. Arthur began using this no-man's land as a refuge at the tender age of six. It would remain his haven for years to come.

The tricky part: getting past the weather-beaten shack on Old Post Road that sat only yards away from the trail's beginning. Nobody in the neighborhood had ever visited that house, but based on the structure's dilapidated exterior, it didn't require a fertile imagination to picture what the inside looked like. Although the building was condemnable, someone lived in it. No one knew his name—he was simply called "the old man." Rumor had it he suffered from shell shock as a result of fighting in one of the world wars.

The old man had no telephone nor did he have a television. No one knew if he even had a radio. Everyone did know he had a drinking problem. As proof, there were empty liquor bottles scattered on his weed-infested lawn and, sitting on the rickety porch by the front door, a few large grocery bags from the top of which sprouted more empties.

Whenever the local fire department's siren blasted, the old man began to scream, mixing his howls in with those of the neighborhood dogs. Even when unprovoked by the siren, the old man's sporadic ranting inside his hovel could be heard near and far. He'd yell a combination of real words and nonsense syllables with such force that, even though he never had visitors, it sounded as if he was having a heated argument with somebody. Adults in the neighborhood said he was crazy. "Crazy" translated to "he could kill you" in kidspeak. Whether on foot or bike, children sped up passing his place, terrified he'd come rushing out after them. Arthur was no exception. In the youngster's world, the old man topped his own father in the fear-provoking department. Or maybe it was a tie.

The old man was a shadowy, mythlike figure, in large part because, aside from his screaming soliloquies behind closed doors, he kept an extremely low profile. Every once in a while he'd go to his mailbox, but that was done only under the cover of darkness. Having no car, he was forced to make an extended public appearance when walking many miles round trip to purchase a few groceries and replenish his liquor supply. Even then he managed to remain a man of mystery. Night or day, winter or summer, when making one of those treks, he always wore a long pea coat with the collar up, a wool cap pulled almost completely over his eyes, and a scarf to cover whatever of his face the cap didn't. He kept himself so well camouflaged, an eyewitness could only have described him as being of average height and average weight.

Other kids kept themselves as far away from the old man's place as possible, having no reason to go near it. Arthur's situation was different. Though warned by his parents to steer clear of the shack, entering the woods that sat near it had already become his life's calling at a very early age. His fear of the old man stood in the way as an occupational hazard. Getting past the shack in one piece was always a nerve-wracking experience, and an impressive accomplishment. Risky work indeed, the price to be paid in order to buy the temporary safety the woods provided, a price the young boy was willing to pay. Whenever Arthur made it to the path, he breathed a silent sigh of relief for having again successfully dodged certain death and reached his wooded haven.

Once on the winding unpaved trail, every stride along it was a step further away from the civilized world. Just fifty yards in from Old Post Road and poof!—the youngster vanished from sight. Another hundred yards and his loudest screams would go unheard by humanity. If Arthur followed the path to its end, a distance well over half a mile, he'd arrive at a small bluff that overlooked the Long Island Railroad tracks. On the other side of the tracks sat a parallel bluff that promised more wilderness behind it.

A youngster Arthur's age had no business wandering alone in the woods. Nevertheless he gravitated to them, finding solitude where others his age would see only danger. Sometimes he took his canine protector, Rex, with him, but countless other times he dared enter this treed realm alone.

Every time Arthur set foot on the dirt road it was for the single purpose of escaping from 21 Lowell Place, his private house of horrors. Although delivering on the promise of providing a respite from his father, the woods, in turn, could envelope the youngster in its own menacing eeriness, sometimes playing games with the youngster's head. A bird's chirping or the occasional plane passing overhead were often the only tangible, and nonthreatening, signs of life other than his own. However, at the slightest noise of undetermined origin, Arthur's imagination might get the best of him. When it did, he'd start thinking he was being stalked at times by some unknown person, at other times by ghosts, none of them holy. He'd not dare scan his surroundings, afraid of confirming his own worst fears. Beads of sweat would break out on his forehead, the palms of his hands would get damp, and his heart would begin pounding ferociously. He'd become dizzy, almost to the point of passing out. If he made the mistake of staying out until it had gotten dark, the experience became even more terrifying. He'd start running frantically, hell-bent on getting back to Old Post Road. Fleeing at breakneck speed, he'd listen intently for any footsteps that might be closing in on him. An animal's noise, a falling branch, rustling leaves, even noises he himself was making—any or all could trick the youngster into believing his unseen nemesis was about to grab him. Sometimes Arthur convinced himself he was not going to make it out of the woods alive. His inner voice would scream Give up! He'd start crying and gasping for breath. By the time he burst out onto Old Post Road, he'd be bawling like a baby.

Once he learned how to ride a bicycle and could cover ground on the trail more rapidly, Arthur felt a bit safer. Even so, whether traveling along the path or entering the deep woods, he always kept a sharp lookout, ready to shift into high gear on bike or foot. He was prepared to give it his all if the bogeyman, or anyone else, came shooting out after him.

Why would Arthur keep visiting these woods and subject himself to such torture? For one thing, the all-out panic attacks were rare. Most of the time in the woodlands, he was able to calm himself by comparing the relative safety of the woods to what he had escaped from back at home. In his world, fear of the unknown was often less terrifying than the known. Though a few of his walks ended with him desperately running from phantoms, most of the time Arthur enjoyed an overwhelming rush of joyful liberation in these woods. Many of his most pleasant memories growing up were a product of his self-imposed isolation deep within this forest.

Arthur had created ways to pass time in the wilderness. What might have bored another child sufficed for this youngster. When alone in the woods, he fought to convince himself he was having a good time and succeeded. Why? Because a much more unpleasant alternative was always waiting for him at home.

Sometimes in the summer, he only got as far as the first patch of wild blueberry and blackberry bushes. He'd park himself on the ground within reaching distance of as many berries as possible and get to work. Arthur never wanted to go berry picking with his sisters. Who wants to put berries in a pot for a later date when your mouth was immediately available?

Frequently Arthur left the trail and entered the woods, in search of adventure. After all, the youngster never knew what he might find.

On one trek, he came across some junked cars that had found their final resting place. One of them still had a usable front seat that Arthur sat on so he could make believe he was driving a car, one that no longer had an engine.

On another jaunt, Arthur discovered a ramshackle tree fort. He tried to climb up and perch himself inside it, but the very first of the decayed wooden steps leading up to it proved too untrustworthy, even for someone with Arthur's sense of daring. It was probably for the best. Had he survived the ascent, a couple of the fort's floor planks were dangling precariously and might very well have spelled doom for the young boy.

An additional point of interest for this youthful sightseer: a pond. Rex liked to swim in it during warm weather. Arthur preferred to throw rocks into it, trying to hurl them as high as possible to make the biggest splash. At other times he would try to see how many skips he could make a stone take on the water's surface.

In another part of the woods, he stumbled upon a large trench, an old rusty shovel lying next to it. Had someone been digging a shallow grave and quit? That thought entered Arthur's mind, but didn't remain for very long. Instead, he declared the general area a battle zone and the trench a foxhole. He would sit in it and peek out cautiously, scoping the countryside for any invading forces. If he'd try to send Rex out on reconnaissance missions, his dog always refused to go unless Arthur accompanied him, which he invariably did. In the trench, he kept a collection of toy soldiers and tanks he had stolen from a neighbor's son. He knew that kid would never dare come looking for them in these woods.

Other times, Arthur might travel the entire length of the path up to the railroad tracks. He'd climb up and take a seat on a huge ball-like mound of dirt held together by the roots of a fallen tree. There he'd wait to greet passing trains. The Long Island Railroad was famous for running pitifully late; since Arthur had no schedule to consult and no train to catch, they all went by right on time in his world. The engineer always returned Arthur's wave, and as an extra treat, sounded the train whistle.

One of Arthur's favorite ways of entertaining himself in the woods was playing baseball, by himself. He'd find a suitably sized stick and, using stones as baseballs, hit them, sometimes for hours. Of course, if he decided to play this game, he had to walk to the end of the trail because the best stones for hitting were along the railroad tracks. If he found an especially good stick, very durable and just the right thickness for his grip, he'd hide it in the nearby bushes for future use. Over the years, he collected a huge arsenal of these "bats." He always played at least one nine inning game in a huge jam-packed stadium built by his imagination, pitting his beloved Dodgers against some other team. Every once in a while, a timeout had to be called so a train could pass through the ballpark.

While Arthur was engaged in his baseball game, Rex would run off to do dog research. If he came back to his master and found him still playing ball, the dog took a seat along the pretend first base line and watched. If the game dragged on, Rex, not a baseball fan, invariably lost interest and went back to his own exploration of the surroundings.

Courtesy of Arthur, the Dodgers had an incredible record in the games they played in Suassa Park. There they would amass well over a thousand wins and zero defeats. If about to lose, they'd always somehow miraculously come back in the bottom of the ninth. If necessary the game went into extra innings, just so the Dodgers could win. Although no Dodger batter ever struck out, Arthur made sure plenty of opposing hitters did.

There were also some questionable umpiring calls on foul balls that should have been fair and vice versa; they all worked in the Dodgers' favor.

Whenever he could, Arthur took refuge from the house he lived in by visiting this wooded sanctuary he had made his second home.

# # #

An early Saturday morning in mid-August, 1953. This was one of those sanctuary-seeking days. Arthur, now nine years old, charged out of the house, fresh from a scorching bath hours earlier. Rex, just as glad to get out, followed right alongside his youthful pal. Reaching the end of Lowell Place, they turned right onto Old Post Road and safely scooted by the old man's place. Twenty yards later they left the paved road and entered the path. The day was sunny with muggy heat. Arthur had cleaned out the blueberry crop days earlier, so he pressed on. Not up to walking all the way to the tracks, he veered into the woods. Rex looked like he was up for a reconnaissance mission or two, so this would be a trench day. Arthur had come prepared, wearing his faux combat belt complete with plastic knife, rubber hand grenade, and cap pistol—the latter now the cheap model of some unknown cowboy.

Before they got to their battle post, Rex spotted a rabbit and vanished into the brush chasing after it.

The young G. I. bravely marched on alone through the battlefield, keeping a sharp lookout for enemy combatants that could be lurking anywhere. He entered a thicket, just past which he knew lay his destination. He began wading through thick brush. Nearing the trench, he heard muttering. Arthur's gut instincts shouted Take off!, but curiosity and bravado got the best of him. He had to see who had the nerve to trespass on "his" property. With all the foliage in full bloom, Arthur couldn't quite make out the uninvited visitor. When he got as close to the edge of the dirt pit as he dared, the young boy stopped and peeked from behind a small tree. There inside the trench sat—the old man! Terrified, Arthur staggered backwards, stumbling over a bush. Losing his balance, he fell hard to the ground. Quick as lightning, the youngster scrambled back to his feet, ready to run for his life before he was spotted. Too late.

"Kid!"

The young boy stopped in his tracks. He turned around and faced the trench, but said nothing, fear stealing his breath and paralyzing his vocal cords. He fought to keep his knees from collapsing under him. How did Arthur know it was the old man? By the pea coat, wool cap and scarf, all of which were lying in the dirt on one side of the grizzled spectre. On the other side lay an empty paper bag. In his hands, the old man was holding the biggest bottle Arthur had ever seen.

"Hey, c'mon kid. Hurry it up!"

The old man patted the dirt next to him. When Arthur hesitated, the old man jumped to his feet.

"Hey, you. Get the hell over here. Don't play games with me, you little fucker."

Still frozen in place, Arthur stared wide-eyed at his host with a mixture of fear and awe. The old man was wearing a frayed thermal shirt and brown slacks that were shiny in spots. He had on weather-beaten black boots that hadn't seen polish in years. His head was covered by thick scraggly black and gray hair that blended into a thick scraggly black and gray beard. A patch covered his left eye. Years ago in battle, half the flesh had been ripped from his face; what remained looked gruesome.

The old man half sat, half fell to the ground, all the while holding on to his bottle for dear life.

"C'mon, sit down here, goddammit!"

Just like that, the youngster's wooded retreat had become his hell. The monster in front of Arthur wasn't some product of his imagination. He was face-to-face with the madman everybody had warned him about, with no one for miles to save him. If he took off running, he'd soon be in the old man's clutches. But if he remained, the same would surely happen. Arthur feared for his life, a familiar uncomfortability.

"What's the problem...cat got your tongue? Sit down!"

Desperately fighting to overcome his panic, the young boy had to think quickly. Having been able to placate his father on the very rare occasion, why not put that talent to use now? Why risk the old man's vengeance by running? Better to buy time, do what he wanted and try to keep him happy. A plan built out of desperation and not likely to work, but it was all Arthur's young mind could come up with.

Following orders, he sat down in the trench, not next to, but across from his host. The old man excitedly waved and shouted past him, as if he were trying to flag down someone standing behind the young boy. Arthur turned around to see who it was, but no one was in sight.

The old man grabbed the liquor bottle with both hands and lifted it to his mouth. After taking three huge swigs, he slammed the bottle back down on the ground, twisting it into the trench's loose sand. While the fearsome figure wiped his mouth with the back of his hand, the young boy sitting across from him wondered how many other people had ever seen the face he was looking at.

The youngster whirled around and took another glance over his shoulder, just to be sure nobody was sneaking up on him. Then he turned back and stared in fear-stricken fascination at the sinister-looking stranger in front of him. The two began an unlikely conversation, initiated by the old man's gravelly voice. "Don't strain your eyeballs, sonny."

Finally, the cat let go of the young boy's tongue. Staring at the old man with a face filled with an equal mix of fear, awe, and wide-eyed curiosity, Arthur naively blurted out, "Are you a pirate, mister?"

After a hearty chuckle, the old man began singing out of key. "Yo-ho-ho, and a bottle of sonsabitchin' wine..." He pointed to a sheath fastened to his belt. It held a huge hunting knife. He continued his tone-deaf crooning. "Yeah, I'm Blackbeard and I'm gonna slice you up into a million pieces if—"

He stopped himself in midsentence, furrowing his brow. On second thought he decided the youngster's question wasn't to his liking. Staring menacingly at Arthur, he screamed, "No, I'm no goddamn pirate, ya little shit. What are you, some kind of wise ass? Bad things happen to wise guys. I don't like wise guys, ya understand?"

The old man got up and angrily rushed at the young boy, coming to a stop just inches from his target. Arthur looked up at the older man, towering over him menacingly. A thought flashed across the young boy's mind: who was more frightening, his father or this grotesque behemoth? Before he could answer his own question, the old man demanded his full attention. He took his knife out, and after brandishing it in front of the young boy, began using the tip of the blade to pick at the dirt under his long, unkempt fingernails while he stood hovering over the youngster.

Though Arthur had only a child's vague concept of mortality, it was sufficient to convince him he should have run off minutes earlier. Now, because he hadn't, his life was at the mercy of a sick monster. Feeling helpless to do anything, he sat and waited for his fate to be decided.

The old man looked up from his self-manicure and shot the young boy a menacing look. "Well, you goin' to answer me?"

At first Arthur didn't respond, fearing that anything he said would only agitate the old man further. Finally, he cleared his throat and, not remembering the original question, meekly replied, "Yes, sir."

Done cleaning his nails, the old man put away his blade and awkwardly seated himself on the edge of the trench, still only yards from his terrified guest. Arthur's level of panic lessened to a more manageable level.

Feverishly scratching his head, the old man focused his lone piercing eye on the youngster and studied him intently from head to toe. He spotted the young boy's holster.

"Whatcha got there? That a real gun you're totin'?"

Pointing to the holster, Arthur bragged, "Yup. Official Roy Rogers."

Sensing an opportunity to show off, Arthur put his fear on hold. He jumped to his feet, pulled out his pistol, stuck his forefinger through the trigger guard, and began awkwardly twirling the weapon. The gun flew out of his hand, landing at the old man's feet. He grabbed Arthur's six-shooter and gave it the once-over.

"Hmm... Impressive. Here you go, sonny."

He held the gun out to Arthur, who stayed put, not daring to reach for it.

"Just wanted to make sure the safety catch was on. Ya don't want to go shootin' anyone by mistake. Heh, heh."

Working up all his courage, Arthur inched just close enough to reach out and retrieve his pistol from the old man's extended hand. The young boy quickly backed off to a safer distance and sat down again.

The old man jabbed himself in the chest with his index finger. "Ernest. And you? What's your name?"

"I'm Arthur."

Pointing at the toys lying in the trench, the old man asked, "Is that your arsenal?"

"Yes, sir."

"Those are a couple of sharp-looking tanks. What rank are you, soldier?"

"I don't know."

"You don't know? Bah! What kind of soldier are you? You better shape up. You know why?" The old man pointed to the woods. " There might be Krauts out there."

"What's a Kraut?"

"You know, Jerries, Germans."

"I think I'm German. Well, not me maybe, but I think my mom and father are. My sister told me they talk German when they don't want us to know something. It sounds funny, except when my father's real mad at me."

"You're German? You don't wanna be a German. They're fuckin' pieces of shit. What's your last name?"

"Berndt. B-e-r-n—"

"That's enough! Well, I'll be damned. Here I am sittin' out in the woods with a goddamn Heinie kid, a little fuckin' Nazi. This is some kind of bad fuckin' joke. I'll tell you what, sonny. A few years ago you and me woulda been shootin' at each other."

"Why?"

"War, that's why. Fuckin' war. That's the only explanation a G.I. ever gets."

"Did you ever shoot a real gun?"

The old man grew silent and hung his head, deep in thought. Then, head still down, he burst out, "Shit, Jesus fuckin' Christ almighty. I shot a kid—a kid, a goddamn fuckin' kid!"

"Did he shoot back at you?"

The old man looked up at Arthur. "He couldn't. He was dead. Probably was around your age, maybe a little older. Had no choice. He had a Kraut uniform on. Kill or be killed. That's what the Sarge always said. That's the way he looked at it. But a kid? I never thought in a million years..."

Again, the old man looked downward, as if studying the ground. Then he raised his head, and with the back of his hand rubbed at a tear that had nestled in the scarred remnants of his cheek. "That's enough of that shit." He guzzled heartily from his bottle.

The young boy brashly changed the subject. "Why is your face like that?"

"Betcha never saw one like it."

"No, sir."

"Pretty, isn't it? Yeah, I've always had the women chasing me. But it's none of your goddamn business, sonny boy. You got that?"

"No...yes, sir."

The old man leapt to his feet and, holding his head high, assumed the posture of an orator, dramatically gesturing with his hands. He moved his lips, but uttered nothing. Arthur, shaken and baffled by this display, stayed put. After a few minutes, the old man's silent sermon ended and he plopped down on the ground, even more clumsily than he had the first two times.

The two then sat in an uncomfortable quiet, eventually broken by the older of the two.

"Christ, you're just a little kid. What the hell ya doing out here all by yourself? You hiding out from the bad guys?"

Did the old man know about Arthur's father and why the young boy spent so much time in the woods? Fearing he'd been exposed, the young boy's face turned bright crimson. To avoid further embarrassment, Arthur answered the old man's first question.

"I'm not by myself. My extra big dog is with me."

"Where the hell is he? If he's so big why the fuck don't I see him?"

"He's right around here."

"Yeah, sure he is."

"Uh huh. Anyway the woods are neat. I like it here."

"Oh yeah? Well, me too. Less troubles out here, at least sometimes. I can... almost... stop thinking. I was a kid once (Arthur had a hard time believing that). You in school?"

Before the youngster could answer, the old man threatened, "Don't try to get smart with me, sonny. I know what you're up to. I can read your mind. I know what you're thinking. I know what everybody's thinking."

Arthur took the old man at his word, figuring anyone who looked like he did could do anything he chose to. The young boy kept his mouth shut, and waited until the old man's face rearranged itself into a slightly friendlier look, though no matter what expression he wore, it had a frightening aura. Their conversation resumed when Arthur regained his courage to speak, hoping against hope he wouldn't say the wrong thing.

"I'm a pretty big kid. I'll be in the fourth grade next year. I'm on the honor roll, too."

"Good boy. Get good grades."

"Okay."

He'd been called a good boy! For a fleeting moment the youngster enjoyed the pleasant—and unaccustomed—warmth of such praise, even though it came from such a fearsome ogre.

The old man's body began shuddering. Letting out a stream of unearthly groans, he doubled over and retched. Nothing came out of his mouth. He pulled himself together and pointed to the bottle in his hand.

"Don't ever drink this shit..." He paused and proceeded to take a few lengthy gulps. "...it'll rot your fucking guts out."

Arthur's guard was still up, but that didn't stop him from asking, "How old are you?"

"51, 52, 53...how the hell would I know?"

"I'm nine...but I'm kinda already almost ten." The youngster counted out loud, using his fingers. "It's only six more months and I'll be ten."

"Oh, very young. Ya lucky sonsabitch." He grinned, showing a mouth devoid of all but a few teeth.

The conversation screeched to a halt. The old man became mute, his body stone rigid. He'd locked himself into a statue-like pose, hands clasped and wrapped around the back of his neck. His bloodshot eye stared blankly off into the distance, not at, but rather through Arthur, as if the young boy had evaporated. What had happened to Arthur's un-heavenly host? Was this a chance to run, or was the old man playing games with him? The youngster didn't dare to find out, so he stayed planted in the trench with his frozen companion. The two sat enveloped in an eerie silence, deep in the bowels of a forest that had betrayed the young boy. Every so often, the lifeless calm was briefly broken by a bird's singing or the rustling of leaves. Then deadly stillness returned.

The two continued to sit for what seemed like forever to the youngster. Off in the distance, a train passed by, its engineer not sounding the whistle since Arthur wasn't there to greet him. How badly the young boy wished he could have been.

Finally the old man snapped back to life and the conversation continued. "Sonny, you're damn lucky you didn't try anything."

Acting as if he hadn't heard the comment and its threatening tone, Arthur asked, "Did you ever go to school?"

Ernest paused, searching for an answer.

"Long ago. Okay as a student, I guess. I got a diploma. What did it get me? Shit. You stay in school, go to college. No army for you."

Without any warning, the old man initiated an unsettling string of rapidly changing facial expressions. The youngster had never seen anything like it. Arthur always felt uneasy when he couldn't gauge an adult's mood and these rapid-fire facial transformations defied his best efforts. At first the old man's forehead wrinkled into an expression of pained confusion that every so often was broken by a demonic grin. Then he flashed a disapproving scowl; that one reminded the youngster of his father. Finally he doubled over, grimacing. Though no one was hitting the old man, the thought struck Arthur that was how he, himself, looked the time he got kicked in the stomach at home.

Ernest's face became drawn and he began having a conversation, apparently with someone other than Arthur. "You think you're funny? I don't think you're so funny."

The old man let out a hearty laugh. Arthur didn't get it; no one had cracked a joke.

"Sometimes, they're funny. Sometimes, I want to kill them."

The word "kill" sent a new wave of terror shooting through the young boy. He didn't see anyone around for the old man to kill except him. Out of the corner of his eye, the youngster spotted the old shovel. For just an instant he remembered the time his father threatened him with a fireplace poker. The image lasted only seconds, but when it vanished, Arthur again glanced at the shovel, now suddenly seeing it as a threat to his life. He prayed it wouldn't attract the old man's attention. The boy's mind continued scrambling to make sense of what was going on and figure out a plan of escape.

The old man planted his bottle in the dirt, grabbed his head with both hands, and began rocking forward and backward.

"They follow me everywhere. I can't get peace and quiet! I want peace and quiet, just once in my life, goddammit!" The old man grabbed his booze and guzzled. After slamming the bottle to the ground, he stared at Arthur and pleaded, "Christ almighty, I need to stop thinking for just a few minutes. I can't take it!" as if imploring the young boy to free him from his pain.

His screaming propelled the youngster's fear to even greater heights. Arthur was swimming in a bizarre pool of feelings; he felt sorry for the same man he was afraid of. On the one hand, the youngster thought he might be making a new friend. On the other hand, he wasn't sure if this was the kind of friend he should have. Whatever the case, his parents would never allow it. Rather than make a run for it, he summoned up the courage and asked to leave. "I have to go home now or I'll get in trouble."

The old man shot Arthur a steely cold stare. "Why now? Something wrong with me? You don't like me?"

"I have to find my dog. Besides, I don't wanna get in trouble. I'm not supposed to talk to y—" He bit his lip, fearing he had said too much.

The old man's icy look vanished, instantly replaced by a wince of pained disappointment. "Oh, okay. I get it."

"Good bye, Mr. Ernest, sir."

"Yeah, sure. Go on. Get the hell out of here. Get lost, you bastard! You stinkin' Heinie!"

Arthur got up. Was this an occasion to shake hands? He didn't have the courage to. Instead, the youngster climbed out of the trench and began walking into the woods towards the dirt path. Before going very far, he turned around for two very different reasons: to wave a friendly goodbye and to see if the old man was coming after him. He wasn't. He was preoccupied, staring into his bottle.

Fearing that if he broke into an all-out run the old man would chase him, Arthur instead walked, but briskly with a purpose. As soon as he was out of the old man's sight, the young boy took off running as if his father were chasing him. Along the way Rex bolted out of the wilderness and scooted up alongside him. Perfect timing. The youngster wasn't sure if his dog and the old man would have hit it off.

A verbal fight broke out far behind them. Arthur stopped running and stood listening. The young boy recognized the old man's shrieking voice. He couldn't hear whomever the old man was arguing with. Rex expressed interest in the quarreling with a couple of halfhearted barks, but obediently stayed with his young master rather than investigating further.

When he came out onto the dirt road, Arthur stepped up the pace to an all-out sprint. As he neared Old Post Road, he got winded and slowed down to a walk, still faintly hearing the old man off in the distance. The second his foot hit the paved road, Arthur felt home free. It was only then that he became aware of the scrapes and sore butt that had resulted from his earlier tumble. Nothing he couldn't handle.

On the way back home, he didn't have to worry about successfully scooting by the old man's shack, knowing it was empty. Even arriving at his own house was less disheartening than usual. For this one day, home felt less threatening than the woods. There was something oddly comforting about facing the more familiar devil in his life.

# # #

For weeks Arthur wondered what had happened to the old man. Had that argument with person(s) unknown gotten physical? Was the old man all right? Then one day, while riding in the car with his mother, he spotted the old man heading for town, wrapped up in his usual garb. The young boy felt a sense of relief, one he knew better than to share with his mother. This was an experience he would never reveal to anyone, not even those his age. From then on, Arthur no longer joined in when other kids told grisly made-up stories about the old man. How could they know what he was like? They didn't even know his real name.

More than a month passed before the youngster summoned up the courage to return to the woods. His father helped him in that effort. Early one morning, Arthur had wet the bed and tasted an especially brutal pummeling. The beating hadn't sated his father's foul mood which carried over into the rest of the day. The woods beckoned. Arthur figured at that point he'd rather take his chances with the old man down the street than the one he lived with. Just to be on the safe side, he took Rex with him.

To his surprise, he didn't experience the customary triumphant thrill after safely passing by the run-down shack. Entering the path, the young boy initially worried about running into the old man, but that fear quickly disappeared. In this forest that sometimes could be so frightening, Arthur felt a measure of comfort in sensing that another human being, however troubled, might be nearby, especially since Arthur had survived their first encounter.

The first crop of blueberries had arrived, making that day's trip into the woods short and (literally) sweet.

It wasn't long before Arthur was back to risking a run past the dilapidated shack on a regular basis. The old man wasn't the only one desperately seeking solace inside the forest.

# Chapter 29

HAVING DODGED THE LEGAL system and survived his encounter with the old man, Arthur spent a good deal of the remainder of the summer of 1953 playing imaginary baseball games in the road in front of his house or in the woods.

That fall, Arthur entered the fourth grade. For the youngster, this would be a school year of firsts, although he began it by exercising an old habit—stealing from his mother. He varied the amount of money pilfered from a dollar to never more than three, in an effort to make sure his thievery would go undetected.

One morning in late October started off in typical fashion. Arthur sat impatiently in the living room, waiting for his mother to go upstairs and ready herself for work. When she did, he went to the dining room and pulled her chair out from under the dining room table, itching to rifle through the pocketbook she always left lying on it. He couldn't believe his eyes—no pocketbook. He ducked under the table to see if it had fallen on the floor or was sitting on anyone else's chair. Still no pocketbook.

What happened? Had it been lost? No, he would have heard about that, maybe even been accused of stealing it. Had she left it in the car overnight? If so, would he dare sneak outside while his mother was upstairs, enter the auto, and snag some money? Could he do that without being caught? Arthur couldn't muster up the guts for such a brazen act. Glumly, he traipsed back into the living room and blankly stared at some TV show, wondering if there was even going to be lunch money. When his mom came downstairs, she went to the dining room cabinet, and, reaching up, pulled her pocketbook off the top of it. She counted out thirty cents for Arthur's cafeteria meal and handed it to him.

Busted! His mom had figured out her son was back to his old thieving ways and had begun leaving her pocketbook out of his reach. A bittersweet experience. On the one hand, he had to start detoxing from sugar; on the other, his mom had kept her discovery to herself, sparing Arthur from his father's brutality.

# # #

At the same time Arthur had to give up sweets of one kind, he found sweets of another—Brenda Watson. Arthur was smitten from the moment she entered the classroom. The daughter of military parents, she had lived in several states before moving to New York. Arthur hoped and prayed she'd make Port Jefferson the final stop. Maybe to others her height, weight and overall appearance were all rather unremarkable. But for Arthur, there was nothing typical about her. Her bangs, her freckles, her beanpole figure—she was the complete package. The fact that she had lived in such far-off places as South Dakota and Virginia only added to her allure, giving her a worldly sophistication that the other girls in his class just didn't have.

Although he was too bashful to engage in direct conversation with Brenda, Arthur tried to get her attention in other ways. He'd write notes to his heartthrob during class, many of them, out of shyness, unsigned. The problem: since the students were seated alphabetically, the two blossoming lovebirds sat at opposite ends of the classroom. The love letters Arthur sent had to pass through a lot of hands before they reached Brenda. While some notes managed to run the gauntlet, most of the missives found their resting place in the hands of this or that student, generating snickers and never arriving to their intended destination. It wasn't long before not only Brenda, but most everyone else in the class knew exactly how Arthur felt about her. This didn't dampen Arthur's feverish writing campaign. He was far too much in love to let embarrassment dissuade him from sending more notes. His heart was an open book, which virtually everyone in the classroom had read and reread.

Brenda didn't answer any of these notes in writing. One time, after reading Arthur's letter and when the teacher wasn't looking, Brenda responded with a tentative wave that sent Arthur on an express flight to heaven.

The notes that never reached Brenda? Some were torn up and discarded, others stuffed into some student's book, desk, or pocket, headed for a fate to be determined later. One day the worst possible scenario occurred. Tommy raised his hand and told the teacher he had been given a note. Mrs. Doherty walked to his desk, looked over the note and decided to read it to the class:

*Brenda,*

*You are neat. I think so. Good luck on the arithmetic test. It should be easy.*

*Arthur*

Arthur's face turned fire-engine red. Brenda's did, too. Ms. Doherty told Arthur her class was not the place for note passing. Arthur obediently, though reluctantly, stopped sending love letters to the girl of his dreams.

Not to be denied, the young boy quickly concocted other ways of getting Brenda's attention. Whenever the class went outside for recreation, he waited to see where Brenda went—the swings, seesaw, slide, etc. That's where he went. He wasn't much of a conversationalist, contenting himself with just being near the object of his affection. At lunch break and playing Elimination, whenever Arthur caught the ball he automatically looked to throw it at Brenda. What clearer message of affection could he send? Ignoring other potential targets, he'd pursue her until close enough to let the ball loose. If he hit Brenda, his heart went gaga. If Brenda caught the ball, Arthur dejectedly dropped out of the game and waited impatiently for a new one to begin so he could resume his pursuit of her. For Arthur, life didn't get any better than chasing his flame around the playground, aiming to give her a love tap with the Elimination ball. One time, Brenda was able to catch it. She threw the ball right back at Arthur, nicking him on the elbow. Though forced out of the game, Arthur's heart went aflutter. His dream girl had cared enough to eliminate him after he'd already been eliminated! Caught up in playing this mating game, he was the most disappointed kid of all when recess ended.

Near the end of the school year, Ms. Doherty made an announcement. Brenda Watson would be leaving school in a few weeks because her father was being transferred by the military to Kansas. Arthur experienced his first taste of unrequited love.

Without Brenda, playing Elimination would never be the same.

# Chapter 30

TWO WEEKS AFTER HIS teacher's devastating announcement regarding Brenda, the school held its annual recreational event, Field Day. There were three-legged races, softball throwing contests, a relay race on an obstacle course, a handball tournament, potato sack races, all sorts of athletic challenges. It took place on one of the last scheduled school days and the entire student body, except for kindergarten, participated.

Arthur chose to take part in the relay race. The first half of the race entailed a short sprint, and then required stepping nimbly through car tires laid out on the playground. Following that, contestants had to jump over low hurdles, run and weave through a series of slalom polls, and crawl through a tunnel made of a wire frame and covered with drop cloths. All that completed, the runner had to do a 180-degree turn and run fifty yards back to the starting line.

Just before the contest began, Mr. Phillips, the gym teacher, selected members for two competing teams. Arthur watched as his team lined up alongside the opposing squad. The seventh runner on his squad, he began counting back seven kids on the opposing team. He hoped he'd be running against someone slow so he could look good. *Oh no, he was pitted against Ronnie Simpson!* Ronnie was easily the most athletic kid in the fourth grade. Arthur's heart sank. He knew this was his last chance to impress Brenda Watson and now that wouldn't happen.

In the moments leading up to the start of the race, the boys on both lines joked with their teammates while mocking the opposition. Mr. Phillips blew his whistle. "Okay. Listen up. Make those lines straight. The next time I blow this whistle, the race starts. Billy and Glenn will go first. Don't anyone take any shortcuts or you'll have to come back and start over right from the beginning. Your team won't be too happy about that. I'm giving both of you (Billy and Glenn) a piece of cloth. When you get back to the starting line, hand yours to the next runner. Don't let it drop—you'll lose time."

Billy complained. "Mr. Phillips, they only have ten runners, we have eleven. That's not fair."

After thanking Billy for the heads-up, Mr. Phillips scanned the spectators. He spotted Steve, a fourth-grader, and a heavy one at that.

"Hey, Steve. Get over here. Come on. Get on Glenn's team."

Steve, all eighty-seven pounds of him, reluctantly accepted the invitation, greeted with groans from his new teammates.

"All right, teams. Get ready... Get set..."

Since this was the final event of the day, all eyes shifted onto this race. Kids from all grade levels were shouting encouragement to various members of each team.

"...Go!"

Mr. Phillips blew his whistle and the race began. Billy and Glenn took off, over 200 students cheering them on. After successfully negotiating the tires, the hurdles, the poles, and the tunnels, the first two runners got to the turnaround point in a virtual tie. On the return trip, Glenn pulled slightly ahead. He passed the cloth to his anxiously awaiting teammate Baxter. When Billy arrived seconds later, his cloth was grabbed by Charlie.

Arthur, filled with adrenaline-fueled competitiveness, cheered for each of the runners on his team that ran ahead of him. He hoped that by the time it was his turn, his team would be so far ahead, he'd wind up finishing the course before Ronnie had even started.

When the fifth runner on each team finished, the race was a dead heat. Now Skinny, on Arthur's team, faced off against Salvatore. Skinny was way faster than his opponent, so Arthur looked forward to starting with a big lead on Ronnie. Imagine, beating Ronnie Simpson, and impressing Brenda Watson to boot! Everything was going as planned until Skinny tripped and fell high-stepping through the last tire. He got back up, rubbing his knee. Salvatore caught up and passed him. Everyone on Skinny's team yelled at him to get back to racing. He did, but now with a slight limp. Meanwhile, Arthur paced back and forth, ready to grab the cloth. Maybe Skinny would manage to overtake Salvatore; maybe Salvatore would fall. A poor sport like Arthur was not above wishing ill on an opponent. Neither happened. Well after Salvatore had handed his cloth to Ronnie, Skinny limped up to Arthur, who was impatiently chomping at the bit. By the time Arthur started running, Ronnie already enjoyed a sizable lead. Kids on Arthur's team, ever the optimists, cheered him on, even though they knew his mission was impossible.

Benefiting from a head start, Ronnie reached the car tires first, but midway through high-stepping them, he caught his foot inside one and fell onto the next one. By the time Ronnie had struggled to his feet, Arthur had closed the gap and was only two tires behind his opponent. Finishing the tires and with Ronnie holding an ever-narrowing lead, the boys sped on to the hurdles. Arthur, excellent at jumping, cleared all six in rapid fashion and was now breathing down Ronnie's neck. Next they had to run zigzag style through a series of fifteen slalom poles. The minute he began wending his way through them, Arthur proved to be quite agile. Maybe all the practice dodging his father at home was paying off. For the first time in the race, he drew even with Ronnie. As they made their way past the last poll, Arthur had eked out a razor-thin lead. Next the tunnel. Arthur, less beefy than Ronnie, had an easier time going through the tunnel and his head poked out first at its other end. They both scrambled to their feet and turned for home.

The rest of the race was a sprint back to the starting line, running alongside all the obstacles they had handled on the way out. Students were lined up the length of the course, cheering on the two boys.

Arthur, brimming with confidence, sensed for the first time in the race that he could beat Ronnie. He fought to hold on to his slim lead. Despite this all-out effort, halfway home, Ronnie drew even with him. With twenty yards left, Ronnie edged ahead. Pushed by his fleet opponent to run faster than he had ever before, Arthur was sprinting at a pace he'd never imagined possible. Not ready to give up, the young boy reached down inside himself, determined to go even faster, sensing victory was within his reach. With ten yards to go Ronnie still led, but Arthur refused to admit it was over. The youngster dug down for one last desperate spurt of energy. So did Ronnie. He crossed the finish line just ahead of Arthur.

Arthur had lost to Ronnie by a few feet. By the time the entire contest was over Arthur's team lost by some thirty yards, but Arthur had won the race within the race. During his run he had whittled his team's then ten-yard deficit down to only a couple of feet, and done it against the great Ronnie Simpson. Adding to the sweetness, during the race Arthur had picked Brenda's voice out of the screaming crowd. She had been shouting encouragement somewhere around the tire section. In addition, later that afternoon, Ronnie paid Arthur one of the greatest compliments he'd ever gotten in his life: "You run pretty good." Coming from a world-class athlete like Ronnie Simpson, that was high praise indeed.

# Chapter 31

WHILE IN THE FOURTH grade, Arthur got into trouble for fighting with another student who had called him a "Heinie." Though Arthur didn't know exactly what the term meant, based on its use by the "old man," he sensed it was an insult. Arthur also had had his mouth washed out with soap by his teacher after shocking everyone by using the word "godammit" in class.

Despite such distractions and his ill-fated obsession with Brenda Watson, Arthur continued to excel academically. Since the first grade, he had been the best student in his class, except for Kathryn Thomas. The young girl always thwarted Arthur's attempts to win the annual medal awarded to the best student from each school grade. She'd won it in the first grade; Arthur had been the runner-up. As a second-grader, Arthur had improved his overall average, but Kathryn stepped up her game too—Kathryn first, Arthur second. In the third grade, although Arthur had come this close, his feminine rival triumphed again. Each year August Berndt made sure to remind his son that second place was not good enough.

A week before school ended, Mrs. Doherty told her fourth-grade class she was going to announce the winner of the medal. To heighten the suspense, she decided to first reveal who the runner-up was. Arthur waited for the inevitable. Good but not good enough, as usual. His father would rib him for again being unable to outdo Kathryn. Rather than covet the medal, Arthur had come to resent it.

"Now, this is of course one of the very best students in the class, and she has been all year. Coming in second is Kathryn Thomas."

The class let out a collective "Wow!" shocked the presumptive favorite wasn't the winner. Arthur was no exception in the surprise department, but he also felt an excited rush of confidence. Since Kathryn hadn't garnered the medal, the winner had to be either his classmate Donald or himself. Just like that, uncertainty reared its head. He second-guessed himself and assumed the worst. No doubt he'd surpassed Kathryn only to come up short against a new rival.

"And now, for the winner of the medal... and, I believe it's someone that's been trying to win it for some time...Arthur Berndt."

Arthur, exuding pride from every pore, hammed it up. He arose from his seat and took several exaggerated bows. The class let out a cheer, all except Donald.

When school ended that day, Arthur rushed to get home, something he rarely ever did. Bursting through the front door, he ran to his mom in the kitchen, not even stopping to pet Rex.

"I won the medal."

"Oh, Art. That's wonderful. Magnificent."

"Don't tell dad. I want to tell him."

"Okay. He'll be very, very proud of you."

Arthur changed his clothes and went outside to play with Rex in the backyard. A half hour later he heard his dad pull into the driveway. For once, August's arrival didn't make his son cringe. Arthur ran to the front stoop and stood there waiting for his father. For the first time in his life, the young boy had done something that would earn his father's praise.

August hopped out of the car, lunchbox in hand, and walked up the stoop, where his son awaited him in celebration.

"Guess what, Dad."

"What?"

"You have to guess."

"No, I don't. Okay. I guess you got in trouble again. No, you wouldn't look so happy. What is it?"

"I'll give you a hint. It's about school."

"Well, school's almost over. Let me guess. You got the runner-up spot again."

"No. I won the medal."

August scrutinized his son skeptically. "You're not kidding around with me, are you?"

"Nope."

"God damn! Hey, it's about time."

The two went inside. Marguerite was waiting for them.

"You heard about your son?"

"Yes, I did."

"Well I think this calls for a special dessert tonight. Whaddaya want, Art?" The youngster beamed from ear to ear. His father hardly ever called him by his nickname.

"Can we have ice cream?"

August asked, "What kind?"

Mother and son crooned in unison, "Vanilla, chocolate, and strawberry."

"Let's go get it!"

"Hot dog."

August and his son drove down to the supermarket and Arthur picked out a half gallon of Breyers Neapolitan. The ride to and from the store was a surprisingly comfortable one for Arthur. Normally opting for the back seat of any car his father was driving, today he was sitting up front. Though technically on land, he was traveling in uncharted waters, enjoying a surprisingly calm cruise and basking in the warmth of his dad's hard-earned and rare approval.

A week later, school was over for the year. Three days after that, the scholarship awards ceremony was to take place, as it did every year, at the high school. Marguerite took her son shopping for the occasion. Arthur got to pick out a pair of Buster Brown sandals to go with a new shirt and shorts. All the while, his mom proudly let the store clerks, and anyone else within earshot, know that her son was the top student in his class.

Friday. The day of the ceremonies had arrived. Scheduled to start at 6:30 P.M., by the time the entire program ended, it would be way past Arthur's bedtime. He'd be getting a taste of what it was like to be a big kid.

Late that afternoon, Arthur took a bath, this one not in scalding water. After that he dressed himself. Then he waited in the living room, watching TV while his parents got ready for the big event. Liz hadn't arrived home yet from college. Ruth, an accomplished musician, would be playing in the school band providing music as part of the evening's festivities. But that night, Arthur was the center of his parents' attention, for once in a positive way. Perhaps the youngster had reached a new stage in his life. One that included a ceasefire between his dad and him.

On the way to the high school, dad and mom sat in the front seat of the car, Ruth and Arthur in the back. Marguerite turned and asked her son, "Well, how do you feel? Important?"

"Yup."

His father asked, "What if they ask you to give a speech? What would you say?"

"Thank you."

"That's it? Nothing else?"

Arthur thought about it. "Maybe 'Thank you very much.'"

Ruth chimed in. "When I won my medal in the sixth grade, I thanked my teacher and mom and dad." Translation: *I'm my parents' favorite, a well-behaved daughter that always does the right thing, so unlike my trouble-making brother.*

His sister's comment touched off a wave of resentment that stung the young boy for a few seconds, and then vanished when Marguerite said, "Arthur, you should be very proud of your accomplishment. I know I am."

August added a dash of pessimism. "Yeah, but that Thomas girl has three. You've still got some wood to chop to catch up with her."

Arriving at the school, the Berndts left the car and, along with hundreds of other adults and children, filed into the high school. Inside, it looked like half the population of Port Jefferson had been stuffed into the gymnasium that served double duty as an auditorium. The atmosphere reminded Arthur of the circus he had once gone to, though this time, he was going to be part of the show.

Ruth headed for the band area where the other student musicians were already congregating. Early arrivers had filled the opened folding chairs sitting on the gymnasium floor closer to the stage, so Arthur and his parents sat in built-in bleacher seats, farther from the stage. Having learned from their own children about Arthur's achievement, a few adults sitting nearby congratulated August and Marguerite. Marguerite proudly chatted with the well-wishers while August uncomfortably shook a few hands.

The lights dimmed, except for those shining on the large stage. The high school principal, Mr. Jansen, walked out onto the stage and approached a microphone. He asked everybody to stand while the school band played the "Star-Spangled Banner." When the music ended, the principal greeted the audience and then proclaimed, "You folks all know I'm a man of few words. Let's get down to the business of celebrating our students."

As it was done every year, awards would be given out in order from the first grade up to the twelfth.

"Okay. Starting off...The winner of the medal from Mrs. Spear's first-grade class is Nancy Wells. Nancy, come on up here."

As the audience energetically applauded, the young girl got up from her seat, walked down the aisle between the rows of chairs, climbed up the steps and walked across the stage to Mr. Jansen. He draped the medal, complete with lanyard, around her neck and shook her hand. The youngster curtsied, an unexpected gesture that generated a sympathetic "Aw!" from the audience. She then retraced her steps back to her seat next to her parents.

"Now, there is a young lady with good manners! Next, our second-grade winner from Mrs. Goward's class, Patricia White."

Arthur's surroundings faded into the background. Overwhelmed with panic, he heard nothing but his inner voice. It warned him that he would soon have to take that same long walk up to the stage that the other winners were taking. More than a thousand eyes would be watching him. He'd never be able to handle all the attention. Arthur's head began swimming. His brain screamed at him, *Run for the nearest door and get out of the building as quickly as possible!* He knew he couldn't. He'd have to see this through, to not upset his mother and, more importantly, not anger his father. Arthur pulled himself together, determined to deal with his uneasiness no matter what.

"...and let's give another round of applause for Charles, this year's best third-grade student."

Those words from the principal signaled that Arthur would be called next. He looked at his parents. His mom was beaming. She was witnessing her son's finest academic hour. His father was wearing one of his less angry expressions. Arthur couldn't let them down. Yet, inside the youngster there was a growing unease bubbling closer and closer to the surface. It wasn't just nervousness about all the attention he was about to deal with, there was something else. He just couldn't put his finger on it.

"Okay. Let's move on to our winner from the fourth grade, Mrs. Doherty's class. The winner of the medal as the best fourth-grade student is... Arthur Berndt."

There was no turning back. Arthur pulled it together and forced himself out of his seat. He got a "Good boy!" from his mom, silence and a halfhearted smile from his dad, as he passed them to get out into the aisle. With legs of rubber, the young boy wobbled a bit coming down the bleacher steps and then began navigating the open aisle that separated the two large clusters of occupied chairs on the gymnasium floor. Along the way, he got so distracted watching people to his left applauding for him that he bumped into a chair on his right. That got a chuckle from some in the audience. Finally, he reached the steps leading to the stage, and, after climbing them, walked onto the stage, over to the principal. Glancing into the audience, he could barely make out his mother waving to him while his father was standing, reaching to shake hands with someone behind him.

Arthur found most adult males intimidating. Standing well over six feet tall with a rotund build, Mr. Jansen cut an especially imposing figure to Arthur. Nevertheless, when the principal extended his hand, Arthur boldly grabbed it with his and exuberantly shook it up and down.

The principal was impressed. "Nothing shy about this youngster. Arthur, you're a big boy. Do you want to wear the medal now or take it with you in this box?"

Arthur said nothing. Instead, he yanked the box from the principal's hand and threw it. The crowd roared with laughter. *This kid is a real comedian.*

Mr. Jansen walked over to where the small box had landed, picked it up and came back to Arthur. "You know folks. I think this young lad is very excited about winning his medal. Almost too excited." Again, the audience laughed. The principal removed the medal from its container.

"Arthur, let me put this medal around your neck. If you don't like the box, you don't have to keep it."

Not waiting for the boy to answer, the principal tucked the box under his armpit and then slipped the medal around Arthur's neck. The youngster was wearing his hard-earned trophy, but not for long. No sooner had the crowd begun applauding when Arthur yanked the medal off and heaved his award with such force it skidded off the stage, into the band pit.

The audience recoiled, gasping in unison. Something was very wrong.

The world went temporarily black for Arthur. The next thing he knew, his father and mother were on the stage. He heard his father say "Let's get him the hell out of here."

Arthur knew he was in trouble, big trouble. He didn't need to be convinced to get moving. He'd do anything to stay out of his father's reach, anything it took to avoid the embarrassment of so many people seeing him get hit. He scrambled across the stage and down the steps, retracing the path he'd taken just minutes before. However, now there was no applauding, only stunned uncomfortable silence. The entire audience was transfixed by the sight of the youngster hurrying to exit the building, with his father and mother in close pursuit. Some in the crowd were now on their feet, straining to get a better view of the bizarre proceedings. Climbing up the stairs past the bleacher seats, Arthur saw a little girl looking up at the woman next to her and asking, "What did he do, mommy?" Seconds later, he recognized a neighbor talking with the man alongside her. "Poor Marguerite. She has so much trouble with him." The man responded, "Well, what do you expect? They're all damn krauts."

Ruth had left the band area and rushed to catch up with the other members of her family. Through the exit the four went. When they got outside the school, August unleashed a flood of expletives in both English and German. Arthur had heard every one of them before, but tonight his father spit them out with extra force.

The Berndts piled into their car and headed home. It was a short drive, but long enough for Arthur to endure a conversation about himself he didn't want to hear. His sister remained silent, always the safest course of action during one of their father's tirades.

"That kid is a goddamn bastard. He's crazy."

"I don't understand it. I just don't understand it." Marguerite turned around and asked Arthur why he had done what he'd done. She got no answer.

"See, he can't even explain it himself. Forget the goddamn medal. You know, they have special places for kids like him." August turned on the interior light and, after adjusting the rear-view mirror, glowered into it, staring at his son. "You're too young for jail so a reform school will have to do. I think I'll do some investigating. Whadda ya think, wise guy? How'd you like to go somewhere special?"

Marguerite began crying.

"See what you did to your mother. You proud of yourself?"

Arthur knew better than to answer any of those hot-button questions. Doing so would only stoke the flames of his father's fiery anger to even greater heights.

When the car turned onto Lowell Place, his father's damning dialogue mercifully ended. Now Arthur faced a bigger problem. He was terrified of going into the house with his father in such an ugly mood. The young boy knew he'd have to face his father eventually. He just couldn't muster the courage to handle it at the moment.

The car pulled into the driveway. Before it came to a full stop, Arthur opened his door and jumped out, bolting onto the street and breaking into an all-out sprint. He heard his father get out of the car and take off in hot pursuit. The young boy's new sandals furiously clattered under him, accompanied by the dull thump of his father's dress shoes hitting the road behind him. Arthur went into a higher gear, knowing he was doomed if his father caught up to him. The sky was overcast and the pitch-black night, scarcely illuminated by a light from this or that house, only made the youngster's task more daunting, and frightening.

"Ow! Dammit!" Arthur knew what that meant. His father's bad knee was giving him trouble. Hoping his father might give up the chase, the young boy, taking no chances, scooted into a treed lot that sat at the end of the street. He clumsily pushed his way through the thick brush and deeper into the night's blackness, getting as deep into the woods as possible, suffering cuts and scrapes from unfriendly foliage along the way.

Arthur came to a stop and stood—a silent statue—well hidden by the night and the protective layer of thick woods surrounding him. He fought to control his heavy breathing, afraid it might give him away. He didn't know if his father had seen him duck into the woods; he didn't even know if his dad was still giving chase. He listened for clues. Rustling in the woods would be big trouble, a sign his father, bum knee and all, hadn't given up, and the chase would continue. A scary prospect because the young boy didn't know how much more run he had left in him. All the youngster could do was sit and wait for his father to make the next move.

Then Arthur heard something in the distance that was music to his ears. The neighbor living directly across from 21 Lowell Place, Mr. Guschel, was having a conversation with August. That meant Arthur's father had ended the pursuit. Arthur's execution had been delayed—but not necessarily canceled.

"Gus, I saw your son in action tonight. You have my condolences. That kid's a handful."

"He'll get his."

Arthur sat down on a tree stump to rest and sort out his situation.

There was no way the youngster could face his father this night, no way he'd have the guts to be under the same roof with him, especially since he had bested his father in a footrace. That fact had only ramped up the elder Berndt's ire to a more extreme level. On the other hand, the youngster knew he couldn't handle sitting in the woods all night either. He'd always had a fear of the dark, a fear of being attacked by someone or something he couldn't see until it was too late. What to do?

While fretting over his dilemma, the youngster could hear his father off in the distance and inside the house, ranting and raving at the top of his lungs. After a while, things quieted down. Then Arthur heard his mother, half calling, half crying from the front door, "Art, come home. Come here, please. You can't stay out there."

Ignoring his mother's pleas, the young boy concocted a plan. He'd stay outside until all the lights were off in his house and everyone was asleep. Then he'd quietly sneak in and go to bed himself. He'd have to face his father in the morning. The young boy wasn't sure he'd ever seen his father this angry, so why not postpone a trip to hell? If that meant staying in the woods for a few more hours, so be it. He squatted down and waited for time to pass.

After what seemed an eternity, he slowly and stiffly got up from the crouched position he'd been in and ventured back to the edge of the lot where it met the street. Before leaving the woods, he peeked out and looked up and down the road, hoping to make sure the coast was clear. There were no house lights on anywhere, so he would have to venture out of the woods' darkness onto the road's darkness. A few scattered stars in an otherwise overcast sky provided the youngster only the scantiest light. Arthur stumbled out onto the pavement and headed towards his house. 21 Lowell Place was totally dark, a sign that no one was up, a good sign to Arthur. He couldn't risk having his footsteps heard on the gravel driveway, so the young boy walked silently across the front lawn, the lawn his father always warned him never to walk on. He went up onto the front stoop. The screen door was closed but due to the unusually hot weather, the storm door was wide open.

Then it struck Arthur. What if his dog gave him away? Rex always greeted his youthful master exuberantly. Would Arthur be able to calm his canine pal before the dog's friskiness woke anybody? That was a chance the youngster would have to take.

Arthur took off his sandals and carefully opened the screen door, making as little noise as possible. He cautiously stepped inside. Quietly closing the door behind him, he turned around and walked over to the stairway that led up to his bedroom. He hesitated, deciding his next move. If he walked up the flight of steps in the dark he might slip or fall, making noise and giving himself away. For safety's sake, the youngster decided he'd crawl up the stairs. Arthur placed his knees on the first step and his hands on the second. The young boy felt a sense of exhilaration. He was doing it! He was just a flight of stairs away from a temporary reprieve. Arthur would worry about tomorrow...tomorrow.

"Make a fool out of me, you goddamn bastard..." The words shot out of a totally dark living room. Arthur couldn't see who had spoken, but knew the voice all too well.

The youngster immediately changed plans. He scrambled off the stairs and ran into the dining room, intent on getting to the back door and out of the house again. He banged his knee on a dining room table and fell to the floor, but quickly scrambled to his feet, desperate to evade his still invisible pursuer. The young boy rushed into the kitchen, closer to his goal.

Nearing the back door, he found a chair had been propped up against it to prevent him from entering the house. Now it served to delay his escape from inside the house. Just as he began pulling the chair away from the door, he felt a hand pulling at his shirt. Instinctively going from escape mode to one of self-protection, Arthur sunk to the floor and covered his head with his hands.

"Get up!"

Arthur refused. August began kicking his son, at the same time yelling at him to stand up. From the basement, Rex was letting loose a steady, mournful wail in protest...

*...Arthur no longer heard his father. He was in the woods, walking alongside a pond he often visited. He gathered up sticks that*

*were perfect for Rex to retrieve. His dog, knowing what was coming, did a happy dance, his feet already in the water. Arthur flung a stick and Rex ran full blast into the pond. He launched into a dog paddle, reached the stick, grabbed it with his mouth and, after making a U-turn, swam back to shore. Filled with the pride of a job well done, he scooted up to his young master, waiting for further direction. A simple "Drop!" was all the dog needed. Arthur picked the stick up and threw it even farther than he had the first time into the pond. Rex was already on the way before the stick hit the water—*

A direct kick to the stomach brought Arthur back to reality. He saw stars and thought he was going to vomit, but didn't. The young boy started crying, but that didn't stop the pummeling. What *did* was the kitchen light being turned on. Marguerite screamed, "Stop it. Stop it now! For God's sake!"

August shot back angrily, "He made a fool of us. Maybe you don't give a shit, but I do."

"You're his father. You're doing the same thing to him your mother did to you. This is too much. Whatever he did, this is too much."

Glaring at his son, August commanded, "You. You get up and get to goddamn bed." Arthur got to his feet and, as quickly as his trembling legs would allow, hustled upstairs to his room. Behind him, he heard his parents arguing.

"You coddle the kid."

"And what do you do? Why be so hard on him? What are you proving? He's my son. For God's sake, he's your son, too. Did you forget that? "

"Sometimes I'd like to. I'm disgusted to admit he is. When he's not pissing in bed, he's pulling crap like this."

"Like I said, you're treating him just like your mother treated you. I don't see any difference."

August Berndt glowered at his wife. "Don't ever bring up my mother, you understand?" He stood silent for a few seconds and then defended himself. "I'm handling him the way you handle a troublemaker. What the hell would you do? Got any bright ideas?"

"I can't take much more of this. That's all I know."

Marguerite left her husband in the kitchen and went upstairs. Before going to bed she checked on her son, sitting cross-legged on his bed and sobbing.

"Are you okay?"

"Yeah." Arthur used the backs of his hands to rub his tear-filled eyes.

"I'm going to have a serious talk with your father. But, Arthur, why in heaven did you do what you did tonight? Please tell me. Your father and I both want to know."

"I don't know, Ma." He wasn't lying. Earlier that evening, on the way to the ceremony he'd been troubled by vague unacceptable thoughts. Then on the stage with the principal, those thoughts, for the briefest of moments, had crystallized. Sensing he'd entered a world of tabooed thinking, he quickly escaped from it. Whatever memory he had of his forbidden thinking was locked inside his subconscious for the time being. Arthur had refined the art of keeping secrets so well he could even keep them from himself.

Marguerite fluffed her son's pillow. The young boy lay down, resting his head on it. His mother rushed to the laundry closet, grabbed a clean washcloth and returned to dab the sweat off her son. "You *have* to know why you did this. Well...it's too late to talk about right now. Tomorrow. Good night, son. Sleep tight."

"Good night, Ma."

Marguerite opened both of the room's windows as much as possible and left the door ajar, hoping to make the sultry night air a bit more bearable for her son. She turned off the ceiling light and uttered one more "Good night."

Arthur, still drenched in sweat and aching from the evening's activities, lay on his bed. Though worn out, he was too agitated to immediately fall asleep.

From the basement, Rex was still barking sporadically. Arthur heard his father let the dog back up from the basement into the house. Rex scooted upstairs, went into Arthur's room, and jumped onto the bed. Unusual for a dog that had been trained to sleep in the living room. Arthur was grateful for his pal's show of concern.

From his parents' bedroom he heard his mom sobbing. Downstairs, his father opened a beer. The youngster felt that all-too-familiar guilt for causing his parents to argue.

Exhaustion finally overcame the young boy. He fell asleep, but not before praying to God that, for just this one night, he wouldn't wet the bed.

# # #

The following day, Marguerite got a phone call from Mr. Jansen's secretary. The medal Arthur had tossed away had been retrieved.

Marguerite covered the receiver and called to her husband upstairs, "Gus, they have the medal. We can pick it up."

Her husband shouted, "What the hell do I want with it? If he doesn't want it why should I?"

Marguerite got back on the phone. "I'll be there. It'll take me about five minutes. You're on the first floor, right?"

Fifteen minutes later, Marguerite was back home with her son's award and the container he had also tossed away. She put it on a wooden ledge that sat high atop the clothes rack in the bedroom closet she shared with her husband, out of their son's reach.

The entire incident surrounding the medal was never again discussed in the Berndt household.

# # #

During July and August, Arthur completed his third consecutive summer of Red Cross swimming lessons. He continued to be warned about staying away from older children, and because of his growing reputation as a troublemaker, children his age were discouraged by their parents from associating with him. As a result, when not swimming, he spent a great deal of time wandering around the neighborhood or in the woods, with or without Rex.

In September 1954, Arthur gladly began the fifth grade. He always felt a bit less lonely and a lot less afraid in school.

# Chapter 32

"DO YOU WANNA GET free candy?"

Of course Arthur did. What kid in his right mind wouldn't? His newfound friend from the fourth grade and now fifth-grade classmate, Ronnie Simpson, put this question to him one morning while they were waiting in their classroom for school to officially start.

Ronnie said, "It's too late today. Come to school extra early tomorrow. I'll meet you out on High Street." He pointed at Arthur's parka. "Wear that same coat."

The following day, Arthur set out for school a half hour early, telling his mom that he and several other students had agreed to get to school early to work on a class project.

It was a cold midwinter day. As directed, Arthur was wearing his parka jacket, complete with hood and deep warm pockets. He walked to school a bit more briskly than usual and wound up at the designated meeting spot a half hour or so before class started. Ronnie was already there to greet him. "Come on. Follow me."

They headed on foot towards downtown Port Jefferson. On the way, Arthur pumped Ronnie for more details. How much candy? What kind? Why was it free? Ronnie's standard response: "You'll find out."

Ronnie was a year older than Arthur, having started school at a later age than his fellow classmate. Arthur wasn't sure why, but according to his dad, it must have had something to do with bad parenting. Ronnie was much taller and more well-built than the average fifth grader and a very take-charge kind of kid. Most of the other children considered him a bully. He had taken a liking to Arthur in the fourth grade and decided they should be friends. It was an invitation Arthur thought best not to refuse. He had seen Ronnie in a couple of scuffles, and his opponents always came out of them wondering why they had ever accepted Ronnie's solicitation to do battle.

When the two reached East Main Street, they continued walking until Ronnie came to a halt in front of Brown's Pharmacy. Arthur had never visited this store, not thinking he had a reason to. Had he known that the drugstore gave away candy for free, he'd have started going there a long time ago.

Ronnie peeked in the store window. "Okay, let's go in."

Before Arthur did, he had to make one thing clear. "Hey, Ronnie. I don't have any money. I don't even have lunch money." He pulled a brown bag out of his coat pocket. "My mom gave me this lunch today. I can't buy anything."

"You won't have to."

Still sounding too good to be true, Arthur, skepticism and all, flipped down his jacket hood, took off his mittens, and still holding his lunch bag, followed his friend into the store.

The interior of Brown's had the same old-fashioned flavor found in several other buildings situated throughout the village of Port Jefferson, some of which were built in the 1800s and early 1900s. It featured a patterned creamy white tin ceiling, overhead lights and fans operated with drawstrings, and a worn creaky wood floor. The store had but a single aisle, its entire shopping area only a bit larger than a one-car garage. Walking towards the back, the boys passed various display cases and racks of over-the-counter medical and cosmetic products. At the very rear stood the pharmacy counter, loaded with more products. Behind the counter, Mr. Brown, the pharmacist, was busying himself among his medicinal potions, filling prescriptions.

The boys never made it all the way to the back. Ronnie stopped them in the middle of the store. To their right, nestled in uncovered cases, sat the "free" candy.

The selection wasn't nearly as extensive as that in the Crystal Fountain, but it did have one especially attractive feature: all the candy was displayed out in the open, easily within reach of even a fifth grader. But Arthur wouldn't be reaching for any. He had no money. He turned to look at Mr. Brown, still hunched over a table concocting some elixir, his back facing the boys.

Arthur felt something drop into his jacket hood. Before he could check to see what had happened, he felt something else land in it. Then, something more. After a few moments of confusion, he realized what was going on. Ronnie was filling up his hood with candy, with the store owner just feet away. Ronnie, quite criminally talented, managed to keep one eye on the candy, the other on Mr. Brown, all the while never missing Arthur's hood with the goodies he was tossing into it.

Mr. Brown turned around from his work, looking directly at the youngsters. "Do you boys want something?"

Arthur was sure they'd been snagged, but Ronnie calmly said, "Yeah. I'll take a pack of Juicy Fruit."

"Righto."

Mr. Brown walked from the pharmacy area, continued along in back of some racks of pharmaceutical goods, and came up to a small open counter area where the cash register sat. The two boys met him there. Arthur was certain the owner would see all the candy stuffed into his jacket hood and there'd be big trouble. The youngster got ready to run for his life. At that moment, he wished for all the world that someone else—anybody else—was wearing his parka. It felt like a straitjacket.

Mr. Brown eyed Arthur. "Whadda ya got there, youngster?"

Panic. The young boy had had his doubts all along about this operation. He could think of nothing to say.

"Hey! What's that you got in your hand?"

"Oh, it's my lunch." *What a relief!*

To Arthur's amazement, Ronnie paid for the pack of gum, Mr. Brown rang up the sale and the two boys left the store untouched. They even got a hearty "So long!" from the store's owner.

The youthful shoplifters hustled up to the end of Prospect Street. As soon as they turned onto High Street, Arthur took off his jacket and the two boys visually feasted on their spoils. They divvied up the sweets, with Ronnie taking some of the preferred catches like Tootsie Pops and Hershey bars. Arthur didn't complain. No need to rile Ronnie and, besides, this had been his idea in the first place.

The two hurried back to school, just beating the bell. In the excitement, Arthur left his lunch bag on the sidewalk where the boys had sorted out their inventory. It didn't matter. He feasted on his ill-gotten gains throughout the school day whenever the teacher wasn't looking. Arthur promised to meet up with his co-conspirator the following morning and return to their newfound source of cheaper than dirt-cheap candy. On second thought, maybe it wasn't so newfound for Ronnie. Arthur got the impression from Ronnie's cool confidence throughout the heist that this wasn't the first time he had pulled off such a caper.

Arthur had to admit that, although it wasn't legal, the candy was indeed free. Envisioning a never-ending string of visits to Brown's Pharmacy, he told his parents the class project was going to be at least a month-long venture, maybe longer. The thought crossed his mind that if he purposely lost his coat, he might be able to get one with an even bigger hood. Was this precocious antisocial thinking? Was Arthur on his way to becoming a criminal, or had he already arrived?

The spree went on for months. This was something new for Arthur. He was getting a fresh supply of candy every school day without having to steal any money from his mother. And technically, *he* wasn't stealing the candy, he just happened to be a kid wearing a jacket with a spacious hood. Either Mr. Brown didn't see what was happening right in front of him, or he had a huge soft spot for kids, at least these two. This was daylight robbery at its finest.

When March rolled around and the weather began to warm up, Arthur, to the bemusement of his mother, still insisted on wearing his parka. After all, the parka was vital to the success of this ongoing shoplifting operation. “I really like it” and “It’s my favorite” were the best he could come up with to justify his ongoing love affair with a coat.

The thievery continued.

# # #

Arthur had never thought he’d live to see the day—he was getting sick of candy. He simply was getting more than his fill. Besides that, all the sugar was again wreaking havoc with his appetite as it had back in the third grade, and he was starting to lose weight again. Ronnie admitted that he too had more sweets than he could handle.

The two boys decided to branch out, putting into action a novel business plan that Arthur had cooked up in a fit of entrepreneurship. Why not sell some of the candy to other kids? “With money, you can buy lots of other stuff, like baseball cards, Wham-o sling shots—they’re the best— BB guns, water pistols.”

They began offering great prices on “all your favorites” in their classroom. Soon enough word got around the entire school that candy could be had from Arthur and Ronnie at bargain prices. Meetings were set up to conduct business on the High Street sidewalk after school. The two thieves didn’t drive very hard bargains. If a student claimed that what they had for sale wasn’t really his or her favorite, the prices were slashed even further right on the spot. What did Arthur and Ronnie care? They hadn’t paid a cent for any of their merchandise. Every sale was one-hundred-per-cent profit.

# # #

St. Patrick's Day. A day of celebration nationwide. Locally, Ronnie and Arthur marked the observance with a celebration of their own. They made over eight dollars that day in candy sales, a personal best. By now they were eating almost none of their snatched sweets, a fact which boosted their total sales to new heights.

A few days later Ronnie and Arthur got called into Mr. Strauss's office. He had been an easy-going teacher and now he was an even easier-going assistant principal. He was known to never use the paddle that the principal, Mr. Tolleson, occasionally did.

"Boys, I've heard you two are quite the candy salesmen."

Arthur boldly asked, "Would you like to buy some?"

Mr. Strauss laughed. " No, that's not why I called you in. Where's all the candy coming from?"

That question left Arthur tongue-tied. Fortunately, his partner in crime immediately launched into a story so polished Arthur figured he'd been saving it for just this sort of special occasion. Ronnie explained that his uncle was a candy representative that went from town to town, stocking stores with candy. As part of his job, he was given lots of samples to keep. He didn't want them so he gave them to Ronnie, his favorite nephew. The assistant principal might have punched holes in Ronnie's story, but he chose not to.

"So where does Arthur come in?"

Ronnie had a ready explanation. "Art's my friend. I let him help me sell them."

"Well, look. We can't have you selling candy in the school or right outside the building either. I applaud your initiative and salesmanship, but you'll have to conduct your business after school hours and somewhere else. Understood?"

With the loss of their built-in customer base, sales immediately dwindled. The boys took all this very philosophically. Ronnie said he could sell candy to some kids that lived near him downtown, so they should hit up the pharmacy a few more times, split those sales, and then take a vacation. Besides, it was getting warmer and pretty soon Arthur would look suspicious entering Brown's in his bulky parka. The last few visits to Brown's would be like a farewell tour. Next winter they'd reopen for business.

Hadn't Mr. Brown noticed he was constantly running out of candy without selling much of it? Was he that elderly that he couldn't keep track of his inventory and thus remained unaware that he was getting ripped off? If that was the case, he might be put out of business by a couple of schoolkids. Or was it only a matter of time before he did the math? Arthur and Ronnie weren't old enough to concern themselves with logic.

Near the end of March, one particular school day started out much like so many had for the two boys over the past several months. Before class began, Ronnie and Arthur rendezvoused on High Street, took the short walk to the pharmacy and went in, with candy on their minds and larceny in their hearts. However, this time, immediately upon entering, the two boys stopped in their tracks.

There, standing next to Mr. Brown, was a uniformed police officer. The two men turned and stared at the boys. As if on cue, Arthur and Ronnie looked at each other, spun around—perfectly synchronized like a well-choreographed dance team—and headed back out the door. They left Brown's that day "empty-hooded," and together hotfooted it back to school without exchanging a word.

That was it for this school year; plans for next year's robbery binge were canceled indefinitely.

# Chapter 33

ALTHOUGH THEIR CANDY-SNATCHING DAYS were over, Arthur and Ronnie continued to be friends.

Arthur had begun showing signs of athletic ability back in the fourth grade. He continued that trend throughout the fifth and felt more and more worthy of being in Ronnie's company. When choosing up sides during gym class, the two boys presented themselves as a package deal, ensuring they'd always be on the same team. Thanks to Ronnie's imposing stature, all the other boys thought better of complaining about the arrangement. Ronnie had that kind of quieting effect on his classmates.

If playing softball, Ronnie and his protégé always batted one, two. When the game was touch football, Ronnie, being a natural leader, played quarterback, and Arthur was always his primary pass receiver. This presented Arthur with a challenge since any ball thrown by Ronnie had a lot of zing on it. Arthur usually had the guts to absorb the painful high-impact passes, thanks in part to the "physical conditioning" he received at home, and thanks in part to his need to look good in Ronnie's eyes. Basketball was Arthur's weak suit. If he was on Ronnie's team, his job was not to handle the ball or shoot, but to position himself in order to get rebounds. It was an easy job because when Ronnie did the shooting, there weren't too many rebounds to get.

Living miles apart, the boys never associated outside the classroom. Inside the school, it was a much different story. Arthur continued to excel in his classwork, purposely straddling a line by not doing well enough to earn the medal while still earning grades that would not provoke his father's rage. Ronnie, on the other hand, had never been a good student. He spent most of his time in the classroom being disruptive—talking, throwing things at other students, purposely dropping books to make noise, and anything else he could do to irritate the teacher. Rarely did he get through a school day without spending some part of it in the principal's office; on occasion, such a visit included a paddling. Friend or no friend, Arthur felt a sense of relief watching Ronnie head to the office. At least someone else was getting a beating, not him. And what about at home? If there was a bad report from school, wouldn't his friend get hit for real by his father just like Arthur would? The only time Arthur had seen Ronnie's dad was in the third grade when he came into the classroom to give his son some money for lunch. He'd reached into his jingling pocket and pulled out a fistful of coins, the most Arthur had ever seen in anyone's hands, and he gave it all to Ronnie. At that moment, Arthur thought Mr. Simpson had to be the richest man in the world. And one of the biggest, too. An ex-marine, he stood well over six-feet tall and had the build of a football lineman. Surely he was giving his son a whipping every time the school called with complaints about his behavior. Though curious, Arthur saw no reason to discuss the matter with Ronnie. He never talked to anyone about his beatings, and he assumed nobody else would talk about theirs.

As the school year progressed, the two got into the habit of making mostly amateurish animal noises—dogs, cats, elephants, etc.—while the teacher, Mr. Mason, was at the board, his back to the classroom. In fact, Ronnie could do pretty good imitations of a chicken and a horse. Another favorite pastime of theirs was passing nonsense notes to each other when the teacher wasn't looking, just to see if they could get away with it. If one of these missives was snagged by the teacher while in transit to Arthur or Ronnie, both would deny passing the note, instead blaming some other student for taking it from one of the two boys' desks. Of course, students weren't supposed to be writing notes period—whether intended for distribution or not. So after Mr. Mason completed a handwriting analysis, he gave the exposed culprit a lengthy written assignment to be completed on the spot. If Arthur was convicted, he'd willingly do the work, fearing his failure to comply might lead to a phone call home. On the other hand, Ronnie, a smug look on his face, almost always blew off the teacher's demands and off to the principal's office he'd go.

Whenever Ronnie was called on to read in class, he'd stumble his way through a few written passages. When he was done, Arthur would immediately volunteer to read, and, careful to not show up his pal, purposely mispronounce a few words. His misguided effort to emulate his pal as a show of moral support failed to impress the teacher. Puzzled and frustrated by Arthur's under-reading, Mr. Mason would reprimand him: "Arthur, you can do better than that." "What's wrong with you today?" "Pay better attention." "Keep your mind on what you're reading."—all criticisms Arthur was willing to endure in his effort to deepen his friendship with Ronnie.

If the class had a spelling bee, Ronnie was always one of the first to be eliminated. Arthur would hang in for a while and then blow a word he knew. The youngster would do anything to not show up his friend.

# # #

Each day a student was selected by Mr. Mason to clean the blackboard erasers. That was prized duty. First of all, you temporarily got out of class. Second of all, you got to walk all the way down to the basement and go into Mr. Dockery's workroom. Third of all, he would let you flick the switch to start the stationary vacuuming machine on which you were allowed to rub the erasers until they were free of chalk. Mr. Dockery was a corpulent sixty-something man with a ruddy face and thick white hair. Besides being the school maintenance man, he served special duty around Christmas time, dressing up as Santa Claus and visiting each classroom in the school, giving out a box of candy to each kid as he "ho-ho-ho-ed" his way throughout the building.

One particular day, Mr. Mason, as was his custom, asked the class for a volunteer to do eraser duty. Before he finished his question, Peter raised his hand. So did Ronnie. The teacher picked Peter. Ronnie had a fit. Peter happily leapt out of his seat, ready to grab the erasers and escape the classroom. As he headed up the aisle towards the front of the room, Ronnie stuck out his foot and tripped him. Peter got up and, after some pushing and shoving, the fight was on. After Ronnie, Peter was the second-biggest kid in the class. Nevertheless, this skirmish quickly turned into a rout. While most fifth-graders contented themselves with wrestling during a scuffle, Ronnie began swinging his fists, connecting on Peter's chin and ear. Mr. Mason rushed to break the fight up. No doubt, Peter was glad he did.

"Well, just for that, neither of you are going. You both know very well I don't allow fighting in my classroom. Paula, you take the erasers. Peter, go to the principal's office. Ronnie, you'll go when Peter comes back."

Peter objected. "Hey, he tripped me."

Mr. Mason looked at Ronnie. "Is that true?"

"He's lying. It's his fault. He doesn't even know how to walk right."

The teacher turned to the class. "Did anyone see what happened here?"

Even though everyone had, the question was greeted with silence. No one ever snitched on Ronnie Simpson.

# # #

Days later, the class had a spelling test. Arthur was prepared for it. Ronnie, true to form, wasn't.

Mr. Mason made the announcement. "There are going to be thirty words." That elicited a groan from his class. "I'll say the word, use it in a sentence, and then say the word again. When we're done, raise your hand if you want me to repeat any of the thirty. Warning! Only one request to a customer so pay attention the first time I give you these words. All right, let's begin, and keep your eyes on your own paper. Number one is geography. Geography deals with the study of the earth's surface. Geography."

All the students got down to business, writing their answers. Except for Ronnie. He kicked the back of Arthur's chair. Arthur turned to look at his friend. Ronnie shrugged his shoulders. Translation—I need help. The teacher spotted Arthur twisted around in his chair.

"Arthur, what the heck are you doing? I told everyone in the class to keep to their own business. That includes you. Frankly, if you have to copy from Mr. Simpson, you're in big trouble. Did you forget to study for this test? "

"Yes, I did. I mean, I studied for it."

"Well then, turn around. Your answer sheet is in front of you, not in back of you. Write down your answers and stop holding up everybody else."

Addressing the entire class, the teacher got back to business. "Okay, let's see if we can finish this without any more interruptions. Number two. Mammal. A mammal is a warm-blooded animal with a backbone. Mammal."

Halfway through the test, Mr. Mason began to have a coughing fit. He grabbed a lozenge out of his desk drawer, popped it into his mouth, and continued giving the test. After a few more words, the cough returned.

Between hacks the teacher managed to give orders to the class. "Put your pens down, turn your papers over, and sit quietly. I'll be right back."

With that, Mr. Mason dashed out into the hall and headed for a nearby water fountain. This was just the opportunity Ronnie needed. He reached past Arthur, grabbed his test paper, lined it up with his own sheet on his desk, and began feverishly copying Arthur's answers onto his paper. Arthur sat at his desk, nervously staring at the front door, afraid the teacher would pop back into the classroom at any moment, but also afraid to ask Ronnie to give back the paper he had taken.

"Ahem." Arthur turned around and saw Mr. Mason. The teacher had reentered the room through the rear door, and was standing directly behind Ronnie's desk. Ronnie, unaware of the teacher's presence, continued busily copying answers. Mr. Mason snatched up both their papers.

"Okay, boys, the party's over. I've had it with the two of you. Ronnie, you go to the office."

Ronnie got up and, with a smirk on his face, slowly sauntered past the teacher and out of the classroom, presumably headed for the principal's office. Presumably, because with Ronnie you just never knew when he might decide to walk right past the principal's office and out the building.

"Arthur, you just sit quietly—and I mean quietly!—at your desk while the class finishes the test. You won't need to. You've earned a zero." While heading towards the front of the room the teacher stopped, turned around, and added, "Arthur, when your partner in crime comes back, you go to Mr. Tolleson's office. By the way, I don't know why I didn't do this sooner. I'm moving you as far away from your friend as possible. In fact, get your things and switch seats with Betty, right now."

This incident brought things to a head. Arthur's parents were contacted by the school and an evening meeting was set up to include Mr. Tolleson, Mr. Mason, Arthur's parents, and Mr. Simpson (a widower). The principal and teacher both declared that the two youngsters were poison together. Because Ronnie dominated their relationship, scholastically Arthur was underperforming intentionally while Ronnie was failing miserably. The solution: the two had to be separated. There were only three weeks left in the school year. Mr. Mason promised to do his best to keep the pair apart during that period of time. He asked for the parents' help. At that point, Ronnie's father had to leave to start his shift at the local hospital. As he left, he said he'd "have a talk with my son." He offered to shake hands with Arthur's father, but August would have none of it.

With Ronnie's father gone, Mr. Tolleson turned to the Berndts. "I've got to tell you. We need to stop this before it goes any further. Frankly, I don't know how else to say this. From what Mr. Mason here tells me, Ronnie's been leading your son around like a puppy."

August turned to his wife and said, "I told you he's got no backbone."

The principal continued. "I know you've had some problems with your son up there in your neighborhood—"

Marguerite interrupted. "He's a good boy at heart. But sometimes we just have trouble controlling him. He can give us fits at times."

August sneered. "I'll say."

Mr. Tolleson suggested a solution to the problem. "Well, in school Art has always been a very good student, very good academically. Every once in a while he's gotten into some kind of trouble but it never was really a big issue until he began associating with the Simpson boy. I'm strongly urging you to keep your son away from Ronnie. I'm going to call Ronnie's father tomorrow and give him the same advice. These two are absolutely no good together. They may have their problems on their own, but together...it just gets much worse."

Mr. Mason chimed in. "I can vouch for that. They've made this year a nightmare for me. I know why Ronnie is a troublemaker. He can't do the work. I don't know what's eating Arthur. Maybe he's just a follower?"

August asked no one in particular with disgust, "Jesus Christ. We have to watch who he pals with at home and now in school, too? Can't you people run a classroom?"

Mr. Tolleson responded. "Mr. Berndt, I understand how you feel. Kids are tough. Ask me. I've got three of them. But I'm confident we can resolve this matter. And you just might see improvement from your son at home. That's my guess."

August shouted angrily, "I'm not counting any chickens before they hatch. He's a goddamn embarrassment. Christ, of all the kids to hang around with he picks one of them damn—"

Embarrassed, Marguerite cut off her husband's rant and told the two educators, "We'll talk our son. He's got to make better friends."

August added, "Anything would be better than that Simpson kid. I'll take care of this the minute I get home. "

The principal disclosed that Ronnie was going to be left back due to his poor academic performance, so the two would be in each other's company far less, at least in school. Both principal and teacher strongly recommended that Arthur also be kept away from Ronnie when outside the school. As the meeting ended, the principal and teacher reaffirmed their concern that Ronnie was headed down the wrong path and Arthur was tagging along.

The drive from the school back home gave August Berndt time to fuel his anger. He stormed into the house while Marguerite put the car in the garage. Arthur, already in bed, was startled out of his sleep by his father's threatening voice coming from downstairs. "Get down here!"

Sitting up, Arthur rubbed his eyes and then dutifully got out of bed. He descended the staircase and went into the living room, where his father was waiting for him.

"So, you're goofing off in school. That's not what you go there for."

"I'm sorry, Dad."

"Sorry doesn't cut the mustard. You stay away from that Simpson kid, you hear me?"

"I won't...I mean I will. I promise. I won't be with him ever again."

"I'll say you won't. You made me have to listen to that crap from those people. You're an embarrassment."

His mother entered the living room and stood silently watching her husband and son, a look of apprehension on her face. Arthur wondered if there was any chance she'd intervene. He didn't hold out much hope.

August continued. "And what the hell you doing with this Simpson kid? I met your so-called friend's old man. Whadda ya turning out to be, some kind of nigger lover?"

Though Arthur didn't understand the question, his gut warned him to answer with a hearty "No!"

"You're damn right 'No!' Not in my house you won't. You keep away from that kid, you understand? And anyone that looks like him, for that matter."

"Yes...yes, Dad." A thought popped into the youngster's head. "But, Dad, what about Jackie Robinson?"

"What about him?"

"You always say he's a really good ballplayer."

"Yeah, so what does that have to do with anything?"

"Well, his skin looks like Ronnie's."

"Sure, they're both niggers. Robinson is okay on the ballfield, but that doesn't mean he's okay off it. Wouldn't want him moving into my neighborhood. I'm sure he knows his place."

"Oh."

"Now, get back to bed." The look of apprehension vanished from Marguerite's face; the look of disgust remained on her husband's.

Arthur wasted no time scrambling upstairs and back into bed. Just before dozing off to sleep, he thanked his lucky starts he's had to endure nothing more than a lecture.

# Chapter 34

THE NEXT SCHOOL DAY, Arthur didn't hang out with Ronnie as he usually did before class started. He sat at his desk, ignoring his friend's attempts to get his attention from across the classroom. At lunch time, Arthur hurried to the cafeteria, got his lunch, and annoyingly crammed himself alongside another studet at an already fill table, guaranteeing there'd be no room left for Ronnie.

After finishing his lunch, Arthur went outside to play. As he stood deciding where to go in the playground, he felt a tap on his shoulder. He turned around. It was Ronnie.

"What's wrong with you?"

"Nothing."

"Well, let's get into the softball game."

"I can't."

"Why?"

"I don't feel good."

"See, I told you there was something wrong with you."

Arthur hesitated before responding. "I... I can't play with you anymore."

"Why not?"

"I don't know. I just can't."

"What for?"

"Well, my father says I can't ever be with you."

"Why?"

"He says we get into too much trouble."

"Oh, you mean in class?"

"Yeah."

"So, we can still play ball and do other stuff."

"No, I can't. I just can't. Besides, my father said something about my kind and your kind don't belong together."

"What does that mean?"

"I don't know. He says I'm German and you're a coon."

"You're a German?"

"I don't even know exactly what a German is. It's some country far away and I've never even been there, but my father says I'm one anyway."

"Well, my father fought Germans. He says they're bad people. They do bad things."

"I don't have to be German if I don't want to."

The two youngsters stood facing each other in a brief awkward silence. Then Ronnie spoke up. "My dad met your dad. He say's your dad is crazy."

Arthur's face reddened. At first he said nothing. Then he decided to stick up for his father. "He is not."

"Is to."

"Yeah? Well, I bet your father is worse."

Ronnie walked up even closer to Arthur until the two boys were only inches apart. "Say that again. I dare ya."

Not waiting for Arthur's response, Ronnie shoved him. Arthur shoved back and immediately regretted doing so. He felt he had a duty to vouch for his father's sanity. After all, if his father was crazy, what would that make him? But he was heading toward a fight he'd never win. Arthur hoped the playground monitor had spotted them and was already rushing to intercede. No such luck.

Then it hit Arthur. An unexpected, but very welcome wave of relief. Ronnie was big all right, but nowhere near as big as Arthur's father. And nowhere near as scary. The youngster was confident he could deal with the punishment about to be dealt him. He was sure he'd handled worse. Besides, once this fight started, a teacher would quickly break it up. Not like at home, where there was no referee—not even his mother—guaranteed to keep his father in check.

The two remained standing face-to-face. Ronnie's chest was puffed out, making him look even more fearsome. He pushed Arthur again. Out of character, because usually by this time in a confrontation Ronnie would have dispensed with the small talk and been throwing punches. Instead he asked, "So, we're not friends anymore? You don't wanna be friends?"

"I didn't say that. I just can't get caught by my dad. He'll get mad and...do something."

"Well, I'm going to play ball. I don't care. If you won't be my friend, I won't be yours either."

To Arthur's relief, Ronnie scurried over to the softball area where kids were choosing up sides.

Arthur sat down on a swing and spent the rest of lunch recess watching the ballgame from a distance. He was determined never to again be caught hanging out with his onetime buddy. The chill between the two boys lasted throughout the remaining weeks of school.

# Chapter 35

THE FINAL DAY OF school lasted only two hours. Books were turned in, desks cleaned out, and final report cards distributed. Before dismissing the class, Mr. Mason couldn't suppress a snide remark about needing the summer off himself after dealing with Ronnie and Arthur for an entire school year.

Class ended at 10:30 a.m. Arthur walked down to Anderson's Market and, with the few coins he had, purchased a Popsicle and a couple of Tootsie Rolls. Leaving the store, he set out along Main Street, heading home. On his way, he passed by the First Presbyterian Church. Hearing a commotion coming from behind it, he decided to investigate. He walked along the sidewalk past the rear of the church and spotted a group of kids his age playing softball in the fully fenced yard that lay between the church and a house. Ronnie had organized the game with classmates at school that morning, not inviting Arthur.

Arthur lingered, leaning on the chain-link fence separating the sidewalk from the makeshift ball field. He wanted to play, but wasn't sure if it was safe to since Ronnie was there.

Kids from both teams coaxed him. "Hey, Art, come on and play."

"Yeah, we need a second baseman."

"So what? We need another outfielder, and you guys already have all the best hitters anyway."

Ronnie, on the heavy hitting team, stayed out of the conversation. Arthur wanted to play and figured if he wasn't on Ronnie's team that counted as staying away from him. He joined the weaker squad. His first time at bat, Arthur popped out to the shortstop. His second at-bat, he beat out a slow roller that the third baseman bobbled. When he reached first base, Ronnie, the opposing team's first baseman, was nearby waiting for him. Arthur did his best to ignore his former friend.

The game proceeded. Arthur stood with a foot on the bag, with Ronnie just a few feet away, ready to field his position. Over them hung a dead uncomfortable silence.

Arthur cheered on Tommy, the next batter, hoping he'd quickly get a hit, not only for the team's sake, but for his own. A base hit would enable Arthur to move to another base, away from Ronnie. He figured the farther away, the better.

Try as he might, Tommy couldn't put the bat on the ball and struck out. Next up: Sal. But, before he got to the plate he stopped to tie his sneaker laces. For Arthur, a fateful pause in the game.

While waiting for Sal, Ronnie made a peace offering to Arthur. "Hey, we're going to play ball here a lot this summer."

Arthur responded with an aloof "So?"

"Do you want to play on my team?"

"I don't know if my dad would let me. No, he wouldn't."

Ronnie persisted. "Well, we wouldn't get in trouble playing ball, right?"

At that moment, a dark green four-door Dodge passed by the field. Arthur didn't see the auto until all that was visible of it was the back half, the front obstructed by bushes. Still, he was sure he'd seen enough. Certain it was his parents' car, what remained uncertain was who had been driving it.

Arthur began a mental drill he was all too familiar with—damage control. If his mom had been driving, he'd beg and plead with her not to tell his dad. If his dad had been driving, he had to come up with an excuse. Maybe something like: *I was playing ball and Ronnie came along and joined the other team. I couldn't help it. Or, I was telling him that I couldn't talk to him, like you said for me to do, when you drove by. Or, I told him he had to play on the other team. That way he wouldn't be near me a lot.* Arthur couldn't fool himself. He knew none of these excuses would save his hide.

Though the game continued, it had ended for Arthur. The youngster lost all interest in softball, far too preoccupied with what lay in wait for him at home. He left the playing field and reluctantly began the walk to his house, barely hearing his teammates' cries of "Quitter!" behind him. He had a two-mile trek ahead of him, during which he hoped to concoct some means of worming his way out of this jam.

As hard as he struggled to create the perfect alibi, he couldn't even come up with a good one. He would just have to see this through to the end. If his father had spotted him, he had all too good an idea what he was in for. If it was his mom that had seen him, he might escape his father's wrath. What if neither had seen him? Dare he dream that miracle? While barely holding on to a flickering hope for the best, Arthur braced himself for the worst. When it came to situations like this one, he preferred to be a pessimist. That way he could never be disappointed.

The closer he got to his house, the slower he walked. The thought of facing the music got harder with each step he took. He turned off Hawthorne Street onto Lowell, stopping in his tracks. There sat the car in the driveway. Who had been driving it? The young boy would soon find out.

Arthur considered ducking into the woods and sitting there for a while, partly to concoct an alibi, partly to just buy time. Was it better to get punishment over with or put it off as long as possible? That was a question the youngster had grappled with far too often in his life. He had yet to come up with a definitive answer.

The young boy decided to take his chances and end the suspense. A last-minute glimmer of optimism bolstered his courage. If his father had caught a glimpse of him playing softball, he might not be mad at all because maybe he hadn't seen that Ronnie was there, too. Even if he had spotted both boys, maybe he'd decide his son hadn't been officially hanging out with Ronnie.

Arthur walked up Lowell Place and turned into the driveway at number Twenty-one. There sat the Dodge. After briefly hesitating, the young boy proceeded until he reached the front stoop. Arthur again paused for moment, took a deep breath, and summoned up all the courage he could. This was a familiar situation for the youngster, but it never got any easier to handle. He opened the front door and entered, as prepared as he could be to meet his fate. The second he entered the house, his heart sank. He heard his father cough in the dining room. Now the young boy knew who had been driving the family car. On top of that, nobody else was home, which always made these confrontations scarier. He knew no one could stop his father when he was meting out punishment yet, rightly or wrongly, the young boy believed his father was somewhat more restrained when there were witnesses. Entering the dining room, Arthur desperately clutched to the hope he had gone undetected at the ballgame. Not for long. August Berndt had a belt in his hand.

"I saw you with that Simpson kid." Arthur heard his dog whining from behind the kitchen door that had already been secured. Things were set up for the young boy to get a beating. Arthur figured he'd plead his case. He had nothing to lose by doing it.

"But dad, I was only playing ball. He was on the other team."

"When I told you to stay away from him, I meant it. Why would you ever want to hang around with one of *them* anyway? What's wrong with you? You just keep disobeying me."

Arthur broke out in tears. "I promise I'll never be near him ever, anywhere. I promise."

"You're damn right you won't and I'm gonna help you keep that promise."

August didn't say another word. He didn't have to. His son knew the drill all too well. With his father behind him, Arthur walked into the dining room. There he lowered his pants and bent over, clutching a dining room chair to brace himself.

Arthur tasted the first lash. The buckle stung. From the record player in the living room came the soothing sounds of Beethoven's Pastoral Symphony, providing background music. From the kitchen, Rex kept whining and scratching against the door. The young boy's best friend couldn't save him. No one could.

# Chapter 36

ARTHUR'S LATEST BEATING AT the hands of his father marked the beginning of his summer vacation.

A week later, Liz arrived home from college with a master's degree in teaching and an ever-worsening drinking problem. While she had been away at college, her brother felt he was missing an ally. He'd always taken comfort when she'd come home during the summers between college sessions. Liz never dared to physically intervene when her father attacked Arthur, but she did her best to stand up for the young boy by voicing complaints about his treatment. Though such protests were largely ineffective, her moral support meant a lot to Arthur.

Ruth continued to excel in academics, music, and athletics. Her answer to the chaos at home was to overachieve and participate in as many activities as possible that kept her outside the house.

Marguerite Berndt had settled into the role of peacekeeper, one she fulfilled with limited success. She had married a man at war with the world. August Berndt was the model of consistency—hardworking, hard-drinking and hard on his family—especially his son.

Anger, coldness, and criticism were vital ingredients in the recipe for cooking up Berndt family values. Add generous amounts of fear and punishment to the mix. Prepare in a pressure cooker. This was the meal served up on a daily basis in the Berndt household. August Berndt was the head chef.

Arthur, now eleven years old, had formed a unique worldview. He knew no matter what, his continual bedwetting would never be excused and guaranteed him several beatings every week of his life. Dropping, breaking, and losing things also could lead to physical discipline. He resented being held accountable for what he had no control over. He decided that if he could get hit for doing nothing, he might as well do something. This led to stealing inside and outside the house. He continually pushed his luck, doing whatever it took to impress whoever his "friends" were for the moment, and enjoying the rush whenever he got away with doing the wrong thing.

Arthur searched for relief from his home life every time he stepped out of his house. He either attempted to gain approval, however dubiously, from nonfamily members, or he headed for the woods and the safety of isolation. Though these coping mechanisms would never serve him well, they were all the young boy had.

With a growing sense that other children were getting treated better than he was, Arthur did all he could to keep his situation a secret and therefore less of an embarrassment. The idea of seeking help never once crossed the young boy's mind, as he was sure he'd never get it. Besides, such personal disclosure might only lead to further shame and further pain at the hands of his father. The dark side of life was to be dealt with alone.

# About the Author

WALTER STOFEEL IS A freeland writer and publisher who specializes in human interest memoir and fiction. His newest book, *Arthur: The Beginning,* is a work of historical fiction that describes a young boy's struggle to survive his childhood. His debut dog rescue memoir, *Lance: A Spirit Unbroken,* has achieved five-star book review status on three continents.

The author has a rich work history that includes teaching GED and substance abuse counseling at local correctional facilities. He lso has experience as a certified mental health screener. For many years, e lived and worked in various South American countries. Most unique ccupation: chipping excess concrete off the undersides of bridges in irginia. All his coworkers were wearing prison stripes.

Mr. Stoffel is a member of the Greater Lehigh Valley Writers Group, ennwriters and Barbara's Writing Group, a critiquing association.

When not writing, he loves to read, travel, work out, and watch bad novies.

The author has a B.A. in psychology and is a credentialed alcoholism nd drug counselor. He lives in Canadensis, PA with his wife Clara, and heir rescued dog Buddy.

Personal accomplishment: after having hip replacement surgery, Valter entered a marathon and finished it—dead last.

# Interview with Walter Stoffel

---

### Where did you get the inspiration for *Arthur: The Beginning*

"My first book (*Lance: A Spirit Unbroken*) was a dog rescue memoir. Th title character suffered years of abuse before getting a second chanc *Arthur: The Beginning* delves into the life of an abused young boy. Tw books, two sentient creatures, two struggles."

---

### So you tend to focus on the dark side of life?

"Why write about the front runners? I believe there is more to be learne from adversity than prosperity. I do try to inject comic relief wherever possible."

---

### Are there any people in *Arthur: The Beginning?* drawn from your own personal experience?

"There is fiction in every nonfiction book and nonfiction in every fiction book. That's the nature of the beast."

---

### You didn't actually answer the question.

"I know."

---

### How did you decide on the genre of *Arthur: The Beginning?*

"I wanted the intensity that nonfiction brings but the greater potential fo creativity that fiction allows. Also, by presenting the work as fiction, real people aren't hurt. Creative writing should be about learning and moving forward, not a pity party or singling people out for attack."

## How did you outline *Arthur: The Beginning?*

I didn't. I tend to be a seat-of-the-pants writer. I visualize a scene and write it. Then I put the scenes I've written in chronological order and tie them together as seamlessly as possible. At least, that's been my style up until now."

## What will the reader take away from *Arthur: The Beginning?*

Hopefully, a strong sense of Arthur's uphill struggle and how he fights for survival his way. Each of us lives our own unique life and handles things in our own way and, like Arthur, we all face challenges of varying degrees."

## What would be your hook to peak a reader's curiosity?

*Arthur: The Beginning*—so gritty and true-to-life you'll forget it's fiction."

Also by Walter Stoffel:

*Lance: A Spirit Unbroken*

# Suggested Reading Guide and Discussion Questions

1. Is Arthur a product of nature, nurture or both? Why do you feel thi way?

2. What are the personality traits of Arthur's that stand out to you?

3. Arthur is living in the 1950s. Would society handle his situatio differently today? If so, how?

4. Imagine you're a therapist. What diagnoses would you give Arthur August and Marguerite??

5. Why do you think Arthur threw away his fourth-grade medal fo achievement?

6. Arthur seems capable of only making "friends" with society's misfits? Why do you think that is?

7. Do you feel any personal connection with any of the people in this book? Why?

8. How would you describe the atmosphere in the Berndt family?

9. Do you know anyone in your life that is or was like Arthur? Explain.

10. What are Arthur's coping mechanisms?

11. Who (or what) provides Arthur the most comfort?

12. What were a few of your favorite quotes from this book?

13. What feelings did this book evoke for you?

14. If you got the chance to ask the author of this book one question, what would it be?

15. What do you think the author's purpose was in writing this book? What ideas is he trying to get across?

16. Did this book seem realistic?

17. Did the book's pace seem too fast/too slow/just right?

18. How well do you think the author built the world in this book?

19. What do you think of the book's title? How does it relate to the book's contents? What alternative title might you choose?

20. How original and unique is this book?

Made in the USA
Middletown, DE
23 November 2019